I'll
Be
Right
There

OTHER WORK IN ENGLISH BY KYUNG-SOOK SHIN

Please Look After Mom

I'll
Be
Right
There

a novel

KYUNG-SOOK SHIN

translated from the Korean by Sora Kim-Russell

OTHER PRESS
New York

Letter on page 62 from Vincent Van Gogh to Theo Van Gogh translated and edited by Robert Harrison, number 150. http://webexhibits.org/vangogh/letter/10/150.htm

Poem on page 297 by Rainer Maria Rilke, from *The Book of Hours.*
Translation © Susan Ranson and Marielle Sutherland 2011.
Published in *Selected Poems* (New York: Oxford University Press Inc., 2011).

Production Editor: Yvonne E. Cárdenas
Text Designer: Chris Welch
This book was set in 10.5 pt Minister Light
by Alpha Design & Composition of Pittsfield, NH.

10 9 8 7 6 5 4 3 2 1

Library of Congress Cataloging-in-Publication Data
Shin, Kyung-sook.
I'll be right there : a novel / by Kyung-sook Shin ; translated by Sora Kim-Russell.
pages cm
First published in Korea by Munhakdongne in Korean in 2010.
ISBN 978-1-59051-673-7 (pbk.) — ISBN 978-1-59051-674-4 (ebook)
1. Students—Fiction. 2. Korea—Fiction. I. Title.
PL992.73.K94I513 2013
895.7'34—dc23
2013011936

Who is that weeping, if not simply the wind,
At this sole hour, with ultimate diamonds? . . . But who
Weeps, so close to myself on the brink of tears?

—Paul Valéry, "The Young Fate"

Can I Come Over?

It was my first phone call from him in eight years.

I recognized his voice right away. As soon as he said "Hello?" I asked, "Where are you?" He didn't say anything. Eight years—it was not a short length of time. Broken down into hours, the number would be unimaginable. I say it had been eight years, but we had stopped talking even before then. Once, at some get-together with friends, we had avoided each other's eyes the entire time, and only when everyone was parting ways did we briefly take each other's hand without the others seeing. That was it.

I don't remember where we were. Only that it was after midnight, summer, and we were standing in front of some steep staircase in a hidden corner of the city. There must have been a fruit stand nearby. The scent floating in the humid air reminded me of biting into a plum. Taking his hand and letting it go was my way of saying goodbye. I did not know what he was thinking, but for me, all of the words I wanted to say to him had collected inside me like pearls. I could not bring myself to say *goodbye* or *see you later*. If I had opened my mouth to say a single word, all of the other expired words would have followed and spilled to the ground, as if the string that held them together had snapped. Since I still clung to the memory of how we had grown and matured together, I was vexed by the thought that there would be no controlling my feelings once they came undone. But outwardly I feigned a look of composure. I did not want to spoil my memories of how we used to rely on each other.

Time is never fair or easy for anyone—not now and not eight years ago. When I calmly asked him where he was, despite not having heard from him in all of that time, I realized that the words I had not been able to say to him then were no longer pent up inside me. Nor did I need to pretend to be fine in order to mask any tumultuous emotions. I mean it when I say I asked him that question calmly. What happened to those words that once drove me to wander aimlessly, my mind filled with doubt and sadness? Those bitter feelings? Those aches that speared my heart whenever I was alone? Where did they finally trickle away to that I should be holding up so well now? Is this life? Is this why the relentless passing of time is both regretful and fortunate? Back when I was caught in the whirling current and could not swim my way out, someone I have since forgotten told me: *This, too, shall pass.* I suppose this was proof. That advice applies both to those who suffer and to those whose lives are filled with abundance. To one, it gives the strength to endure; to the other, the strength to be humble.

The silence lengthened between us. Too late, I realized that I had gotten things out of order. I should have said hello first. It was strange. Saying things like *long time, no talk* or *what's new?* felt too awkward. And though I figured he was probably taken aback by the way I immediately asked where he was, I wasn't comfortable enough yet to ask how he'd been. Asking someone where they are the moment you answer the phone makes sense only if you spend a lot of time together. But there we were, he on one end of the line and I on the other, for the first time in eight years. Time is always bearing down on us; nevertheless, had I understood in my youth that we can never relive the same moment twice, things might have turned out differently. Had I understood that, I would never have said goodbye to someone, and someone else might still be alive. If only I had known that the moment you think everything has ended, something new is beginning.

I turned to look out the window.

While the silence between us continued, the window slowly filled with the morning light of winter. Yesterday's weather forecast said it would snow today, but I didn't believe it. It was early, the light of dawn still lingering. The time of day when you would normally hesitate before calling someone who was not family or otherwise very close to you. Calls at this time were either urgent or brought bad news.

"The professor is in the hospital," he finally said.

"Professor Yoon?"

"I thought I should tell you."

I blinked and looked away from the window. His words—*I thought I should tell you*—swirled before my eyes like snowflakes. I concentrated on his voice, as if clinging to it, and narrowed my blurry eyes to slits. To my surprise, snowflakes were casting their shadows on the lowered blinds.

"He's been in the hospital for about three months now."

I'd had no idea.

"I don't think he has much longer."

Three months? I let out a deep sigh. Resentment toward Professor Yoon welled up in me and subsided. I had not seen him in three years. As his illness progressed, Professor Yoon had insisted on being alone and refused visitors—just as my mother had done. He had become a lone figure in a room that could only be reached by passing through countless closed doors. In the face of death, he wanted to be strictly and faithfully alone.

Early one winter morning three years ago, I set out to visit Professor Yoon, but I never made it. I never tried to visit him again. That morning, on the first day of the new year, I had felt like paying him a holiday visit. Though I knew he was having trouble breathing and could not sit up for long periods of time, I wanted to see him in person, however briefly. The sky was dark that morning; large snowflakes had begun to fall. I wasn't good at driving. I usually assumed it was my fault whenever something went wrong with the car. The snow turned heavy, and the wind was blowing from the north. The car began to skid and then plowed into a snowdrift. Since Professor Yoon's house was not far, I left the car where it was and began walking the rest of the way. My cheeks felt frozen, and tiny icicles dangled from the hems of my pants. As I walked, I glanced back to see that the mountainsides were blanketed in white. The wind was swirling mounds of snow into the air and sweeping it down into the folds of the mountains. It was getting harder to see. I told myself to keep going, but I became more and more frightened. Each time I heard a snow-laden branch snap and fall to the forest floor, my stomach dropped with it. Finally, when a large dead tree could no longer take the weight of the snow and collapsed with a boom, I turned back with a defeated heart.

What stopped me from reaching his house? Getting back was no easier. After giving up that night, I never got up the nerve to try again. Each time I thought about him, the idea that I would never be able to reach him spread through my mind like a shadow. And it seemed I was not the only one. One friend told me that he had driven to Professor Yoon's house in the middle of the night, but as he got closer, he could not bring himself to go the rest of the way and drove to the top of a hill instead, where he looked down at the lights of the house before going home. He said he circled the house a few times and left, biting his lip the whole way. Why couldn't we just barge into Professor Yoon's house like we did in the old days? The phone still in my hand, I got up from the desk, went to the window, and pulled open the blinds.

Outside, white flakes were drifting down.

I was not surprised to hear he was dying. I had been nervously expecting to get that news someday. I just did not know it would be today. The snow had started off so light that I could have counted it by the individual flakes, but it grew heavier as I stood in the window. In the yard of the house across from mine, a Himalayan cedar tree that had remained a lush green even in winter was turning white. There was no one out. The local neighborhood bus, which I had never once ridden in the four years that I'd lived there, was heading through the side streets, gliding carefully along the snowy roads.

Though I tend to confuse things that happened yesterday with things that happened ten years ago, and am prone to standing in front of the open refrigerator, trying to remember what I was looking for, only to sheepishly close the door again after bathing in the cold air, I could still remember seeing Professor Yoon for the first time all those years ago like it was yesterday. I was twenty at the time. Back then, I could look at a single book title and think of a dozen other books related to it. On that first day of college, the March sunlight was streaming into the classroom when Professor Yoon walked in. I had my head down on the desk as he walked past. His shoes caught my eye. They were so big that his heels slipped out of the backs with each step. It looked like he was wearing someone else's shoes. Curious, I lifted my head and immediately felt ashamed. How could anyone be that skinny? The problem was not the shoes. No shoes in the world would have fit him. He looked like a plaster skeleton.

I looked up at his eyes instead. They gleamed sharply behind his glasses. He turned to look out the window. The shouting of the student demonstrators outside had been disrupting classes. Tear gas wafted into the room, carried on the still-cold March wind. Before class began, someone had struggled to shut the hinged windows. Professor Yoon stood in the window for a long time, watching the demonstrators. He did not move, so we all gradually joined him at the window. Riot police were chasing a group of students. White clouds bobbed above their heads in the frigid air. That day, Professor Yoon had just one thing to say to us: *What is the use of art in this day and age?* I could not tell whether the question was aimed at us or at himself, but I saw his keen eyes grimace in pain. In that moment, when I first began paying attention to his eyes, a sharp, unfamiliar pain pricked at my heart. Back then, how could I have known what was in store for us? Or that the strange prick I felt that day would still be with me even after all these years? Though my memories of our time together have faded and lost their edge, his eyes still haunt me. Each time I picture them, the same old pain returns. That pain pierces my heart in a thousand places, bursts through the skin, and peppers me with the same question.

What are you doing with your life?

When I was twenty, each time I asked myself that, I left the university and walked for hours around the city, eyes streaming from the sting of tear gas in the air. Has nothing changed since then? Even now, whenever I picture his eyes, I have to get out of my house and walk—I pick any road and follow it to the end. Neither society nor I have changed for the better; we have only become more imperfect in different ways. When the bridge over the river that cuts through the city collapsed and a bus carrying girls to school plunged into the river, when I saw an airplane crash into a tall Wall Street building one morning, when I sat in front of the television on the first day of the new year and watched for hours in disbelief as flames engulfed Sungnyemun Gate, I asked myself the same question: *What are you doing with your life?* I drove in circles around what was left of the burned city gate in the middle of the night until I felt like returning home again. Now as then, whenever I feel like giving up, I walk around the city. Through the depression and loneliness, the same thought arises: *If only he were here.*

Which of us was the first to let go?

At some point, I realized I would have to live without him. I was nervous and afraid, but the time had come for me to go it alone. Even afterward, images of him clung and would not let go. Like that night we spent in some seaside village on a remote island. How were we able to walk all night like that? And while getting caught in cloudbursts. We took a ferry from Incheon so far out into the sea, and yet I've completely forgotten the name of the village. We hadn't planned on going there. We just jumped on Subway Line 1 at Seoul Station for some reason. The fact that it was Line 1 doesn't hold any meaning; I am only assuming that was how we got there because I remember passing Bucheon Station. He wore a white short-sleeved shirt, which means it was probably midsummer. The subway train was so packed that it was hard to stand up straight. I was tired, and it must have been one of those days when I was not in the mood to talk. Each time the train stopped, a crowd of people surged in, filling the car with the smell of sweat. As he stood there swaying, brow furrowed, I said, "Let's go somewhere far away." Or maybe it was his idea. We got off the subway at Incheon and took a bus to the ferry terminal. We did not care where the ferry went as long as it was as far as possible from the harbor. The ferry carried us across the sea. As we stood at the side of the boat and took in the breeze, whatever it was that had me feeling so worn down did not seem to matter anymore. We stared at the sea. I had never gone that far from the coast before. Since he had grown up in a beach town, the experience was probably different for him than it was for me. It was not easy to get to the island. The ferry ride took two hours, and when we reached the island, the tide had come in, making it impossible to go all the way to shore. Someone brought a small motorboat out to us from the village dock. After everyone boarded, we headed for the island. I saw children fishing way out in the water. I frowned, worried they might be swept away at any moment, but someone told me they were standing on an embankment and were not actually in the water. They said I would be able to see it once the tide was out. The boat let us off on another submerged embankment. I hiked up my skirt, and he rolled his pants up to his thighs, and together we waded along the embankment to the island.

That day, we walked as far around the island as we could. It must have been the rainy season, because more people were sitting on the beach than swimming in the water, and the farther we got from the dock, the fewer people we ran into. We could smell salt on the air, and a line of trees next to the beach shook violently in the wind. We stood on the beach and put our arms around each other as the sun slipped into the sea. In the blink of an eye, the crimson disk disappeared below the horizon. Afterward, he turned moody. Though he had kept trying to cheer me up while I was feeling down, now he was the one not saying a word. I grew quiet. As we walked along the beach together in silence, we came upon a dead seagull carried in on the tide.

"A bird!" I murmured.

He started digging a hole in the sand to bury it.

"What's the point?" I asked. "The tide will just wash it out."

"All the same!"

When I think of the way he said that, I cannot help but smile. That phrase always used to remind me of him. Whatever the situation, he would say, "All the same, it's better that way!" He took a notebook out of his bag, tore a sheet of paper from it, and wrote, *Rise again, dear bird.* Then he rolled the piece of paper around a stick and planted it in front of the bird's grave.

Did we eat anything that night? I don't remember eating, nor do I remember being hungry. That night, we walked until the whole island was dark, as if we were trying to find out where the water ended. That was probably the first time I watched the sea grow black as darkness fell. The black water climbed over and over itself until it reached our feet and retreated.

"Jung Yoon!" Whenever he called me by my full name, it meant he had something on his mind.

"What is it?"

"Let's remember this day forever."

That's it? Unimpressed, I mumbled under my breath that if you wanted to remember something, you ought to have a memento. I heard a rustling sound in the dark. He slipped his journal out of his bag and into my hand.

"I call this my Brown Notebook. I use it to jot down my thoughts. I want you to have it."

He put his hand around my wrist and pulled me toward

him; I let him put his arms around me. He pulled my hand down to his crotch and said, "You can have this, too." He sounded so serious that I couldn't help but laugh. With one hand on his notebook and the other on his crotch, I felt a strange sadness wash over me, and I whispered in his ear, "Can we go somewhere farther away?" But I knew there was nowhere else.

Who can foresee the days that are yet to come?

The future rushes in and all we can do is take our memories and move forward with them. Memory keeps only what it wants. Images from memories are sprinkled throughout our lives, but that does not mean we must believe that our own or other people's memories are of things that really happened. When someone stubbornly insists that they saw something with their own eyes, I take it as a statement mixed with wishful thinking. As what they want to believe. Yet as imperfect as memories are, whenever I am faced with one, I cannot help getting lost in thought. Especially when that memory reminds me of what it felt like to be always out of place and always a step behind. Why was it so hard for me to open my eyes every morning, why was I so afraid to form a relationship with anyone, and why was I nevertheless able to break down my walls and find him?

In my first year of college, I used to stare at the front gate of the university every morning and debate whether or not to go inside. Often, I would turn around and walk back down the hill I had just climbed. Even now, I cannot say what was wrong with me. For three months, during the end of my nineteenth year and the start of my twentieth, I kept the window of the small room in the apartment where I lived with my older newlywed cousin covered with black construction paper. It was only a single sheet, but it turned the room as dark as night. In that darkness, I left the light on and passed the time reading. There was no reason for it. I just had nothing else to do and nothing I wanted to do. I read an entire sixty-volume literature anthology, in order, each volume of which contained over twenty short stories printed in letters smaller than sesame seeds. When I finished, I looked out the window to discover it was March. When I think about it now, it seems so long ago. To think that in the happy home of two newlyweds there was a room that was kept as black as night! When I came out of that room, it was to attend the matriculation ceremony at the university, which was the freest place I had ever experienced in this city. Now Professor Yoon is in the hospital, Myungsuh is out there living a life that has nothing to do with me, and there is another whom I will never see again. But had I not met them where and when I did, how could I have made it through those days?

I watched the snowflakes grow heavier and collected my thoughts. I reminded myself that the only reason he had called after eight years was to tell me Professor Yoon was dying. I muttered to myself not to lose sight of that. First and foremost, I needed to get to the hospital. We are always crossing and recrossing each other's paths whether we realize it or not. Long-forgotten memories kept cropping up and surprising me, like pulling on the stalk of a potato plant after the rain and seeing endless clusters of potatoes pop out of the soil. Even if I never thought of him or heard from him again, the fact that we had connected with each other, however briefly, still made me sad.

He broke the silence. I held the receiver, unable to say a word as he told me about Professor Yoon. Then he asked, "Can I come over?"

At this hour?

I thought it was over between us, but he asked it so casually: *Can I come over?* How long had it been since I last heard those words? Back when we were together, he used to say those words to me all the time over the phone. *Can I come over?* He would even call from phone booths to say, *I'm on my way.* Whether rainy, windy, cloudy, or clear, each day passed with those words ringing between us. Back then, he and I were always waiting for each other. It was never too late at night for him to come see me, and there were no limits to when I could see him. We would tell each other to come over any time, day or night. We each get one life that is our own. We each in our own way struggle to get ahead, love, grieve, and lose our loved ones to death. There are no exceptions for anyone—not for me, not for the man who had called me, and not for Professor Yoon. Just one chance. That's all. If youth were something we could do over, I would not be standing here today, answering my phone and listening to his voice for the first time in eight years.

I hesitated a moment and then said, "No, I'll figure it out."

He sighed and hung up.

My last words to him left me feeling lonely. They were my words, yet they sounded strange to me. I should have told him I would meet him at the hospital. It was a harsh thing to say. He had said the same words to me once, many years ago. By then, we were past the point of always knowing where the other one was and what we were doing. I had asked him what he was planning to do about something, and he snapped, "I'll figure it out." It seems that whether we are aware of it or not, memory carries a dagger in its breast. I had not been dwelling on his words all that time, and more than enough time had passed for me to forget about it completely, but in an instant, my subconscious retrieved his words and turned them on him. I was not the type to rebuff a friend like that. And if someone I had been feeling close to were to speak to me that way, I would likely start keeping my distance. His words had been roaming around inside me all that time, like lost puzzle pieces, before finding their way back.

I returned to my desk and spent the morning slumped in my chair. After the difficult memories finally subsided, I was left with a cool breeze.

Was it August? Or September? We were filling a basket with crab apples from the tree that grew in Professor Yoon's yard when a cool breeze blew over us and we laughed. The tiny tree was barely tall enough to peek over the wall, but it was heavy with crab apples. Professor Yoon watched from the living room window as we filled the basket. I have forgotten why my college friends and I had gotten together to pick crab apples, but we must have been happy and at peace then, considering the way our laughter gushed forth.

"Will these days ever come again?"

My friend had meant it in an offhand way, but the comment cut deep.

"Not the same days," someone said sadly.

We gathered up the laughter that had poured forth so easily a moment before and, to avoid one another's eyes, looked at Professor Yoon gazing out the window at us, each of us lost in our private thoughts. Maybe we had already foreseen the future. After we finished picking the fruit, we returned to the living room and sat in a circle. Professor Yoon had fallen asleep with a book on his knee. Someone set the book down carefully on the table. Curious to see what he had been reading, I picked it up. It was *The World of Silence*. It looked old: the pages were yellowed and folded back. With my hand on top of the book, I stared at Professor Yoon's socks hanging loosely on his too-thin feet.

Though I knew I should go to the hospital, I could not bring myself to leave my chair. I felt like I was floating, and I kept dozing off. By the time I was able to sit up straight and examine my desk, it was already noon. Books I was in the middle of reading were scattered about, and a memo pad lay facedown beneath some papers I had been editing. Two pencils sat askew in a pencil case I had bought at the Picasso Museum in Barcelona's Gothic Quarter. I stared at the dove carrying a leaf in its beak engraved on the side of the case and then began to straighten up my desk. I closed the poetry books that were sitting open and put my scattered pens and pencils back in the case. I crumpled up the discarded papers covered in underlines and tossed them in the trash, removed the paperweights from the thick books that I had shoved aside in the middle of reading and gathered them off to one side, and returned the books to their shelves.

For some reason, straightening up my desk always reminds me of death. Once, I had tidied up and was heading out of the room when I glanced back at my clean desk. Suddenly frightened, I went back and messed it up again. Growing old does not make us any better at loving one another or understanding the meaning of life or death. Nor does knowledge come with the passage of time. Compared with when I was young, I am worse now at loving another person, and news of someone's unexpected death shocks and upsets me each time. Nevertheless, I hope that when I die, I will be writing or reading a book at my desk late one snowy night and I will simply put my head down and close my eyes forever. I want that to be the last image of me on this earth. I brushed away the traces of death that clung to my fingertips each time I put a book on its shelf and finished tidying up. To get ready to go to the hospital, I lathered my hands with soap and washed my face, changed into clean clothes, and checked the mirror. On my way out the door, I paused involuntarily and glanced back at my desk.

As if it had been waiting for me, the telephone rang again.

CHAPTER 1

Parting

When I turned twenty, I returned to the city and made five promises to myself:

Start reading again.
Write down new words and their definitions.
Memorize one poem a week.
Do not go to Mom's grave before the Chuseok
    holiday.
Walk around the city for at least two hours every
    day.

My mother passed away before the end of my first semester of college.

The first thing she did after she found out she was sick was to send me to live with my older female cousin in the city. I was in middle school at the time. For my mother, sending me away was her way of loving me. She said I was too young to be tied down to a sick mother and that I had too much to live for. Everybody has to say goodbye eventually, she told me, so you may as well start practicing. I cannot say she was right. I think that if we all have to say goodbye eventually then the best we can do is try to stay together as long as we possibly can. But it's not that one of us was right and the other was wrong. We just saw things differently.

Up until her illness took a turn for the worse, I used to get her medication for her at a big hospital in the city, where she had once been admitted. Every Wednesday, I ordered her pre-scription at the pharmacy, sat in the waiting room, and waited for the number written on the piece of paper I was given to appear on the electronic display. When my number popped up with a ding, I pushed the slip of paper through the window. After a brief wait, a basket with a week's worth of my mother's medication was pushed back to me. I repeated this trip to the pharmacy every Wednesday to purchase my mother's pills and mail them to her. Each time I called to tell her they were in the mail, she said, "That's my daughter!" Always in the same unchanging voice. *Good work, daughter! Thank you, daughter!*

Four days before she died, she sent me a package. It contained a ring she always wore and some perilla leaf kimchi.

"Perilla leaf kimchi is your favorite." She sounded cheerful over the phone. "I've looked forward to leaving that ring to you!"

I didn't know she would die so soon.

Whenever I thought about the fact that she had packed perilla leaf kimchi for me and then took off her ring, wrapped it in paper, and sent it to me before dying, I rubbed my eyes hard, as if to dig them out. There was no more medicine for me to pick up on Wednesdays, yet every Wednesday morning I could be found sitting in the waiting room of that hospital. It was my Wednesday routine. I no longer had a number to wait for, but each time the pager dinged, I looked up and watched the display change. After a while, I would tell myself it was time to get to class, and I would leave the waiting room. But before I knew it, I would find myself heading toward the train station instead and boarding a train. Some mornings, I even made it to the steep road that led up to the school only to turn around and head for the station. There, I would buy a ticket for the first train out.

There were always empty seats on the train in the middle of the day. I could sit wherever I wanted regardless of the seat number printed on my ticket. Some days, I was the only person in the entire train car. I would stare out the window until the conductor announced that the train had arrived at the station in the small town where I was born. Along the way, when the river appeared, I turned my head and stared until I could not see the water anymore, and when distant mountains suddenly slid into view, I leaned back in my seat. Once, a flock of birds appeared from out of nowhere and flew across a field. I watched them until the train went into a tunnel, and then I shut my eyes tight even though there was nothing to see anyway. I was always famished by the time the train stopped. I would slurp down a bowl of noodles in a shop in front of the station, and only then would I realize where I was and murmur to myself, *Mama, I'm back.*

My mother's death was not the only reason I decided to take a break from school. I was studying at a university for the arts. The campus had a freewheeling atmosphere that was characteristic of art schools. Some people fit right in, while others were left out. I was in the latter group. I doubt anyone there even knew what my voice sounded like. The male students were more interested in protesting or drinking than in going to class, and the female students were busy preening or being dramatically depressed. It was the kind of place where, in the middle of an ordinary conversation, you could burst into Hamlet's or Ophelia's lines and nobody thought anything of it. There, it was considered a performance and a mark of individuality to sing incessantly or to sit in one spot and stare at someone without blinking. Even if you weren't trying to spot someone doing something unusual, someone would catch your eye nonetheless. With my ordinary looks, I felt as if I was always alone. Everything they said sounded to me like a foreign language from some far-off land. But that was not the only reason I decided to take a leave of absence. Back then, I would have been the odd one out no matter where I was.

One day, one of my male classmates disappeared. He was a friendly guy whom everyone called Pedal, because he had this powerful walk that made him look like he was pedaling his legs. The day he stopped coming to school, he came running up to me where I was seated on a bench. He told me his younger brother was in town and that he had to send money home with him right away. He talked me into giving him all of the cash I had on me. He even took a book of poems from me—a collection by Emily Dickinson that Dahn, my childhood friend, had given me when I left home. Later, I found out that Pedal had borrowed money, as well as a fountain pen, books, and notebooks, from more than ten other girls that same day and then disappeared without a trace. Too late, it was discovered that he was not even a registered student. But while my classmates were exploding with rage, saying it was unbelievable that he had been taking classes with them for several months and that they needed to do something about it, I left to apply for a leave of absence.

The night Dahn had given me that book of poems, he showed up at our front gate and called out my name. Dahn and I snuck through the darkened alleys of our hometown, where hundreds of thousands of our footprints were stamped in the dirt, and walked to an open field on the edge of town. We sat next to each other beside the railroad tracks. A night train chugged and rattled past us. The light coming from each of the cars was luminous. If not for the chugging of the engine, it could have been just glowing windows racing through the dark.

"We have to go to college." Dahn sounded like he was making a pledge.

I was too surprised to respond.

"I'm going to be an artist," he said.

I felt like I was going to burst. The night breeze blew toward us over the field and seemed to carry our hopes with it, departing before us into some distant time. When Dahn and I parted ways that night, he handed me a paperback book of poetry. He said that he had just finished reading it and so was giving it to me. It was too dark for me to make out the title.

"They say that when she died, she left over seventeen hundred poems stashed in a drawer," he said. "Her first collection was published four years after her death."

"Who?"

"Emily Dickinson."

"*E-mi-ly Di-ckin-son.*" Even after sounding out the syllables, I still did not recognize the name. Dahn had always known from a young age what he wanted to do; he thought deeply about things and conducted himself differently from our peers. He read different books, owned different things, and had a different way of speaking.

"She seemed to see things that were not of this world," he said.

"Not of this world?"

"Things we can't see. Like death . . . and so on."

It was the first time I had heard someone my age talk about death or things that were not of this world. That was probably why Dahn always seemed like he was a few years older than he really was. When I got home and flipped to the first page of the book, the first thing I saw was Dahn's handwriting.

> I began to tread softly . . . Poor people shouldn't be
> disturbed when they're deep in thought.
> —Rainer Maria Rilke, *The Notebooks of Malte Laurids Brigge*

I liked Dahn's handwriting. It looked scribbled, but the style was so energetic that it reminded me of the hoofbeats of a galloping horse. I stared at the quote and realized it was goodbye. I put the book in the bottom of my bag.

Because I could not stop for Death,
He kindly stopped for me;
The carriage held but just ourselves
And Immortality.

When I read Dickinson's poetry, I pictured my mother's face. I wanted to savor the poems, so I read them slowly, going over each one five times. When I finished the book, I took my first subway ride to a large bookstore on Jongno Street, clinging to the strap the whole way to keep from swaying. The first book I spent money on in this city was *The Notebooks of Malte Laurids Brigge*. With no clue as to what it was about, I selected it because it was the title Dahn had written in the book. On the subway ride back, I opened to the first page.

Here, then, is where people come to live.

As I stared vacantly at the first sentence, a single tear fell from my eye, a tear that had refused to come even when I left home. Was I, too, one of those who had come to live? This city was not kind to me. It had tall buildings and many houses and countless people, but no one to greet me gladly or take my hand. Too many wide and narrow streets made me lose my way frequently. And I had no intention of getting to know the people of this city. I grew accustomed to not greeting people when I met them and behaved like a young exile.

The cousin I lived with in the city served as my legal guardian until I finished high school. She got married around the time that I started college. At that point, it made sense for me to move out, but I had nowhere else to go. Even though my mother had sent me away, she did not want me to be alone. I stayed with my cousin in order to reassure my mother, who was still fighting her illness. But once she passed on, it became harder for me to stay there. My cousin's husband was an airline pilot, which meant he was often gone on long flights to places like Paris and London, but he was not gone all the time, and I did not want to intrude. I would have preferred to stay with my mother, even if only for a short time before starting college, but she refused to let me. By then, she did not have a single strand of hair left.

The next line in *The Notebooks of Malte Laurids Brigge*, "I'd have thought it more a place to die in," was ringing in my head when I applied for a leave of absence, the first semester not yet over. I had no friends, so there was no one for me to say goodbye to before returning to my parents' house in the countryside. When I moved out of my cousin's apartment, she gave me a look of regret and asked if I really had to go.

"Sorry," I said. It was not the right way to answer her question.

"Sorry? What are you sorry for?"

"Everything."

I meant it. I felt especially sorry toward my cousin. Sorry for not smiling more, sorry for taping black paper over a window in a newlywed's house, sorry for not being nicer, and sorry for forcing her to look after me because I had lost my mother. I had noticed the sympathy that flashed in her eyes whenever she looked at me. After all, we had lived together for over four years. She urged me to stay, telling me to think it over once more. I told her I had already made my decision. She asked me again if I would change my mind. I shook my head. With a sad look on her face, she gave me a long hug.

"Come back anytime, if things get tough."

From my cousin's body came the fresh scent of a newlywed woman. She smelled like strawberries, leaves, a peach. The moment I caught that sweet scent, I knew I had made the right decision. Though the space I had taken up was only one small room, it was still a newlywed's home. To think that I had taped over the windows of that room and forced them to mind how they laughed or smiled around me. To think that, even then, my cousin had never once frowned at me. Once, her husband asked me, "Isn't the room too dark?" I told him it was fine, and he never brought it up again.

My year at home was dull and boring. Dahn had also left for college and was living in another city, and my father's daily routine never varied, whether I was there or not. Seasons changed: new buds appeared, typhoons passed through, persimmons swelled, heavy snow fell. In the space of a year, my father's back grew more stooped, and he turned into an old man. He had grown accustomed to taking care of himself during my mother's long illness, so things were no harder for him than they were before she was gone. Nevertheless, he grew old quickly. My aging father grew even more taciturn. I wondered sometimes if my presence in the house made him uncomfortable. I would go to bed late and struggle to wake up the next day; meanwhile, the first thing he did every morning was visit my mother's grave. He laid fresh sod over it and even dug up her favorite crepe-myrtle tree that grew in the courtyard and replanted it close to her grave. I accompanied him a few times but otherwise avoided going with him. As I walked behind my father on the way to her headstone, he looked like a house that was caving in. So instead, I timed my visits for midday or when the sun was setting. That way, there was no chance I would run into him.

My mother had not been afraid of dying. Rather, apologetic.

It rained continuously for several days and then stopped. When it did, two things happened.

My father returned from town, took off his shirt, and tossed it up on the porch, and then, dressed only in a sleeveless undershirt, he grabbed a shovel and went back out the front gate. A pack of cigarettes had fallen out of the shirt he had tossed. I grabbed the cigarettes and found a lighter and went to the back of the house. The backyard was overgrown with pumpkin and taro leaves. I squatted down and looked at the green taro leaves that had unfurled after the rain. Then I took a cigarette from the pack, put it in my mouth, flicked the lighter, and raised it to the cigarette. I kept looking nervously in one direction, worried someone might catch me, but my father suddenly appeared from behind me. There was no time to mask what I was doing. My father's eyes met mine just as the flame touched the cigarette. He stopped in his tracks and eyed me for a moment, and then he turned around and walked away without saying a word. I prepared to be scolded harshly. I even thought that if we argued, it might take away the silence and solitude that had drawn a heavy curtain between father and daughter. But to my surprise, he did not say a word at the dinner table. I thought maybe it was painful for him to see me lighting a cigarette and he had chosen to pretend he saw nothing instead. A strange anger rose up inside me. I wanted him to scold me. That way, I could smoke without feeling guilty. I started to clear the table, but he suddenly asked if I wanted to dye my nails.

"Dye my nails?"

"I don't know if you remember but once, when you were little, I dyed your fingernails with balsam flowers."

Did he? I looked down at my hands where they held the dinner tray.

"When you unwrapped the orange dye from your fingers in the morning, you screamed, 'My nails are bleeding!' You ran to the well and stuck your hands in the cold water. You were so little . . ."

On summer nights when my mother was sick, my father crushed up balsam petals, put them on her fingernails, wrapped them in plastic, and bound them with thread. She had asked him to do it for her. He said he wondered if the balsam was the reason the anesthesia did not take well during her surgery. After clearing the dinner table, I watched as he placed the crushed balsam flowers on my fingernails, and I asked weakly, "Dad, does dyeing your nails with this really stop anesthesia from working?" He murmured, "I'm not sure."

I thought, *I'm sorry, Mama. I won't smoke again, Mama.*

That night, I tied string around my fingertips and went with Dahn to the field on the edge of town. Dahn was home for a visit from the southern city where he was attending college. We walked over the railroad ties in the dark. Since moving south for college, Dahn had become taciturn, like my father, and his brow seemed permanently furrowed. His chin was unshaven and he refused to smile, as if he had made up his mind to not be nice to anyone. Not even me.

"Dahn," I said, and turned him around by one shoulder in the dark. We were separated by endless rows of black railroad ties. "Would you like to see my mother's grave?"

I didn't think he would agree so readily. He nodded right away and said he would stop by his house first to get his headlamp.

"Headlamp?"

"I use it for night hikes or anytime I go out walking late at night."

"Do you mean the thing miners use?"

"That's an actual helmet. Mine is smaller. I have trouble sleeping so I use it in the dorm to sketch by. If I leave the lamp on, my roommate can't sleep. I keep the headlamp in my bag and use it outside, as well."

Did he really just say he wears a headlamp in the middle of the night to sketch by?

This Dahn who talked about sketching by the light of a headlamp because he could not sleep seemed like a stranger to me. We left the train tracks and walked to his house in silence. Our shadows crisscrossed each other on the wall. Dahn snuck into his house and came back with his headlamp. He tried to put it on my head.

"No, you wear it," I said. "Walk ahead of me."

Dahn put the lantern on. When the light flicked on over his forehead, he looked like a different person. We cut through a field and headed toward the mountain where my mother was buried.

"You handled it well," he said.

"What?"

"Your mother."

Feeling a sudden pang in my chest, I hooked one of my fingers, still bound with cotton thread, around Dahn's pinky.

After Mom died, I stopped reading books.

My cousin called and tried to get me to go to church, but I did not want to listen to anyone. I did nothing the whole year. On days when the rain came streaming down or when I felt like a potato pulled from its vine, I would go downtown and slip into the theater that showed double features, slump down in my seat, and return straight home afterward. I kept my mother's ring, the one with the pearl shaped like a tear, in my pocket at all times. In the middle of napping, I would wake with a start and hurriedly shove my hand into my pocket, searching for the ring. I would relax once my finger grazed the pearl, but it also made me feel sorry for the way I'd treated my mother. Once, after she had become sick, we got into an argument and I raised my voice at her. I was so bitter and angry with her that I imagined I was dead and pictured her looking inconsolable with grief. The ring reminded me of that. I could never take that moment back. I felt sad and hated myself for having wished her pain. But I could not bring myself to wear it. Doing so seemed like admitting that she was dead, and I was afraid of that.

When we reached the foot of the mountain, Dahn hung back.

"What is it?" I asked.

"Spiders."

To get to the grave, we had to take a mountain path, and along that dark path, spiders would be building webs in the air, waiting with bated breath underfoot, or crawling on rocks.

"You're afraid of spiders?"

The light from Dahn's headlamp bobbed up and down in the dark.

"They scare me more than riot police."

I giggled involuntarily. A grown man afraid of spiders.

"Don't laugh. You make light of them now but you'll be sorry. Didn't you hear about the giant bird-eating spider that attacked a village in Australia?"

"No."

I had honestly never heard of it. But ever since learning about the baby spiders that feed on their mother's body as they grow, I had been unable to like spiders. It was both fascinating and strange to hear the names that came out of Dahn's mouth: wolf spider, tarantula, crab spider, brown recluse . . . Sydney funnel-web spider.

"The strongest are the funnel-webs."

Once he started talking about spiders, he would not stop. He told me that spiders had descended from trilobites, which lived in the Cambrian period of the Paleozoic era, and that spiders had lived underground a long time ago but came aboveground from the Mesozoic era to the Cenozoic. He added that the number of species had increased exponentially during that time, and now it was difficult to comprehend just how many there were. Do fear and love share the same root? I wondered if he was really scared of them. He knew everything there was to know about spiders, the way you take a deep interest in something because you love it so much.

"When did you start being afraid of spiders?" I asked.

"A long time ago."

"But how come I never knew?"

"You couldn't have known."

"Why not? Was it a big secret?"

"You don't love me . . . That's why you didn't know."

I stared at him as he walked ahead of me in the dark despite his dread of coming across a spider. Each word—*you don't love me*—hit me like raindrops falling from the eaves.

"Did something bad happen to make you afraid of spiders?"

"Not that I remember."

"Then what is it? Why spiders, of all things?"

"Why do you have to add 'of all things' after 'spiders'? Would it be any different if I said I was afraid of owls or squirrels?"

Talking about spiders seemed to have put Dahn on edge. But he had a point.

"You should just stare at a spider, head on, with your eyes wide open . . . Maybe you'll overcome your fear."

"I tried that. Someone told me it was all in my head and that I should go see this spider museum way down in Namyangju. Confront some giant spiders and face them down. But the sight of the taxidermied ones alone made me itch all the way down to the skin under my toenails. I felt like my blood was running backward and my whole body was swelling up like one big blister."

"It's that bad?"

"It really is."

I unhooked my finger from Dahn's and looked at him straight on. He stood still, like a man waiting to be sentenced. I opened my arms and wrapped them around him.

"Don't be afraid." Those words were meant for me, too. "We'll be okay, we'll be fine."

The light from Dahn's headlamp, which had been sweeping the ground for spiders, shone on my face.

"Can I kiss you?" he asked.

I didn't say anything.

Dahn's lips hesitantly brushed my cheek, my forehead. After a moment, he brought his lips to mine. They were warm and sweet.

"I never thought you would be my first kiss," Dahn said.

I couldn't help but let out a small laugh. As if I could have known either that he would be my first kiss and that it would turn out to be so unexciting. Against the night sky, the mountain's spine looked like a ferocious animal. Its dark silhouette, like a large black beast lying on its stomach with its mouth open, was growing more distinct. As we got closer to the mountain, I started to feel afraid. I suggested turning back. But though he shook with fear of the spiders that he would never have known were there if not for the headlamp, he was adamant that we go the rest of the way to my mother's grave. Nocturnal birds took flight, moving from tree to tree, as if spooked by the sound of us arguing about whether to turn back or press on. We continued toward the grave. Dahn was so busy shining the light on the path and in the air, checking for spiders, that he had trouble keeping his footing. He kept moving forward, though, even while describing how his knees would go weak at the mere sight of a spider, and how seeing one in the daylight, even from a distance, could give him cold sores. I thought if he was that afraid, he could just avoid looking at them. Why the compulsion to hunt them down with his headlamp? What if he actually saw one? Maybe searching for them with his own eyes was his way of coping with his fear. *So that's the kind of person you are*, I thought. I had learned something new about Dahn. At long last, Dahn guided me through the dark to my mother's grave, fighting off the fearsome spiders along the way.

"We're here."

As soon as we reached the grave, Dahn let out a deep sigh. It was the joyful sigh of one who had conquered his fear.

"Let's bow," he said.

"At this time of night?"

"Isn't that why we came?"

"No," I said.

I told him not to, but Dahn bowed anyway, the headlamp still in place. When he was done, he shone the light on the crepe-myrtle tree and murmured, "So this is where he moved it." He went over to the tree, took out a cigarette, and lit it; meanwhile, the thread tied around my finger came undone. The crushed balsam paste fell in front of the grave with a plop. Dahn's cigarette flickered in the dark. He must have been rubbing his face with it between his fingers, because the ember danced around like a firefly. In front of my mother's grave, I grabbed a fistful of soil, squeezed it together in my hand like a ball of rice, and put it in my pocket. The soil was probably touching my mother's ring. Swayed by a sense of emptiness that made me want to grasp on to something, I looked over at Dahn where he was fidgeting beneath the crepe-myrtle, the lantern on his head and cigarette in his mouth, unable to set his feet anywhere comfortably for fear there might be a spider beneath the tree as well, and I nearly asked him, *Do you love me?* If I had, Dahn and I might have drifted apart irreversibly. I swallowed my words and stared at my mother's grave. Then and there, I decided it was time to return to the city.

"Students are protesting every day at my university," Dahn said.

I balled up more soil from my mother's grave and put it in my pocket.

"I beat up one of my friends," he said.

"You did?"

"It was someone I met my freshman year. He loved to eat. No matter what he ate, even if it was nothing special, he could make it look like it was the best thing he'd ever tasted. Made you hungry, too, just to see it. We threw him a going-away party because he said he was joining the army, but he wound up in the riot guard instead. He was sent back to our university to put down a demonstration. What luck, right? He gets sent to his own school, of all places . . . Whenever I walked past the riot guard, he would be standing there, drenched with sweat in the blazing sun. A few times, I saw him sitting on the ground next to the police bus, the kind with barbed wire over the windows, stuffing spoiled-looking rice into his mouth. Each time, I thought about how he used to eat so well, and I felt something surge up inside of me. Then one day, he and his buddies were chasing some students, and he fell behind. It was just he and I. I don't know why I did it. When I saw him fall out of rank, I went after him. He spun around and recognized me. Neither of us smiled. We grappled—I don't know who took the first swing—and just started pummeling each other, torso and limbs, blindly . . . He tried to run back to his group, but I stayed right on him, kept him from going anywhere, and beat the hell out of him again."

"Why'd you do it?"

"Don't know. Felt like I was going crazy. Couldn't stand it."

"Stand what?"

"Myself . . . us . . . my situation . . . I mean, *our* situation."

I listened quietly.

"Just because I attacked him doesn't mean I was the only one swinging. I took a beating as well. He punched me in the head, gave me a black eye, everything. He tried to shake me off, but I wouldn't let him get away. I chased him, and then he chased me, and then I chased him again. It was all a blur. All that was left was the urge to destroy. Each time he tried to get away, I chased after him only to get more beat up, but I would not stop. When I finally came to, I was lying in my dorm room. Someone must have carried me there."

I wanted to say something to him, but I could not think of anything to say.

"I can't sleep. I can't do anything." His voice grew so quiet that I could barely hear him. "I've been thinking about leaving school and joining the army."

There was nothing I could do to make him feel better. Nothing other than go to him, take his hand, and swing it back and forth in the dark.

When I told my father I was going back to school, he handed me two bankbooks that my mother had left to me. One was for the money from my mother's life insurance policy, and the other was the one my mother kept before she got sick. He told me to find a place of my own in the city. Both bankbooks had my name printed inside them. I opened the second bankbook: it listed the money my mother had saved up before she got sick. She had deposited a little bit every day, without fail. How did my father keep from spending it? I tried to give the life insurance money back to my father. But he insisted that she'd meant for me to have it. He said, "You're a grown-up now, so you have to look after yourself." While I was packing for the city, I put the bankbooks in the bottom of my bag. Several times on the train, I took them out and tried to count how much money she had deposited each day. I could picture her hands. Some days, it was ten thousand won, others thirty thousand, still others eighty thousand . . . Then one day, something must have happened, because she had deposited two hundred thousand all at one time. I withdrew some cash and rented an *oktap bang*, a converted studio—a shack, really—on a rooftop, in a hilly neighborhood near my cousin's apartment. The first thing I unpacked was the soil from my mother's grave, still clumped together like a ball of rice. Then I put on my tennis shoes and walked to the bookstore on Jongno Street to buy a copy of Emily Dickinson's poetry and an atlas with detailed maps of the city. On the way back, I stopped at a florist and bought a flowerpot. I put the soil from my mother's grave in the flowerpot and opened the atlas. Having returned after a year to this city, I decided it was time I got to know it. In order to do that, I would explore every corner of it on foot.

Haven't been to school in days. Registered for classes, but the only one I feel like going to is Professor Yoon's. The school is still a riot zone. I got there half an hour early so I could stop by the bookstore. I hadn't been by in a long time. The guy who works there looked happy to see me. He said really loudly, "Still single, huh?"

Does it show that I don't have a girlfriend? I asked how he could tell whether I was seeing someone or not.

"It's written all over your face!" he said.

"Excuse me?"

"I can tell just by looking at you that it's been a long time since your last kiss."

He slapped me on the shoulder. I looked through the piles of textbooks, magazines, and new books, but all I wound up buying was this small brown leather-bound journal that I am now writing in. I like the color and how it feels in my hand. I'm going to use it to write down my thoughts and things that happen. Figure it'll go missing eventually. I've left my bag on the subway before. Another time, I slipped my sneakers off at a bar and forgot them there under the table. I lost all of the journals that I filled with chicken scratch in high school. It's like all of the thoughts and feelings that I had scribbled down were lost along with the journals that held them. But I pulled myself together and decided to start writing again. I wanted to give my journal a title to commemorate the event. I thought about calling it "Sae Notes." Sae means "new," but it can also mean "between," as well as "bird." A bird flying freely through the heavens . . . But if I do that, should I call it "Sae Notes" or "Notes of Sae"? That sounds strange. "Wind Notes"? "Spring Notes"? "Proof of Existence"? I spent a couple of hours pondering different names but finally settled on "Brown Notebook." Because the cover is brown. Boring, I know. Why am I even writing this? I have no idea. Not a clue. I just hope that compared with my previous diaries, whatever I write here will be proof of my maturity and growth.

| | |

I took a photography class in high school. I found a book one day by Roland Barthes in which he wrote, "Writing develops like a seed." It was like coming across a window. Later, I found out that Barthes had also written about photography. I read Camera Lucida, which made me want to start taking photos. My father owned a camera, but I had never seen him use it. He would take it out once in a while and stroke it and talk about how if my grandfather hadn't left the bathhouse to him, he would have become a photographer and traveled around the world. I wanted to try my father's camera out for myself. But when I joined the class, there was nothing for me to learn. No one there had ever heard of studium *or* punctum, *which I'd picked up from reading Barthes. They'd never even heard the name Barthes before. I got sick of the* club. One day, the teacher was explaining how to take portraits. I was restless and couldn't take another minute of it. I tried to slip out of the classroom unseen, but the teacher yelled my name and stopped me in my tracks.

"Yi Myungsuh! Where do you think you're going?"

I told him I had to go to the doctor.

"What's wrong with you?"

I wasn't really sick, and I didn't really have to go. I just wanted to get out of there.

"I said, what's wrong with you?" the teacher yelled again.

I didn't know what to say. I hesitated and then blurted out, "My heart is broken."

Even I was shocked by how immature I sounded. I thought, now I'll be a total laughingstock. He'll make me run around the track ten, maybe twenty, times. The photography teacher also taught science. Whenever students disobeyed him in class, he would make them do an army crawl, or cane them, or make them run around the track when the sun was at its hottest until they dropped from exhaustion. I resigned myself to being punished, but the teacher's reaction caught me by surprise.

"Your heart is broken?" He gazed at me abstractedly through his glasses. "Better hurry then. And don't be late for next period."

| | |

I left the campus and climbed the hill behind the school. There, I lay on top of a grave that seemed to have no owner and gazed up at a fluffy white cloud floating in the sky like an island before eventually heading back to photography class. After that day, I never missed a single session. I even became more interested in science, which I had never done well in before. If I had not gone up to the grave on the hill behind the school and watched that cloud drifting in the sky, I probably would have given the camera back to my father.

| | |

Massive demonstration today. This morning, I went to throw the newspaper out, but a picture of some dogs caught my eye and I opened it back up again. It was a story about two abandoned dogs. One of the dogs was blind. Everywhere they went, the dog with good eyesight stayed right next to the blind dog to protect it. When they crossed the street or stopped for a drink of water, the seeing dog stood watch while the blind dog went first. The article said the dogs had even been seen resting their heads together or on each other's bellies when they were tired. Whenever the blind dog stopped walking, the seeing dog would stop as well.

Was it training, or instinct?

They say that a dog will not voluntarily guide another dog that cannot see, and yet such a dog exists. What does it mean? Stormy days continue. I feel as though I've been cast out at school and on the streets with a blindfold over my eyes. I stared long and hard at the photo of the two dogs.

—Brown Notebook 1

CHAPTER 2

Water Crosser

Two hours before class, I put on my sneakers and left my room. I was going to walk to school instead of taking the bus. On my way out, I paused to look at the dirt from my mother's grave that I had put in the flowerpot and thought about what kind of flower to plant in it. Though I had checked the route on the map before leaving, it was a winding and unfamiliar path. The road dead-ended, forcing me to backtrack and take a pedestrian overpass instead. At the top of the overpass, I paused to lean over the railing and look around. Everything looked different from above. I could see the roofs and tops of things and the small alleyways branching off the main street. There were windows and cars and trashcans, rooftops and streetlights, a bathhouse chimney, and far off in the distance, the tops of people's heads as they came and went.

Viewing the world from a different angle made it all look strange and dynamic, as if seeing it for the first time—the sycamores and ginkgo trees planted along the road, the small, shy-looking flowerbeds, the hand-painted theater billboards.

From the overpass, and especially through the thick tangle of power lines, the sky looked vast and endless. I had always looked up at the overpass but never looked down from on top of it. The tops of the cars looked flat and harmless, and the trees were so thick and lush that their branches grazed the windows of the buildings. As I kept going, I came across a large traffic tunnel. I peered inside and debated whether to just walk through. But I couldn't tell how far the tunnel went, and there were no signs indicating that it was open to pedestrians. I strained my eyes to try to see where the deep, dark tunnel ended, but then changed my mind and walked back to a bus stop instead. There, I caught a bus the rest of the way to the university.

School was the same as when I had left.

The drama majors were still posing as if they were waiting for Godot, the photography students ran around lugging heavy camera bags, and the students from the classical Korean music department crowded into the small theater with their stringed *gayageums*, eyebrows penciled in, hair pulled into chignons, and faces drawn into prim expressions. I thought about how I used to peek through the front gate—the campus itself always exuding the excitement of a performance about to begin—and debate whether or not to enter. But instead of making me hesitate, those memories emboldened me, and I strode lightly into the school. I barely recognized anyone. The few boys in my department whom I would have recognized must have been off completing their military service, and even the girls I had gone to class with had permed their hair since then, or started wearing makeup and piling on the accessories, or had work done on their eyes. On my way to the lecture hall, I looked for things that had not changed: the library, the campus bookstore, the school post office, the wooden benches in front of the lotus pond where I used to sit. I let out a sigh of relief at the sight of them. The smell of tear gas in the air was also unchanged.

My first class was Professor Yoon's.

As luck would have it, it was in the same room as before. I went in and sat in the back, where everyone was clustered. Though I had promised myself I would not sit alone, it felt uncomfortable to be staring at the back of a boy's head just inches away from me, so I moved to a seat near the window. In the very last row, a boy and girl were sitting side by side as if they were a couple. Was he a reentry student? He looked older than the rest of us. I didn't know him, but he looked strangely familiar. He was so tall that he seemed to be scrunched into the desk, and his eyes never seemed to leave the face of the girl next to him as they talked. Suddenly he turned to look at me. I pretended to rub my face and turned back around. But something made me turn to look at them again. Something about the girl kept tugging at me. I leaned over to try to get a peek at her face, but even with my cheek practically grazing the desk, I still could not get a good look. Her long black hair spilled forward and hid her face from view. I had no idea what he was saying to her, but she lowered her face each time he spoke.

"Yi Myungsuh."

"Here."

It was only when Professor Yoon started calling attendance that I found out his name was Myungsuh.

The past merged with the present.

Professor Yoon was as thin as ever, as unchanged as the stone steps in front of the library. Even his eyes, deep and keen, which had grimaced in pain when he stood in the window and looked down at the rioting students, were the same as before. Whenever I was alone, my memories from a year ago were hazy and indistinct; now that I was back in the same classroom, the old me was as sharp and clear as if she were sitting right in front of me. Professor Yoon called each name in turn. When he got to Myungsuh's name, he looked up from the attendance sheet.

"Shouldn't you have graduated by now?" he asked, and smiled at Myungsuh from over his glasses.

Myungsuh scratched his head and smiled. It was a bashful smile, but it spread from ear to ear. You couldn't help but smile, too, when you saw it. Nevertheless, the girl beside him kept her head down. I wanted to know her name. I listened carefully as Professor Yoon read the rest of the attendance sheet. Had I missed it? He finished calling roll, but he had not called her name. When he put the sheet away, I looked back at the two of them again.

Yi Myungsuh. I wrote his name down. When was the last time I'd written someone's name in my notebook? I kept casually glancing back at them during class. Each time, I noticed something different—his wavy hair, his strong profile, the way he twirled his pencil—but I didn't learn anything about her. She sat in the same position the whole time and did not lift her head. All I could see was a glimpse of her nose from behind the long veil of hair. I felt intensely curious about her name, her eyes. There was something about her that made me want to find out more. Professor Yoon must have felt it, too, because his gaze kept drifting over to her during his lecture.

Since it was the first day of the semester, we expected the class to just be a general overview of the syllabus. Professor Yoon told us which texts were required and which were recommended reading, and then he listed off the things we had to keep in mind while attending his class, most of which amounted to threats, such as if we were more than ten minutes late we should not even think of entering the classroom, or if we failed to turn in three or more assignments in a row then we would get an automatic F. Several other professors had already given the same speech, so everyone's eyes were starting to glaze over with boredom. Some students even assumed class was almost over and were already packing up their pens and notebook.

Professor Yoon adjusted his glasses and gazed out the window. The shouting of student demonstrators outside burst into the room. Nothing had changed since last year. Professor Yoon glanced around the room.

"Have any of you heard about a man named Christopher?"

Christopher?

The name Christopher reminded me of a book I'd read in high school called *Jean-Christophe*, by Romain Rolland. It was a ten-volume fictionalized account of the life of Beethoven. It was the only book I had ever seen my cousin read, so I read it, too. I was deeply impressed by the main character, who becomes ever more positive in the face of increasing despair. Regardless of what happens, he never gives up on his quest for self-perfection. Filled with a sense of awe and admiration for the main character, I read every volume in a thrall of emotions and held those yellow books printed with his name close to my heart. I even wanted to see the Rhine one day because the title character was born in a small town on the banks of that river. I wondered if Professor Yoon was referring to the same person, but I was not confident enough to raise my hand and say that I had heard about him. I sat up straight and fixed my eyes on Professor Yoon. The walls of the classroom seemed to drop away and leave us all, professor and students alike, standing in the middle of an open field with the wind blowing over us. Nobody said a word, so Professor Yoon continued.

"Christopher is the name of a medieval European saint. Some of you must be churchgoers. Has no one heard of him?"

One student hesitantly raised her hand. She stammered, "I don't know, but . . ."

"Then tell us what you do know," Professor Yoon quipped.

Everyone giggled. The girl stood up and said that she had heard the story from her Sunday school teacher when she was young and therefore did not remember it clearly, but was he talking about the man who was saved because he carried Jesus across a river? It was more of a question than an answer. Professor Yoon nodded. When the girl sat back down, Professor Yoon cleared his throat, glanced around the classroom, and said in a low voice that there was indeed such a legend. The students who thought class was almost over and had begun clearing their desks stared at Professor Yoon. He gripped the podium and began his lecture.

"This is the story of Saint Christopher.

"According to legend, Christopher was a Canaanite. A giant, some say. A man of great strength who was afraid of nothing. He made up his mind to serve only the greatest, strongest man in the world. But no matter where he looked, he could find none worth devoting his life to. Everyone disappointed him. He grew weary of ever finding someone worth serving and became despondent. But here, I'll spare you the boring details and get straight to the most important part. Christopher built a house for himself on the banks of a river and made a living carrying travelers across the water. He was very strong. He owned only a single pole, but he used it to pick his way through even the roughest current and carry people safely to the other side. It was just a pastime to him. He was a boatman with no boat, a man who ferried people with his body."

The world seemed to have come to a stop. In a classroom filled with thirty, maybe forty, students, no one so much as cleared their throat.

"One night, Christopher was fast asleep when he heard a faint voice calling his name. Wondering whom it could be at that time of night, he opened the door. But there was no one there. Only darkness. He closed the door and went back to bed, but the voice returned. *Christopher!* He opened the door again, but just as before, there was only darkness. The third time he heard the voice, it sounded like it was right beside him. He looked all around but saw no one. Thinking this odd,

Christopher took up his pole and headed down to the river. There in the darkness beside the river was a small child. The child told him he had to get to the other side before the night ended, and he asked Christopher to carry him across. The child was so young and his plea so earnest that Christopher agreed to help, despite the late hour. He put the child on his shoulders and entered the river. But the moment he stepped into the river, the water began to rise. In an instant, it nearly reached over the tall Christopher's head. And that was not all. The child, so light at first, grew heavier the higher the waters rose. The weight, like a massive piece of iron, so unbelievable for such a small child, pressed down on Christopher's shoulders. The waters rose inch by inch, and the child pressed down on him with its enormous weight. The once overly confident Christopher began to tremble with fear for the first time at the thought that he might drown. Barely able to keep his balance with the pole, Christopher plowed his way through the water with the child on his shoulders and just made it to the other side. As he set the child down, he said, 'I thought I was going to die because of you. Though you are so small, you were so heavy that it felt as if I was carrying the weight of the world. I have carried many across this river, but I have never carried one so heavy as you.' At that moment, the child vanished and Jesus appeared before him, surrounded by a dazzling light. He said, 'Christopher! What you just carried was no child. It was I, Christ. When you crossed that river, you *were* carrying the world on your shoulders.'"

Professor Yoon paused and looked around the room. I thought at first that he was trying to tell whether we understood the story. But then I thought maybe he had discovered something anew, something he had forgotten, about Saint Christopher. He held his silence for a moment and then resumed.

"So let me ask you this. Are those of you here today Christopher? Or are you the child he carries on his back?"

Professor Yoon's story had started out like a single drop of rain amid the hustle and bustle of students preparing for class to end but turned into a sudden midday shower beating down on us. A clear ray of light from the last of the summer sun slipped in through a classroom window that someone had shut tight.

Professor Yoon studied us expectantly, but nobody offered an answer to his question. The slogans of student demonstrators outside followed the ray of sunlight through the window and pushed their way again into our midst. Over his glasses, Professor Yoon's keen and gentle eyes stopped on each of us in turn before moving on.

"Each of you is both Christopher and the child he carries on his back. You are all forging your way through adversity in this difficult world on your way to the other side of the river. I did not tell you this story in order to talk about religion. We are all travelers crossing from this bank to that bank, from this world to nirvana. But the waters are rough. We must rely on something in order to make it over. That something could be the art or literature that you aspire to create. You will think that the thing you choose will serve as your boat or raft to carry you to that other bank. But if you think deeply about it, you may find that it does not carry you but rather you carry it. Perhaps only the student who truly savors this paradox will make it safely across. Literature and art are not simply what will carry you; they are also what you must lay down your life for, what you must labor over and shoulder for the rest of your life."

Everyone's eyes were fixed on Professor Yoon. Nobody looked out the window. Even the boy in the back row had stopped twirling his pencil. The girl, too, had lifted her head and was listening intently.

"You are Saint Christopher. You are the ones who will ferry the child across the river. It is your fate to brave the swollen waters. Though the waters may rise, you must not stop before the child reaches the other side. So, how do we cross this river?"

It both was and was not a question. Professor Yoon's voice dropped even lower and grew stronger.

"We cross by becoming Saint Christopher to one another. By carrying the child across together. There is no difference between the person who crosses and the person who helps another across. You are not just Saint Christopher, carrying your pole into the rising waters. You are the world and its creators, each one of you. Sometimes you are the Christopher and other times you are the child—you carry each other across the river. So you must treasure yourselves and hold one another dear."

The trust that had been budding inside each of us spread throughout the classroom. Had one of the windows broken at that moment, not even the sound of breaking glass could have disturbed the gentle stillness.

"So, my young Christophers! That is all for today. But before you go, I need a volunteer. Someone to type up the course reader for me."

No one said anything.

"Anyone?"

Saint Christopher, the child, the river, fate, us . . . I had started off taking notes but quickly became too absorbed in his story. I raised my hand to volunteer. I didn't even think about it as I did so. Professor Yoon looked at me for a moment.

"Your name?"

"It's Jung Yoon."

"Jung Yoon." He said my name aloud once. "Thank you. Come to my office after class."

Even after the professor left, everyone remained seated. Finally, I got up to follow him to his office. When I pushed my seat back, the scraping of the chair across the floor echoed in the silent room. On that cue, the others also started to gather up their things and leave. Professor Yoon's office was in the opposite direction of my next class. I glanced behind me. Myungsuh and the girl were walking under a large green zelkova tree that I had just passed.

The girl had a distinctive walk. Anyone who saw it would not easily forget it. With the early-autumn sunlight pouring down on me, I stopped to watch her. There were many students by the tree. They gathered there in pairs or small groups before heading off in separate directions or staying behind to wait for someone. Yet even amid all those people moving at the same time, she caught my eye. She was the one I noticed first, not the boy walking beside her. But as she walked toward me with her bag hanging from her shoulder and a book in her hand, I still could not see her face. She kept her head down and shoulders rolled in as she walked, as if staring at her own heart. Nevertheless, she was beautiful. It was the skirt she wore, a flared skirt with white flowers on a dark blue background, with a white cotton jacket. The brightness of the tiny flowers blooming across her skirt clashed with the rest of her and made her stand out. When she passed the tree, the hem of her skirt floated up in the breeze. Whatever it was that made her different from the others seemed to emanate from that skirt. It was not a popular style for our age group; most wore pants or blue jeans. Even the students who did wear skirts never wore that kind of billowy style.

The boy's walk was just as distinct as hers. He looked like someone who walked on air, rather than someone who lived with his feet on the ground. One foot seemed already aloft before the other had touched down. If she looked like she was sinking into the earth, he looked like he might be whisked away by the wind at any moment. I watched them walk toward me and then turned around.

I reached Professor Yoon's office and was about to knock, but the door was already ajar. I pushed it open. The professor looked up at me. It looked at first like there was a partition between his desk and a sofa, but it turned out to be stacks and stacks of books serving as a room divider. Professor Yoon's desk sat behind the books.

"Come in," he said, the upper half of his body materializing from above the stacks. I saw that he was holding a sheaf of paper. "Have a seat over there for a moment."

Professor Yoon seemed to have been in the middle of something or was busy straightening up his desk; when he sat back down, I heard papers being shuffled. I remained standing and looked around his office. It was drab. There were no plants or picture frames—just books, crammed into industrial shelves designed to hold as many books as possible, and not so much as a calendar or a mirror hanging on the wall. Old books, which looked as if they would crumble to pieces if I touched them, were shelved backward so the titles were not visible. I had never seen books shelved that way before. I reached for one out of curiosity but was stopped by a knock at the door. Professor Yoon and I looked up at the same time. The door opened and in walked the boy and girl I had just seen walking toward me beneath the zelkova tree. They had also been heading to Professor Yoon's office. The professor looked at the two of them and stood and walked over to the sofa, the sheaf of papers still in his hands.

"Aren't you bored of me yet?" Professor Yoon said to the boy. "Seems time we went our separate ways."

He was smiling warmly. Myungsuh scratched his head and grinned, as he had back in the classroom.

"I wanted to introduce my friend to you," Myungsuh said.

"You weren't enough, so you brought a friend? Have a seat. You, too."

Professor Yoon looked at me as I stood in front of the bookshelf. I felt I was experiencing this moment over again, even though it was happening for the first time. When we all sat down, Professor Yoon and I were next to each other, and the boy and girl were across from us. It felt awkward to sit next to Professor Yoon, but it would have been just as awkward to sit next to the girl. She and Myungsuh were like each other's shadow, making the thought of sitting between them inconceivable. It was strange. As we sat there, the feeling of déjà vu persisted, as if we had sat that way before. The boy and I looked each other in the eyes for the first time. His eyebrows were jet black, as if they had been rubbed on with charcoal—the kind of black that made you feel as if you were being sucked into it. Each time his face changed expression, his eyebrows moved first. His friends could probably tell what mood he was in just by looking at them. Below his brows, his thoughtful-looking eyes seemed to smile for a moment before skipping over mine and settling on the girl. The girl kept her hands in her pockets and did not look at me.

"We've been friends our whole lives," the boy named Myungsuh said. "She goes to another university. She's on a leave of absence right now and would like to audit your class. We came to ask your permission."

When I heard him say how long they had been friends, I pictured Dahn's face.

"She's on a leave of absence from her regular school?" the professor asked.

"Yes," Myungsuh said.

"What's your name?"

"Yoon Miru." Myungsuh answered for her, but Professor Yoon kept directing his questions to her.

"Mireu?"

"No, sir. Not Mireu. Miru, as in the poplar tree," Myungsuh said again.

Yoon Miru. I whispered her name to myself, quietly, so no one else could hear. *Yoon Miru. Yoon Miru.*

"Why do you keep answering for her?" Professor Yoon asked. "Are you her lawyer?"

Myungsuh smiled bashfully.

"Why do you want to sit in on my class?" the professor asked.

Miru raised her head. Finally I could see her face. She blinked and lowered her head again. Her eyes were dark, so dark that they seemed to be all pupils. Though she was looking down, I could see her smooth forehead. The bridge of her nose was high and narrow. She had full, bee-stung lips, which gave the contours of her face a graceful beauty. If that were all, she would have been memorable enough for just her pretty face and fair skin. But then she took her hands out of her pockets. I flinched. It was an instantaneous reaction. Her hands. Despite her smooth face, the backs of her hands were withered and wrinkled. They looked like they had been soaking in water for too long. Miru, so pretty with her dark eyes and fair skin, had the hands of an old person. That was the answer to the curiosity I had felt, why I had wondered who she was ever since trying to get a glimpse of her face in the classroom, and the key to the incongruity that could not be explained by her flared floral-print skirt alone. She must have felt my eyes on her hands because she slipped them back into her pockets. Professor Yoon seemed to have noticed them as well. He looked as surprised as I was. An awkward silence opened up between us.

"What happened to your hands?" Professor Yoon asked Miru.

I would never have guessed that Professor Yoon would be so blunt. Her hands were painful even to look at. She took them out of her pockets, lifted them up in front of her, spread her fingers, and looked down at the backs of them. I had not expected her to do that. She stared at them as if they belonged to someone else.

"I burned them," she said.

That was the first time I heard her speak. Her voice was clear and distinct.

"Hot water?"

"No, gasoline."

"That must have been very painful," Professor Yoon whispered under his breath. He did not ask how it happened. Miru turned her hands over, looked at her palms, and said yes.

"But surely you don't regard them as a symbol of who you are?"

My stomach sank when he said that, but Miru looked composed. Beside her, Myungsuh raised his eyebrows and sat up straighter on the couch. He seemed to want to stop their conversation before it went any further.

"Well, Professor, I guess we will take that as a yes," Myungsuh said.

Professor Yoon raised his head but looked at Miru instead.

"Everywhere you go, you stand out."

There was another awkward silence.

"I noticed you, even before I saw your hands. I've never met you before, but you stand out from the others."

An odd tension filled the room.

"Free yourself from your hands." Professor Yoon spoke calmly. "If you want to be free of your hands, then audit my class. If not, then don't waste your time."

Miru's dark eyes seemed to scowl at Professor Yoon. I realized then that the strange energy she gave off was also anxiety. Her eyes flared with nervous energy, and she looked like she might attack Professor Yoon. But almost immediately, they wavered. Her eyes turned to rest on me. Full of questions and pleas, her eyes seemed to be asking for rescue. I reached my hand out to her. Her dark eyes locked on my fingers. Myungsuh stood and gently took her hand. Her wrinkled hand was caught in his big, strong one. Her burned hand disappeared into his, as if that were the most suitable place in the world for it.

"We'll be going now," he said.

Miru stood up. Myungsuh guided her before him to the door and was about to leave when he turned and looked back at me.

"Jung Yoon." He enunciated my full name precisely. "It's been a year."

I didn't think it was strange of him to say my full name that way. Since I had found out his name only during attendance, he had probably learned my name the same way. Nevertheless, when he spoke to me, I felt a sudden premonition that I would soon be walking around the city with the two of them.

"Thank you," he said.

He stood there without leaving, as if waiting for me to respond. I didn't know what he was thanking me for, but I nodded. Finally, he gave a slight bow to Professor Yoon. Miru seemed to be looking at me as well, her scarred hand still enveloped by his large one.

After the two of them left, Professor Yoon and I were quiet for a moment. He had seemed so cold to Miru for some reason, but he let out a deep sigh and turned back into the same person who had told the story of Saint Christopher during class.

"Are you a fast typist?" he asked.

I grinned nervously instead of answering.

"Are you?"

I smiled again.

"You should answer clearly, not just smile, when a teacher asks you a question."

I thought of how his voice sounded when he said *then tell us what you do know* to the girl in class. I had long been in the habit of smiling when I wasn't sure how to answer someone. No one had ever pointed it out to me before.

"I'm sort of fast," I said.

"How fast?"

"Fast enough that I can compose as I type."

"I see. I envy people who can type with all ten fingers. I've tried to learn, but it's too hard for me. I'm what you call a hunt and peck typist. Unlike you, my hands can't keep up with my thoughts. When I try to type, my thoughts keep stopping and looking back as my hands try to catch up."

The professor had a unique way of speaking that was unfamiliar to me, but I sort of understood what he meant.

Maybe what Professor Yoon felt when he was unable to get ahead of or catch up to the thoughts in his head when he typed and instead watched his fingers slowly lagging behind the sentences that had already come into the world was similar to how I felt the night I walked to my mother's grave with Dahn, when I realized I had to break through the lethargy I felt at my parents' house and return to the city. That night, when I nearly asked Dahn if he loved me, after he had told me about the mess he was in after beating up a classmate, I knew I had to come back to the city. That was what stopped me from asking Dahn that question. You should only ask someone if they love you if you love them, regardless of what their answer might be. My decision that night, when I grabbed a handful of dirt from my mother's grave, had brought me back to the city, but my heart had not yet returned and seemed to be roaming around out there somewhere.

I thought, too, about my cousin's husband, who had once said something like Professor Yoon. Each time my cousin's husband returned from a week of flying, the dinner table would be set with his favorite foods. Rice, seaweed soup, grilled dried corvina, steamed egg, toasted dried laver, seasoned spinach, mung bean sprouts, and radish—all of the things he liked. The three of us ate together sometimes. One night, he was too exhausted to eat. My cousin set the grilled corvina on the table and asked if he needed to see a doctor, but he told her not to worry. He said the plane was too fast, his body had arrived first. That he felt ill because his soul could not keep pace with the speed of the plane and was still on its way home, and he would feel better once it had caught up to the rest of him.

Professor Yoon handed me the sheaf of papers.

"It's a collection of works by Korean writers, dating back to the 1950s. There are a lot of pages. Won't it be too much for you?"

"I can handle it."

"After you type them all up, I plan to print copies to use in class as our course reader. I'm sorry to put you up to this, but maybe it will help you study."

Small scraps of paper were stuck between the pages of the manuscript. Some of the pages had Post-its covered with handwritten notes. Professor Yoon took a large envelope from the top of his desk and slid the manuscript inside. His slim fingers caught my eye.

"You can add the comments on the notes to the manuscript according to the directions I wrote down."

I had learned to type while living with my cousin. The landlord's daughter, who was the same age as me, attended a vocational high school and owned a typewriter. She must have owned a great many things, but all I ever thought about was that typewriter. I wanted it so badly that when I closed my eyes, I could easily picture the word *Clover* branded on the front. Whenever I had reason to go into her room, I would stand in front of the typewriter, stretch my fingers, and tap at the keys—*tak tak tak*. She did not like it at first when I touched her typewriter, but when she saw how fond I was of it, she taught me how to type. I learned the positions of all the keys and enjoyed the sound it made when I tapped them. Each time I moved my fingers—*tak tak tak*—the quiet keys leapt into action, and inky black letters appeared one by one on the white paper, like an answer to a question. Later on, the landlord's daughter started bringing it to our apartment so I could use it. Whenever that happened, I felt so excited and overjoyed that I clung to it like it was my mother. At first, I filled the paper with *ga*, *na*, *da*, *ra*, then *me*, *you*, *us* over and over, like someone first learning how to write. By the time I outpaced the landlord's daughter at typing, I was copying the letters Van Gogh had sent to his younger brother Theo. I started typing them because I liked the sound of the words *Dear Theo*.

Careful study and the constant and repeated copying of Bargue's Exercises au Fusain have given me a better insight into figure-drawing. I have learned to measure and to see and to look for the broad outlines, so that, thank God, what seemed utterly impossible to me before is gradually becoming possible now. I have drawn a man with a spade, that is *un bêcheur*, five times over in a variety of poses, a sower twice, a girl with a broom twice. Then a woman in a white cap peeling potatoes and a shepherd leaning on his crook and finally an old, sick peasant sitting on a chair by the hearth with his head in his hands and his elbows on his knees. And it won't be left at that, of course. Once a few sheep have crossed the bridge, the whole flock follows. Now I must draw diggers, sowers, men and women at the plough, without cease. Scrutinize and draw everything that is part of country life. Just as many others have done and are doing. I no longer stand helpless before nature as I used to.

I stopped in the middle of typing to stare at the part where he talked about copying Bargue's plates. He must have meant that he *no longer stood helpless before nature* because he had drawn those plates over and over. I folded up the typewritten paper and sent it to Dahn, hoping all the while that Dahn, who had vowed to never stop drawing, would become an artist like Van Gogh. Now I felt that all of that time I had spent learning how to type had led me to Professor Yoon.

My eyes drifted over to the shelf where the books sat facing in.

"Are you wondering why I shelved them that way?" the professor asked.

"Yes."

"They belong to writers who died before the age of thirty-three. I used to collect them."

Writers who died before the age of thirty-three . . . I savored the words in my head.

"You're probably now wondering why thirty-three. That's the age at which Jesus was crucified and Alexander the Great created his empire and died. After thirty-three, you can't really say you're young anymore. And don't we say that someone has died young if they die before the age of thirty-three? For artists, an early death is sometimes an honor. Their works fill me with awe and sympathy. If you're interested, you may borrow them."

"Thank you."

Professor Yoon walked around the wall of books. Suddenly he asked, "Are you friends with Miru?"

"I met her for the first time today," I said.

He looked at me for a moment.

"I also wanted to thank you."

He was echoing what Myungsuh had said right before leaving the office.

"Thank you for reaching out to her. I was only thinking about how to make her confront her issues, and it didn't occur to me to do what you did. I felt ashamed of myself. She didn't take your hand, but maybe she'll be able to free herself on her own, thanks to you."

Professor Yoon sat down at his desk with his back to me. He looked frail and tired. I watched him for a moment and then put the manuscript in my bag, left the office, and quietly closed the door. I looked at his name printed on the office door, turned the sign next to it to read *out of office*, and walked down the hallway. I made my way over to the big zelkova tree. I thought maybe Myungsuh and Miru would be there, but they were nowhere to be seen. A group of students walked quickly past. I sat on a bench beneath the tree and looked up. The distant sky was passing from summer to early autumn; white clouds like mounds of ice cream floated past. A breeze whispered through the branches. Had the school always been like this? The sting of tear gas in the air was the same as before, but the yew trees planted like a wall around the campus had never looked so green. Some distance away, the students I had just seen in the classroom were sitting on the grass together and talking. Their conversation carried all the way to where I sat beneath the zelkova. They were talking about the story of Saint Christopher.

"So, my young Christophers!" Someone was mimicking Professor Yoon. "Can someone answer the title of this book?"

He was holding up the textbook for Professor Yoon's writing class. It was titled *What Is Art?*

"Not demonstrating!" someone shouted in a self-mocking tone, and the cheerful mood instantly turned quiet. "Of what use is art to us? It can't teach us how to make money or get a job. It can't tell us how to succeed in romance. And it definitely can't tell us whether or not we should demonstrate!" He was speaking in a high-pitched voice, as if to lift the mood, but it didn't help. He fell back on the grass, looked up at the sky, and said, "Remember what Rimbaud said. The best thing in life is getting drunk on cheap liquor and sleeping on the beach."

"So what are you supposed to do after you sober up? What can you do?"

"Find more cheap liquor and roam the streets."

"Idiot!" the student who had mimicked Professor Yoon yelled. "You think you can live your whole life like some old bohemian?" He got up and ran off.

The boy lying on the grass sat up and looked over at the shouting student protesters. I rose from beneath the tree and walked around the old stone buildings on campus and the newer ones with elevators. I had never wandered around campus so intently before. Each time I saw a group of students, I scanned their faces. I didn't know at first who I was looking for. Once I realized I was looking for Myungsuh and Miru, I trudged back to the zelkova tree and sat there for a long time. They were nowhere to be seen.

I had that dream again. I think I hear someone calling me, so I open the door and look out. But all I see are layers of darkness. I take a single step into the dark and stand there. When I told Miru about the dream, she squeezed my hand tight. Told me not to follow the voice. Said if I have that dream again, I should keep the door shut and not go out, as if I could control the dream however I wanted.

"You won't go out there, right?" she asked. She looked so serious that she made me think I had dreamt something really remarkable.

"Only if you promise to stop looking for him," I said.

Miru gave me a hard look. I felt bad. Like I was letting her sister Mirae down. I apologized to her after a while.

"Please don't act like my parents," she said. "I'll never ask you to help me look for him again, so leave me alone."

I listened and didn't say a word. Miru cleared her throat and continued.

"If I don't find out what happened to the man my sister was looking for, I won't be able to live with myself."

| | |

A while back, before the semester started, Miru was reading one of the professor's books. It was a collection of essays that had come out six years ago. Miru suddenly asked me if he was a bachelor. I said that if by bachelor she meant someone who lives alone, then yes. She said she thought she knew why he lived alone. It was strange to see her talk that way about someone she had never met. The book she was reading, which was his only published work aside from two books of poetry published when he was younger, consisted of reveries on poetry, with no mention of his private life. He had not published anything else since that book, including any poetry collections. The only way to read his more recent work was to dig through old magazines in the library. Until Miru brought it up, I had never given any thought to the fact that he wasn't married, even though it was obvious he was a bachelor. I asked her how she knew.

"I think he's seen something," she said, and muttered under her breath, "It must haunt him."

I asked her why she said that.

"Look," she said. "What do you suppose this picture is doing here?"

She showed me the page. There was no mention of the artist, but I knew at once who it was.

"Arnold . . .

I stumbled on the pronunciation of his last name, so Miru finished for me.

"Arnold Böcklin."

She seemed to be turning something over in her head. Then she said she wanted to sit in on his class. I wondered aloud why someone who had stopped going to her own school would want to go to someone else's, but then I thought maybe it wasn't such a bad idea after all. Maybe the professor's class would help her turn her life around. Whenever I told her she should start acting like a normal college student again, she would retort, "You're one to talk!" She was becoming more like her sister every day. She said she would do whatever it took to find the man who had disappeared, the one her sister had failed to find. But how are you supposed to find someone who's dead? I didn't know what to say to her.

| | |

I saw Jung Yoon in class today. I thought that was her first name, but I guess it's just Yoon, and Jung is her family name. Turns out she was taking a break from school. She looks like she's lost weight. But then again, even when she was a new student, she never seemed happy or excited. I wonder what's bothering her. I could tell she didn't recognize me. One time, I walked behind her all the way to school. She was deep in thought, and the feeling coming off her was very strange. She stopped in front of the school. Just stood there without going in. I stopped, too, and waited to see what she would do. How often had I watched her from a distance? I had also watched her once as she was sitting by herself at school reading Emily Dickinson. She stood in front of the gate with her head down, scuffed the ground a few times, and then turned and walked away. She was gone in an instant.

| | |

That day, I didn't see her on campus at all. I found out later that she had applied for a leave of absence. She always kept her distance from others. Come to think of it, I'd never properly spoken to her except for one time when she was a new student. During that first semester, all of the students in our department had gone to Ilyeong on an overnight retreat. Out of all of those students, she was the only one who caught my eye. I still remember the way she looked: black hair falling to her shoulders, black vest over a white shirt, snow-white sneakers, stubbornly closed mouth. While everyone else sat in a circle next to the river and sang, she stared into the glowing flames and refused to sing along. The next morning, I woke up hungover on the floor of the guesthouse next to the others who had passed out drunk and got up and headed outside. The nausea was overwhelming. While I was dry heaving on all fours on the riverbank, I glimpsed her through the haze rising off the river. At first, I thought she had just dipped her face in the water. Her face was wet. When she noticed me watching her, she jumped and hid her face. I realized that she had been crying. Her eyes were puffy, like she had been weeping without restraint. She put her head down and walked away, but I followed her. She stopped next to the pile of wood leftover from the night before. The thick fog had settled over the charred remains of the campfire. She squatted next to the ashes. I sat beside her. She rested her arms on her knees and buried her face in them. I did the same. She lifted her head and rested it on her forearms. I did the same.

"Why are you copying me?" she asked.

"To make you laugh!"

She laughed weakly, as if to be polite.

"Do you know me?" she asked.

"Not yet."

"If you don't know me, then how can you make me laugh?"

She kept using the formal register with me, despite my attempts to get close to her.

"But I just did," I said.

She peered at me through the fog. Her eyes were still swollen. She must have seen me throwing up, because she took an aspirin out of her pocket, handed it to me, stood up, and disappeared into the mist.

— Brown Notebook 2

CHAPTER 3

We Are Breathing

I made the right decision to learn about the city by walking around it. Walking made me think more and focus on the world around me. Moving forward, putting one foot in front of the other, reminded me of reading a book. I came across wooded paths and narrow market alleyways where people who were strangers to me shared conversations, asked one another for help, and called out to one another. I took in both people and scenery.

After I found a way to get to school without having to go through the large traffic tunnel, I enjoyed walking to school as well. I had walked toward the school one day only to find myself back in front of the tunnel again. I looked around, wondering what to do, when I saw a staircase to the right of the tunnel. At the top of the stairs, a narrow, winding path led uphill over the tunnel and through old tile-roofed buildings. The school was only a couple of minutes away by bus, but if I took the path that led over the tunnel, it would be a good twenty minutes on foot. As I walked farther, I came across more staircases.

It felt like a different city up there. A tall, redbrick smoke-stack had BATHHOUSE painted on it in huge white letters. A house that sold clay jars of all sizes sat with its front gate open, and I even came across a sign for the Social Science Library. A crepe-myrtle tree like the one by my mother's grave was growing in an empty lot. But it must have been quite old, because the base of the trunk was incomparably thicker and the branches spread much wider than my mother's tree. At one point, the path became so narrow that I had to step to the side when two giggling girls wearing backpacks passed me in the opposite direction. People up there lived life at a slower pace and did not concern themselves with those who lived below the tunnel. I peeked over a shoulder-high wall to see slices of daikon radish drying on a round straw tray. Bright red chili peppers hung from vines planted in even rows in a blue plastic container. There was even the occasional flowerpot planted with premature chrysanthemums sitting in front of someone's house. In one alleyway, I came upon a long wooden deck placed between two of the houses upon which elderly women were kneading dough and julienning what looked like pumpkin. When I walked by, they stopped what they were doing and stared at me like I was another species. The first time I went through there, I walked very slowly so I could take it all in. But I soon grew so familiar with the place that I could get from one end to the other in ten minutes. Later still, even when I was not on that road, the road was with me. When it rained, I found myself wondering whether the straw tray had been taken inside. I even enjoyed the small pleasure of exchanging greetings with the girls who passed me on the street. I lowered my head when I saw a man mixing concrete. He had taken off his shirt and was dripping with sweat, and the tan lines from his undershirt made me aware of the difficulty of his labor. I discovered that if I took just a five-minute detour on the way from school back to my apartment, I could pass a street lined with used-book stores. I had to take an underpass and detour around a baseball stadium to get there, but it was worth it. I would stroll past the towering stacks of used books and pause to peruse the titles at the very bottom. When I got to know that street, the feeling of being a runaway, which I had had ever since I started walking around the city, finally started to soften.

During the nearly three weeks that I spent exploring the different paths to school, I did not see Miru once. I didn't see Myungsuh, either, except in Professor Yoon's class. Whenever I walked into the classroom, the first thing I did was check to see if he was there. He was always sitting by himself in the back, where he had sat next to Miru on the first day of class. Always in the same seat. I would glance back again at the end of class, but he was usually gone by then. Sometimes while walking, I got so distracted by my feelings toward him and Miru that I lost all track of where I was.

I didn't understand why I couldn't get Miru off of my mind. She haunted me. And when I was not in Professor Yoon's class, I wandered around the school wondering where Myungsuh might be. I didn't have anything to say to him, but I looked for him all the same. After a while, I couldn't tell whether the person I was really curious about was him or Miru.

Then one day, Professor Yoon distributed copies of the course reader that I had typed up. Myungsuh was not in class that day. Professor Yoon set the stack on the podium so everyone could grab a copy on the way out. I stared at the black letters of the manuscript that I had typed, then took two more copies and put them in my bag. I was thinking of Myungsuh and Miru. When Professor Yoon announced to the class that I was the one who had typed the manuscript, I unconsciously glanced back at Myungsuh's seat. I hadn't seen him when I first got there, but he might have come in after me. His seat was still empty. I was disappointed that he wasn't there to hear Professor Yoon tell everyone that I had done the typing. Though that was all I had done, I felt proud to see the printed and bound copies. On the cover of the finished book was the title, *We Are Breathing*. It was in Professor Yoon's handwriting.

Do not write a single sentence that abets violence.

That was the first sentence of *We Are Breathing*.

The first time I pulled the manuscript out of the envelope and read that sentence, I felt my spine straighten. I typed the sentence over and over, once for every year of my age, changing the paper as I went. I became so absorbed in typing that I felt like I was no longer the same person who had brought the manuscript home. Reviews of poems and stories personally selected by Professor Yoon filled the sheets of paper. I started to understand what he meant when he said he was sorry to put me up to it but that maybe it would help me as I studied. The notes tucked between the pages appeared to be an appendix. Post-it notes and arrows indicated where he wanted memos and other brief texts to be added to the manuscript. There were even poems copied down in Professor Yoon's handwriting that I felt I should look up on my own.

The next day I went to a shop that loaned out typewriters. I had seen the shop on my way to the bookstore on Jongno Street. The shortest rental period was one month. I rented a typewriter and lugged it home on the bus. After that, I found myself eager to get home from school every day so I could get back to typing. I could not take the extra ten minutes to walk through the neighborhood above the tunnel or the extra five minutes to visit the street with the used-book stores, so I would find myself on the bus instead.

When I first started typing, I was so loath to leave even a single typo that if I mistyped a letter, I started over with a new piece of paper. But after a while, I started correcting my typos with correction fluid instead. As I typed one page after another, I became more familiar with Professor Yoon's handwriting. At first, I racked my brain trying to decipher some of the letters, marking those pages for later if I could not figure them out. I went to the school library to compare his copies against the original texts. I could have checked with him directly, but I didn't want to. I wanted to give him the completed manuscript without having to ask any questions.

Whenever my shoulders ached at night from all the typing, I rested my arms on the windowsill and looked at the world outside. I gazed down at the light pouring out of the thick cluster of apartment buildings at the base of Naksan

Mountain. My cousin had found the rooftop apartment for me because it was close to where she lived. I traced the buildings with my eyes and tried to guess which of those countless lights was my cousin's apartment. Then I looked up at the sky. It was studded with stars. I tried to spell out the words *do not write a single sentence that supports violence* in the stars. I also looked at Namsan Tower off in the distance. Though it didn't look like much in the daytime, at night it blazed with light and marked its position. It reassured me to know there was something that stayed in one place and did not change, even if it was just a tower. I forgot about it during the day but found myself unconsciously staring at it at night. On overcast nights, when clouds obscured the tower, I poked my head out more often and waited for the clouds to lift. I decided I had to go up there someday. I surprised myself by picturing going up there with Myungsuh or Miru. After what felt like endless typing, I reached the final page. It contained a list of twenty books that Professor Yoon wanted us to read before graduation.

The day Professor Yoon distributed copies of the course reader, I studied the map for a long time before leaving the school. I was in no hurry to get back home. I looked for the longest route and tightened my shoelaces. Finishing the manuscript had left me feeling empty. Now there was no reason to grab the next bus so I could get home as fast as possible. The typewriter, which was not due back at the store yet, still sat on my desk, but a sense of loss surged through me. I felt like I was alone again. It was a strange day. Not only did I feel like I had lost something, but my feelings for Myungsuh and

Miru were growing faint. It was as if my heart had opened up to them while I was typing Professor Yoon's manuscript, but it closed again the moment the typing was done. The longest route back to my apartment passed through the center of the city. Since it was a bustling area, there would be more to see and the streets would be crowded, so I was sure to walk slower and arrive home late.

My plan was to take the underpass in front of City Hall to the Plaza Hotel, head north to Gwanghwamun Gate, east to Anguk-dong, detour around the Secret Garden at Changdeok-gung Palace, and head east again through Myeongnyun-dong on my way back to Hyehwa-dong. Since it was the first time I had taken this route, I double-checked the map and visualized the journey several times, but when I got near City Hall, I could not go any farther. I got caught in a wave of protesters and was pressed up against the glass doors of the Koreana Hotel, unable to move. All of the stores in the area had their metal roll-down gates shut tight. Even the glass doors that led into the hotel were firmly locked. The hotel employees were watching the commotion in the streets from inside. Just a few steps away from the hotel was the underpass. I thought if I could make it to the underpass, I could get across to the other side, and I took a step toward it. Just then, a tear gas canister exploded overhead, and a huge crowd of protesters surged into the underpass to try to avoid it. I was shoved forward with them, but the roll-down gates at the bottom of the stairwell were closed as well. There was nowhere to go, but the people at the top kept pouring in and falling on top of us. The people in front of the security gates began to collapse on top of one another. There was no time to think about how to get out. I fell down with someone and felt someone else fall on top of me.

When I came to, I was lying on the ground behind the Cecil Theater, near Deoksugung Palace. I had no idea how I made it out. I did not even know how much time had passed. I lay still for a moment before trying to sit up. I was short of breath and had trouble seeing. The knees of my pants were wet with blood. I vaguely recalled squinting and sluggishly picking my way toward the light at the top of the underpass. With each breath, my throat had closed up, and when I opened my eyes, tears poured out. I remembered trying to hold my breath and keep my eyes closed as I went wherever my feet took me. Then I remembered collapsing on the ground. I had lain there for some time. I sat up on the cement and looked around me. There was a patch of grass beside me, and a wooden bench. I tried to move to the bench, but a sharp pain in my knee stopped me. I looked down at the dried bloodstain on my pants. I sat down on the bench and tried to pull the fabric away from my knee, but it was glued to the skin. I gave up on checking my knee and just sat there. How long had I been there? I did not even realize my bag and shoes were gone until I felt the gravel embedded in the soles of my feet. My first thought was to try to recall what I'd had in my bag. And then I remembered: the three copies of *We Are Breathing*. I ignored the pain radiating from my knee and walked back down a long alley to the main road. Everything was a mess from the demonstration. The huge wave of people had disappeared somewhere; the street was littered with abandoned bags and shoes

that had been knocked off in the scrimmage with the riot police. I picked through all of it, hoping to find my belongings. I
headed back to the underpass in front of the hotel where I had
collapsed, wondering if I would find my shoes and bag there.
I could hear the sporadic shouts of protest slogans. The demonstration had not ended but had simply been pushed back to
one end of the street. The glass doors to the hotel, which the
employees had locked in fear when the crowds of demonstrators surged through, were sitting open. The worried-looking
employees stood out front. One of them handed me a bottle
of water. I accepted the bottle without even looking at her
and took a drink. The underpass was empty, as if someone
had come through and cleaned it. Even though I could see at
once that there was nothing in the stairwell, I walked down
for a closer look. The metal gates were still firmly locked. Why
weren't we allowed to cross to the other side? I climbed back
up the stairs. The pain in my knee made it difficult. I wanted
to sit down on the ground right there, but one of the riot police stepped in front of me. He must have thought I was trying
to head toward Gwanghwamun Gate, where the protesters
were, because he kept blocking my way.

"My shoes . . . my bag," I said.

He glared at me. His eyes were red. Finally, he pointed to
a small vacant lot between the road and the hotel.

"Go that way. Everything is being collected over there."

The pain in my knee would not go away. I was about to
limp over to the vacant lot when I heard someone behind me
call my name. I turned to see Myungsuh standing there with
a camera hanging from his neck. There he was, right where a

demonstration had just swept through like a flash flood. My mind went blank. How could I describe the shock that I felt? It was similar to what I felt when my father told me he was moving the crepe-myrtle tree to my mother's grave. Somehow, I could not believe the tree could be moved, not even when I watched my father dig it up from the yard, not even when I saw it casting its shade over my mother's grave like a parasol, and not even when the crimson blossoms alighted on the green grass of her grave like butterflies. Each time I saw the tree, I stared at it as if I were seeing it for the first time.

"Jung Yoon!"

I stood and stared at Myungsuh like I was looking at a hallucination. He said my name again. Once I realized he really was standing there, he looked like a beacon of light shining out of the dark. My mother's death, which had been drifting out of reach all that time, sank in at once, and a wave of loss washed over me. I was not prepared for it. Of all things, why did the fact that I would never see my mother again, a fact that had not yet sunk in despite my walking around with her ring in my pocket, have to hit me then and there? *Mama's dead.* I may as well have heard drums beating and a herald delivering the news. I would never hold my mother's hand again. Never curl up against her ailing body and fall asleep. Never hear her say my name. As I stood there in the middle of the city, I brought both hands up and covered my face. The heat drained out of me, and my body turned as cold as ice. Before I knew it, tears were pouring down my face. He ran to my side and threw his arms around me.

"What's wrong?" he asked.

The employee who had been watching us from inside the hotel brought another bottle of water and pressed it into his hand. Even the riot cop who had told me which way to go stopped to look at us.

"Let's go somewhere and sit down," he said.

He wrapped his arm around my shoulders. The only place we could go off the main road was the place the riot cop had pointed out. Once started, my tears would not stop rolling down my cheeks. I wanted to stop crying, but I couldn't control myself. I was embarrassed and tried to shake his arm off, but he held on tight and would not let go. The buildings lining the street, the signs in the alleys, the walls, the asphalt, all seemed to be watching me.

"I'm fine," I said.

Even as I tried to free my shoulder from his grip, the tears kept coming.

"Let me tell you a funny story," he said. "You might have already heard it on the radio. This one clueless college student had a crush on a girl he went to school with. His nickname was Nak Sujang. He looked for her on campus every day but never actually spoke to her. She was dating someone else. But he couldn't help his feelings, and so he always kept one eye out for her, albeit from a distance. One day, he saw her sitting on the grass in front of the library with her boyfriend. They looked like they were fighting. Suddenly the boyfriend got up and left. The girl was crying. Nak Sujang felt really bad for her. What guy wouldn't feel bad seeing a girl he likes crying her eyes out? So he decided to tell her a joke to cheer her up. He was going to say, 'What did one saggy boob say to the other? We better perk up or somebody is going to think we're nuts.' But when he walked up to her, she snapped, 'What do you want?' He was so flustered that he blurted out, 'What did your saggy boob say?!'"

I burst out laughing, tears still hanging from my eyes.

"You laughed!"

He looked like a man and a boy at the same time. He was smiling and posing as if he had just won a hundred-meter race. I swallowed the memory of my mother that had been caught like a lump in my throat. I forgot all about crying and looked at him as I laughed out loud once more.

"You laughed again!"

Each time I laughed, he said it again. He looked like he wanted to keep a tally of my laughter. He looked so silly that I could not stop laughing, even as my tears kept flowing. Is the root of laughter also sorrow? As I laughed, I was filled with both joy and sorrow. People walking by stared at us.

"Jung Yoon laughed!"

The paving bricks scratched up in the demonstration, the glass windows on the buildings, the stairs, the pillars, and the railings all stared at us.

"I made Jung Yoon laugh!"

Had I ever wanted that badly to make someone laugh? I pictured my father's face and realized that I had not made the best use of my time while I was home. Not even once had I tried to cheer up my father, who had lost his laughter when he lost his wife. I pictured Dahn's sad face next. My tears would not stop falling. I wiped them away with the back of my hand and finally took a good look at Myungsuh. He looked as bad as I did. The bottoms of his jeans were soaked, and the back of his shirt was in tatters. I stopped laughing, but we had already grown closer.

"What happened to your shoes?" Myungsuh asked.

He looked down at my bare feet. I looked down at them, too. I was already starting to forget the details of what had happened. The only part I remembered clearly was being swept into the underground passage with the other people, getting knocked down, and falling on my face. The pain in my knee flared up again, and I unconsciously wiggled my toes. He stared at the bloodstains on my knees.

"Does it hurt?" he asked.

"Yes."

"You have to arm yourself properly if you're going to demonstrate. Make sure your shoelaces are tied tight, and wear a mask."

"I wasn't trying to demonstrate."

He gave me a look.

"Let's just go over there and look for your shoes," he said.

"My bag first!"

I was worried about the copies of *We Are Breathing* that were in my bag. If he'd known I had lost my bag as well, he probably would have added that it was a bad idea to bring it to a protest.

"Jung Yoon, you look like a beggar."

At that moment, I was. I didn't have so much as a thousand-won bill on me. At that moment, he was all I had. He stopped teasing and got serious. It turned out that I was not the only one. When we walked into the alley and found the empty lot, there was a small mountain of ownerless shoes, bags, hats, and jackets. Having been blasted with tear gas and water cannons, everything was wet and smelled. Only then did he take his arm from around my shoulder. He looked me over and gazed down at my feet again. This city was full of surprises. I would never have guessed that I would one day be standing in the middle of it while someone stared openly at my bare feet. And not even at clean feet, but at bruised, chafed, dirty feet.

"I see why you were crying," he said.

"I wasn't crying over my shoes."

I had begun talking back to him without realizing it.

"What were you doing here?"

"Walking," I said.

"Walking?"

He didn't seem to understand what I meant, because he stared at me for a moment.

"I need to find my bag," I said.

One by one, other people like me who had sought shelter somewhere began to emerge. At first it was just the two of us, but soon there were many harried-looking people searching for their belongings. Many of them were barefoot, and one was in just an undershirt, while another clutched his arm as if it was broken. We all looked dazed. I joined the crowd and started digging among other people's belongings in search of my own.

"They were sneakers, right?" Myungsuh asked.

"Yes."

"White?"

"Yes."

"And a brown bag with a long strap."

"How did you know that?" I asked.

"Because they're yours," he said.

His words drummed in my ears like rain. He became engrossed in trying to find my shoes and bag. The camera hanging from his neck swayed back and forth. Something seemed to strike him, because he took it off and snapped a picture of the pile of lost objects. He started to hang it around his neck again but handed it to me instead and went back to searching for my shoes. I saw pens and pencils that had spilled out of bags. There were hats, handkerchiefs, makeup, a pair of nail clippers. The stem of someone's eyeglasses was rolling around in the pile, and I even spotted a belt. Scattered about here and there were heels that had broken off of shoes.

"Found it!"

Out of all those countless bags, he had managed to find mine and was holding it aloft. The charm that had been attached to it was torn. He wiped the wet bag with the hem of his shirt and handed it to me. Though it was impossible to get all of the dirt off it, he tried to clean it anyway. I took the bag from him and clutched it to my chest. He started searching again for my shoes. There were no white sneakers to be found. They may have started out as white, but it was unlikely they still were. They were comfortable sneakers with absolutely no distinguishing characteristics. Even if he did find them, I probably would not be able to put them on. Everything in the pile was soaked. I watched intently as he looked for my shoes. The city truly was full of surprises. I had searched for him all

over the school to no avail, only to bump into him here. He
was checking each shoe one by one. When I suggested that he
stop looking, he looked down at my bare feet with a defeated
look on his face. Dusk had fallen in the meantime, and the
light of the streetlamps shone on his face. He took the camera from my hand, hung it around his neck, and squatted with
his back to me.

"Hop on," he said.

"That's okay."

"You can't walk on that knee."

I hadn't told him that I hurt my knee, but the pain had not
let up once.

"Put your bag over your shoulder first."

I stood and stared at him.

"Aren't you getting on?" He glanced back at me.

"I can walk," I said.

"On those feet?"

"I can walk."

"Stubborn."

He scooted backward to try to nudge me onto his back,
but I kept moving back as well.

"I said I can walk. See!"

I started walking out of the alley. The cuts on the bottoms
of my feet all began to hurt at once, and the pain made my
knees wobble. My pants came unstuck from the wound in my
knee; the stanched blood started running down my leg and
seeping through the fabric. When he saw how unstable I was,
he stepped in front of me and offered me his back again.

"Just get on, Jung Yoon!"

As he bent over, his torn shirt opened up in the back. I could see the clear outline of his spine. It reminded me of a mountain ravine. I had a sudden desire to run my hand down it. He looked like he could lift me up and gallop around the city with me on his back.

"Okay, but only until we find a shoe store," I said.

"Understood. Until we find a shoe store."

I climbed onto his back with my bag slung over my shoulder, just as he had instructed. He stepped onto the sidewalk and headed for the main street. I was conscious of my breasts and stomach pressed against him, but he didn't seem to notice. He moved forward without the slightest waver. I wrapped my arms around his neck. The position was awkward at first, but I soon felt comfortable. I could see my bare feet swinging next to his thighs. It reminded me of how my mother used to carry me on her back that way when I was very young. It occurred to me that the smell I had always thought of as her scent was just the smell of sweat. I used to fall asleep with my nose pressed against her strong, warm back. Myungsuh's torn shirt pressed against my stomach. I resisted the urge to rest my cheek against his shoulder and turned to look at the empty lot. The ownerless shoes, bags, shirts, and other belongings were scattered under the streetlights. I felt like I was the only one to survive that chaos. I felt bad for the ones who did not—ones I could not even see—and my heart grew heavy for them. Though we had agreed that he would only carry me to the nearest shoe store, neither he nor I knew where to find one. After a while, he added, "*If* we find a shoe store."

"And if we don't?" I asked.

"Don't worry. I'll carry you all the way home."

The buses had stopped running because of the demonstration, so we had no choice but to walk. When we reached the spot where he first found me, he paused and asked where I lived.

"Dongsung-dong."

"You live in Dongsung-dong?"

"Yes."

"We might have bumped into each other."

"Do you live there?"

"No, but Miru used to."

Yoon Miru.

The sound of her name was like a black curtain being drawn over my heart, like when the day goes dark and a sudden rainstorm beats down.

"Where is Yoon Miru now?"

He didn't answer.

"Where is she?"

I kept asking him where she was, as if I were her *unni*, her older sister. He paused to catch his breath, but instead of answering me, he repositioned his hands to better support my weight.

"We should take the underpass, right?"

He seemed to be avoiding talking about her.

"We can't," I said. "The gates are closed."

We waited at a crosswalk. Though there were no cars, the traffic lights changed in order.

"Where is she?"

"She just got back from the island."

"The island?"

Just as he started to explain, a group of protesters whooshed out of a dark alley and streamed onto the main road. For a moment, we were caught in the middle. Some of them bumped into us. We received a few hard stares, too. I wanted him to set me down, but he only held me tighter. The protesters streamed by so quickly that I could not tell whether they were slamming into us or we were slamming into them.

He started walking again. Finding a shoe store was like finding a spring blossom in the dead of winter. Most of the stores on the first floors of the buildings had their metal security gates rolled down or the glass doors locked with the lights out so no one could see in. A menu board in front of a restaurant had been knocked over. I was glad to see a faint light streaming out of a car showroom. Whenever I walked downtown in the middle of the day and saw the crowds of pedestrians, I wondered what they were doing out instead of being at work somewhere, but now I realized that they were the life force of this city. Without people, the city felt dead. The excitement that had engulfed us when we were being overrun by protesters faded, and we were left with a sad silence. As Myungsuh walked forward, I could smell the sharp scent of tear gas on the air. The sporadic shouts of protesters and the roar of riot police reached my ears. My spine stiffened at the sound of the water cannon.

We passed a locked-up newsstand.

"What can any of us do in this day and age?" he mumbled. He sounded like Professor Yoon. "What do you want to do with your life, Jung Yoon?"

I thought of the copies of *We Are Breathing* in my bag.

"Sometimes I wish we could start off old and get younger as we go," he said.

"What would happen then?" I asked.

"I guess we would both look old right now," he said.

I couldn't imagine either of us looking old.

"I wish someone would promise me that nothing is meaningless," he said. "I wish there were promises worth believing in. That after we've been hunted and lonely and anxious and living in fear, there is something else. Considering the way we are living right now, if we were young at the end of our lives instead, then maybe our dreams could come true."

We passed a bus stop. There were no buses anywhere.

"Don't you think?" He was looking in vain for me to agree with him.

"That means we would die looking our youngest and spend this part of our lives looking our oldest. Is that what you want?" I asked.

He stopped in front of a closed jewelry store. Though I couldn't see him, I could imagine the look on his face.

"I didn't think about that," he said.

I had never thought about what it would be like if I could live my life in reverse. I mumbled to myself, not intending for him or anyone else to hear me, "How does everyone stand it?" Dahn's and Miru's faces came to mind.

"They can't stand it," he said, "and that's why they form barricades, throw paving bricks, and run away only to get caught and arrested. What they can't stand is the fact that nothing ever gets better. Nothing has changed since last year. It's as if time has stopped."

"What do you hope will happen?" I asked.

"I just want something to change. Nothing ever changes no matter how hard we fight, so we become lethargic. Sometimes I find myself wishing that someone would steal all the books, just take them all, every last one, even from the libraries. I wish the schools would close so that no one could go, not even if they wanted to. Everything is the same. It only feels like time is passing, and only the characters change. We are torn apart and chased around. We fight back and get chased some more . . . We all stare at the walls and complain of loneliness. All we have to do is turn around, but instead we keep our faces to the walls. It's depressing to think that this will never change. Things were no different last spring, either."

I listened without saying anything.

"If I hadn't met you," he said, "I might not be able to tell the difference between this day last year and today."

Then he mumbled under his breath, "So . . . let's remember this day forever." I wanted to see his face. I wanted to see what he looked like when he said those words, because the lethargy that he was feeling was mine, too. Maybe we had exaggerated the meaning of our chance encounter that day in an attempt to dispel that lethargy. I took my arm from around his neck and ran my hand over his cheek. Then, one by one, I felt his forehead, his nose, the groove under his nose, his lips, his chin, his ears. Then his eyebrows. He let me touch him.

When I ran my fingers over his eyes, he stopped walking. It must have been hard for him to keep moving forward.

"Yoon." He had never called me by just my first name before. "I never thought I would see you out in the streets. They were fighting dirty today—both the demonstrators and the riot cops. I got separated from my group and was starting to get scared when suddenly there you were. I couldn't stop rubbing my eyes in disbelief. Why did you come out today?" He sounded heavyhearted.

"I didn't want to go home early. I was trying to take the longest route home, and then this happened to me."

I thought of the typewriter sitting on my desk in my empty room. The clacking of the keys echoed in my ears. There are times when I am grateful for the fact of not being asked why. He did not ask why I didn't want to go home. I wouldn't have known how to answer if he had. He took a deep breath and exhaled. I felt his chest rise and fall. I pulled my hand away from his face and rubbed the corners of my stinging eyes. Each time he breathed, my chest and stomach clenched. That tightness also came with the piquant joy of seeing the ocean for the first time, of rising at the crack of dawn in winter and discovering the courtyard white with snow, of scraping a fingernail in disbelief over a grapevine where green tendrils flush with spring curl out of a dried-up and lifeless plant, of looking down at the pink fingernails of a young child. Like seeing white cumulous clouds in a summer sky, or peeling back the skin on a sweet peach and taking a bite, or walking along a forest path and absentmindedly picking up a pinecone to discover the inside packed with white pine nuts.

I hugged him tighter. The scent of his body was right under my nose. It was mixed with the smell of tear gas.

"Do you demonstrate every day?" I asked him.

He didn't answer.

"Is that why you haven't been to class?"

"Every morning, I open my eyes and I ask myself: Should I go to school, or should I go demonstrate? I can't sit still in class, but it's the same when I'm out in the streets. I feel like something is pushing me to join the demonstrations, but I often wind up getting separated from the others, like today. Sometimes I wake up in the morning, blow my nose, and throw the tissue at the trashcan. If it makes it into the can, I go to school, and if it doesn't, I take to the streets. Other times, I stay in my room and wait for someone to come find me."

"I see."

"Sometimes I go to school just because you're there."

I loosened my grip.

"But I didn't go today *because* I knew you'd be there . . ."

"What do you mean?"

"I thought, if I saw you, I might grab you and tell you everything."

I wondered what he meant by that.

"But instead, there you were in the street. I was so surprised."

"You didn't look surprised."

"You immediately started crying, standing there in your bare feet, so how could you tell whether I was surprised or not?"

I liked the way he smelled. His smell made me not want to ask where Miru was. If I got to know her better, would I get to know him, too? It bothered me that he didn't want to talk about her. I had a feeling that if he did, I would have to get off his back and walk home alone on bare wounded feet through this tumultuous, chaotic city. I was suddenly frightened by my overpowering curiosity toward Miru. Would the things I learned bring Myungsuh and me closer, or push us further apart? I used to think that sharing secrets always brought people closer. So I revealed secrets I did not want known in order to feel closer to someone. Oh, the loss I felt when I found out the secrets that I had held dear, that were so difficult to say out loud, that I had kept to myself, were being spread around the next day as if they were nothing! I think that was the moment I realized that pouring your heart out to someone might not bring you closer but in fact make you poorer instead. I even thought maybe growing close to someone was better achieved by empathizing in silence.

The city looked as tangled as a spider's web: the buildings with their countless windows, streetlamps standing in rows, narrow alleyways, and signs so jumbled that you could not tell which shops they belonged to. The streets had been closed to traffic, but the lights kept changing like clockwork. Though there was no one to look up at them, the large billboards filled the air with their glittering colors. I glanced down an alleyway, the darkness too thick to see where it ended. Myungsuh crossed a small intersection, brushed past an empty phone booth, walked beneath an overpass, and crossed another intersection. Though he was headed toward my place, we were like people with nowhere to go.

We must have walked for over twenty minutes in silence.

"Let's stop there," I said, pointing at a flower shop.

The door sat wide open. All of the other shops had their security shutters rolled down or their doors only half open, as if they had given up on doing business. The fistful of soil from my mother's grave was still sitting in a clay pot outside my apartment. I glanced at it each time I left. I had bought the pot with the idea of planting something in it, but I couldn't decide what; meanwhile, the soil was drying out.

"Why here?" he asked.

"I have a flowerpot at home. I want to plant something in it."

I pointed at something green sitting on the doorsill of the flower shop. I had been looking for an excuse to get down, and that was all I found. It looked ornamental, but I did not know what it was called.

"It looks like palm leaves," Myungsuh said.

Despite its small size, it was indeed a palm plant.

"Let me down," I said.

He set me down in front of the flower shop. There was only a handful of soil in the flowerpot at home. I would need to buy more. The shop was barely bigger than a closet. If you weren't paying attention, you might not even notice it was there. Inside, an older woman in glasses was sitting on a stool and gazing out. She stood up when she saw us. I caught the faint scent of mackerel being grilled. There must have been a fish restaurant close by. The smell made my stomach growl.

When I poked my head into the store, the woman came out. I asked her the name of the plant, and she said it was a

table palm. Inside the shop, there were more flowers wither-
ing than blooming. The balsam and hyacinth had lost their
petals, and even the leaves were wilting.

"Are you young folks heading back from a demonstration?"
the woman asked.

We weren't sure what to say. The furrow in her brow
deepened.

"When will this country ever stop rioting?" She sighed. "I
can't open my shop. It's closed most of the time, and there's
so much tear gas in the air that all the flowers have wilted.
Look at this. I was raising two birds in this cage, but they died
yesterday. And look at my face. Even at this age, I have acne
that won't go away. It's from breathing tear gas every day."

Her voice was raspy.

"Take whatever you want," she said. "Everything is so
wilted that it would be wrong to take your money."

Sullenly, she picked up the table palm that I had asked
about and put it in a bag.

"When you get home, transfer the plant to another container and water it. I'm sorry we couldn't leave you a world
where no one has to riot . . . I'm so sorry."

Myungsuh had been staring blankly at my feet when the
woman surprised us with her apology, but he suddenly dashed
across the street to a phone booth.

"This is going to sound as ridiculous as telling you that a
cat hatched an egg . . . You kids may be in the right, but if you
keep this up, the rest of us will have to protest as well. We'll
have to protest all the protesting."

She smiled bitterly.

"You kids aren't doing anything wrong, but we can't live this way."

I didn't know what to say.

"We have to make a living, too."

She was talking to me as if we were related. I didn't know how to respond to her. I hadn't done anything wrong, but I kept bowing my head. I hoped Myungsuh would hurry back. The longer she talked, the more anxiously I gazed at where he stood inside the phone booth across the street.

"We failed this time around, but you have to leave a better world to the next generation."

The woman locked the door to her shop, the melancholy look never once leaving her face. Then both she and the flowers vanished, making me wonder if I had imagined everything. All that was left of her shop was the cold metal roll-down gate. My knees gave way, and I sat on the ground and watched as he finished the call and ran back to me.

He sat down at my side.

"Miru's coming," he said.

Miru.

"I asked her to bring you some shoes," he said.

"That must have been a surprise."

"What size are you?"

"235."

"Same as Miru."

He seemed to know everything about her.

"Where is she coming from?" I asked.

"Myeongnyun-dong."

We were in Anguk-dong. Since the buses had stopped, Miru would have to walk the whole way. That afternoon, when I planned my long route home through downtown, I had assumed it would take me two hours. I had even thought about taking a three-hour walking route instead. But several hours had passed since I left the campus, part of which I spent being carried on his back from City Hall, and I had only just reached Anguk-dong.

"Did Miru move there from Dongsung-dong?" I asked.

"We lived together in Dongsung-dong."

"What?"

"We lived in a house that Miru's parents got for her and Mirae—her older sister," he said.

"Miru has an older sister?"

He started to nod and then stopped and fumbled with the plastic bag. He grabbed my hand and put it on his knee. I could feel the dirt on his jeans.

"To be honest, I don't want you and Miru to become friends. But you two are always asking about each other."

Miru asked about me?

"And you're both persistent," he added. "You look for each other. It's been a long time since Miru showed an interest in someone else. I should be happy about it, but instead I'm worried."

"Why?" I asked.

His laugh sounded hollow.

"I guess we meet who we're supposed to meet. After all, look at how you and I met."

"Why are you being so serious?"

He laughed and asked if he really sounded serious.

While we waited for Miru, we sat against the closed shutters like scattered members of some enemy troop and talked.

"The three of us lived in a house on a hill in Dongsung-dong. We grew up together. Mirae was a year older, but the three of us were almost inseparable. She left for college first and lived in a boardinghouse, but when Miru and I joined her in the city, their parents got us the house. We lived together, but we were just friends."

"I understand."

"You do? Everyone else thought it was weird."

"Why?"

"Because I'm a guy and I'm not related to them."

"But you said you grew up together?"

He stared at me. I was thinking about Dahn. Dahn may have said I didn't love him, but I loved the time I spent with him. He and I could spend time together without having to talk. Even when we ran out of things to say and were both silent, it never felt awkward. We could sit across from each other for hours without saying anything at all. I would read, and Dahn would draw in his sketchbook. It felt completely natural to us. When one of us said something, the other understood ten times as much. That's not something that happens right away. It builds over time while you're growing up together.

"You're different from the others," he said.

"How so?"

"I thought I would have to explain why I lived with two girls, and I even had a speech prepared, but when you said you understood, you took the wind right out of me."

"I shouldn't have said anything, then."

He laughed weakly.

"Why don't you live together now?"

"I'd rather not talk about it."

He, too, was different from the others. The things he said could seem cold, but he said them so gently.

"Who is Miru looking for?" I asked.

"Someone who disappeared."

"Who?"

"I don't have to say, right?"

"No, you're not obligated."

"Obligated?" His voice got quieter. "Even if I don't tell you, you'll find out if you keep spending time with us."

"What do you mean?"

"Miru is almost here."

Something was fluttering in the dark across the street. I took a closer look. It was Miru's skirt. I remembered the day I saw them on the way to Professor Yoon's office. The two of them were walking beneath the zelkova tree, and Miru's floral-print skirt had billowed up in the breeze. It clashed with everything around it and filled me with a strange sense of anxiety. Miru was stepping off the sidewalk and into the street, as if to jaywalk instead of taking the crosswalk. We watched her. She still had her shoulders hunched and her head hanging down. It was strange. Though Myungsuh was right next to me, and though he was the one who had called her, I felt like she was heading for me alone. I unconsciously scooted away from him. Just before she reached us, a white cat leapt down from her arms and walked toward Myungsuh.

He reached out his arms and picked up the cat. They seemed to know each other well. The flowers on Miru's skirt flickered before my eyes, and then there she was sitting between us, before I could get a look at her face. She unzipped her bag, took out a pair of sneakers wrapped in newspaper, and set them down next to me. Myungsuh must have told her everything on the phone, because she did not ask why I was barefoot or why we were sitting there. She didn't even offer the usual greetings. I slipped on the sneakers and began to tie the laces, but she reached out her hands toward my feet. I couldn't take my eyes off her scars. She started to tie the shoes herself but then stood up as if the position was uncomfortable and moved so she was sitting directly in front of me. Then she redid the loose knots, retying them one by one and tugging on the bows to make sure they were tight. She did it so naturally that I didn't have the chance to tell her I would do it myself. I was surprised I didn't pull my feet away. I felt comfortable letting her touch my feet. Her scarred fingers moved between the white laces. Even Myungsuh was watching quietly. Her hands, which had always remained hidden in her pockets or under her desk, were moving freely in front of us.

"These were my sister's shoes," she said.

She sat down between us again. Her voice was clear and subdued. It was as if she had been with us the whole time, rather than having just met us, or even as if we had been traveling together for days and had only stopped for a short rest. I would never have guessed that I could feel so comfortable with them. The tension Myungsuh and I felt each time her name came up had gone away and left me feeling weak. I realized I had been acting silly when I scooted away from him the moment she showed up. Miru's sister's shoes fit like they were my own. It was as if I were a different person from the one who had been talking to Myungsuh just moments earlier. My mother died without knowing this about me, but when I first came to live here, I avoided forming a deep relationship with anyone or anything. Whenever she asked if I had made any friends, I told her I hadn't yet. I felt abandoned. She had sent me away as soon as she learned she was dying, peeled me off of her despite my not wanting to leave her side, so the last thing I wanted was to feel close to anyone. I couldn't bear the thought of telling someone about myself or of spending time with someone. I chose to be alone in order to keep things uncomplicated, to avoid perplexing emotions. My cousin used to say to me, "You don't really believe you can survive in this world alone, do you? No one makes it on their own." Sitting there in the street, I realized that Myungsuh and Miru had succeeded in getting through to me.

"What happened when you went to the island?" Myungsuh asked Miru.

"I didn't find anything," she said.

"Please stop looking."

They both got very quiet all of a sudden. To dispel the awkwardness, I asked if they were hungry. Myungsuh said he was, but Miru did not answer.

"Shall we go to my place?"

They turned to look at me.

"All I have is perilla kimchi," I said, "but I'll make rice. I have plenty of rice. Let's go."

I grabbed the bag with the table palm and stood up. They followed me. Miru picked up the cat. Its snow-white fur moved gently in the dark. Miru ran her scarred fingers through the cat's fur and stroked its neck. The cat stared at me with eyes as blue as the sky at dawn. When we reached the main street, Myungsuh said he was too hungry to walk and flagged down a taxi. The buses were still not running, but taxis had begun to appear. Had the protest finally died down? The streets were deserted; few people were out at night. Myungsuh sat in the front, and Miru and I sat in the back. When she saw me staring at the cat, Miru offered to let me hold it. It was the first time since bringing the shoes that she had looked directly at me. Her dark eyes studied me. I set the plant down on the floor of the cab and took the cat. Its tail stiffened at first but soon relaxed. The soft fur brushed against my cheek. The cat sat in my arms and stared idly out the car window at the darkness and at the trees that lined the road.

"She likes you," Miru said.

"Excuse me?"

"She's sitting still."

I was not fond of cats. A very long time ago, when I had gone to visit my mother and was taking a nap with her, a cat had come along and sat down beside us. The first to awake, I was startled and threw a book at the cat and yelled at it. But it just strolled away coolly. The next day, the cat appeared again, urinated on the floor in front of me, and walked away.

I slipped on its urine. My mother said, "See, you threw a book at it, so it left its pee for you." That memory kept me away from any more cats. When I first moved to the city, there was a cat in my cousin's building as well. I don't know what happened, but the landlord filled the building with tenants and moved out, leaving the gray cat behind. My cousin would often feed it. I asked her once why the landlord left it behind, and she said that cats are more attached to places than to people. And that was why cats are so often found in abandoned houses.

That story of Saint Christopher has been stuck in my head ever since the first day of class. I wanted to know more about him, so I searched through book after book in the library.

1. Because he carried the Christ child across the river, Saint Christopher is still regarded as the patron saint of travelers. Some taxi drivers and truck drivers even keep medals of Saint Christopher on their dashboards like talismans. At the same time that he was an ascetic who sought to realize the will of God through hard work, he was also a messenger with something very important to transport and deliver.

2. In that sense, Saint Christopher is also a Christ figure. The name Christopher is derived from "Christ"; the "ph" comes from a Greek word meaning "bearer." Christ, who carried all of man's sins and agonies with him onto the cross in order to save humanity, was both an ascetic who carried the world on his back and a messenger sent to earth to deliver God's will. When we look at it that way,

then the Christian Christopher can also be seen as a combination of Atlas and Hermes of Greek mythology.

3. Christ shouldered the cross, and Saint Christopher shouldered Christ. If we invert the sentence, then the cross carried Jesus, and Jesus delivered Saint Christopher to the path of salvation. They both had a calling to which they devoted their whole lives, and they both experienced fateful meetings that enabled them to fulfill those callings. In that case, do I also have a calling? A task that I am destined to carry out for the rest of my life? When will the chance to fulfill that calling find its way to me? Though I'm in my twenties now, I feel like I am still fumbling in the dark, trying to make my way forward.

I stole a book from the bookstore. I didn't need it. I don't even want to read it. Yet when I pulled it off the shelf, this unnamable urge shot through me. I walked out of the store with the book in my hand, but no one stopped me. It was anticlimactic. On the title page, I wrote the date and a note: "Yi Myungsuh's first stolen book." It looked incomplete, so I added: "You're not a grown-up until you've stolen a book." But then I felt like I was making a childish excuse, so I erased everything except for the date.

—Brown Notebook 3

CHAPTER 4

To The Salt Lake

I asked Myungsuh and Miru to wait outside before I let
them in. The list of promises I'd made to myself when I
returned to the city was taped to the wall above my desk, and
I thought I should take it down first. The cat came in and
started exploring, as if looking for a spot of her own in this
new place. She leaped onto the windowsill and curled up in
a ball. Myungsuh transferred the table palm from the plastic container to the clay flowerpot and placed it on my desk.
Then he sat down in the chair and tapped on the typewriter.
Miru stood near the kitchen. I call it a kitchen, but it was
really just a sink and a stove at one end of the room, along
with a refrigerator. I washed the rice and put it in the pot.
Then I pulled out the retractable tabletop that was hidden
in the side of the kitchen counter and set it with containers of side dishes from the refrigerator. The pullout table was
short and narrow. I kept it folded away when I was not using
it. The three of us would have been knee-to-knee if we all
tried to sit there. My cousin had made the side dishes for me;

the containers were filled with stir-fried anchovies, brisket marinated in soy sauce, seasoned perilla. The perilla that my cousin had brought was different from the perilla kimchi my mother used to send me: my cousin had simply steamed the leaves and seasoned them with soy sauce. Each time I opened a container, Miru murmured the names of the dishes like she was reciting the titles of books: *radish kimchi, braised lotus root, sauteed burdock root* . . . She marveled at how much food I had and asked if I had made it all myself.

"I have an older cousin who lives nearby," I explained. "She brought it over."

"You said all you had was perilla kimchi."

"I didn't realize how much was in there." I pointed at the burdock and lotus root. "It's the first time I've opened these."

"Why haven't you had any yet?"

"I guess I just don't take it all out when I'm eating alone."

I ate because I was hungry, not for the flavor. My cousin made all kinds of things and left them in my refrigerator, but whenever I ate, I just reached in and grabbed the first three containers I saw. Myungsuh stopped tapping at the type-writer and came over. He transferred the food into smaller serving dishes.

"I have some curled mallow," I said. "Shall I make some soup?"

"Don't bother," Miru said. "This is already too much food."

It was true. The small table was crowded with dishes.

"But we're eating together for the first time," I said. "We ought to have soup."

I grabbed a pot, filled it with water, and placed it on the

stove. Then I took the mallow out of the refrigerator. Even the mallow had been brought over by my cousin.

"I can't believe you have mallow," Miru said. "Here, I'll do it."

She took the big mallow leaves from me. She had the stems peeled in no time. Her scarred hands moved fluidly from stem to stem. I was surprised to see her work. From the way she handled the leaves, stripping off the thin outer layer of the plant and picking out the tougher pieces without hesitation, it seemed she had made this soup often. She added salt to the boiling water to blanch the leaves and then wrung them out hard under a running tap.

"You blanch it first?" I asked.

"That gets rid of the bitterness."

"You must really like mallow soup."

"My sister did. We used to grow mallow in our garden when we were little. First thing in the morning, I would take my basket to go pick mallow with my sister. I was always amazed by how fast the mallow grew back after it was cut. But mostly I liked going out to the garden because I had fun shaking the dew off the leaves. My pants would be soaked with dew by the time we were done."

She had told me not to bother making soup and then wound up making it herself.

"There's some dried shrimp in the refrigerator, too."

Miru found the plastic bag, peeked inside, and rejoiced: "We have shrimp!" She washed the dried shrimp and added it to the pot. When my mother made this soup, she used to just wring the leaves out until the water ran green and then rinse them and add them to the soup. I had never made it myself. It was strange to see Miru so adept at it. Myungsuh must have been hungry, because he grabbed a perilla leaf with his fingers and ate it. Miru gave him a look and handed him a pair of chopsticks. He took them and ate another. They looked so natural together that I stood still and watched them for a moment.

When the soup came to a boil, the cat stood up and arched her back into a deep stretch. Her supple belly grazed the windowsill. She leapt down lightly from the sill and strolled over to Miru, wrapped her tail around Miru's skirt, and gave it a tap. The whole time, the cat kept her face turned away, as if feigning indifference.

"That's how they communicate," Miru said. "This means she likes me. She'll do it to you, too, once she gets to know you."

The cat sat quietly at Miru's feet and looked up at me. The blue eyes seemed to say, "And who are you?" I filled three bowls with rice. It was the first time I had ever eaten with other people in my rooftop apartment. Every single plate and bowl in my cabinet was put to use. Once the table was set, Miru took a blank piece of paper and a pencil from my desk and wrote down the date and the names of every dish on the table: *curled mallow soup, rice, perilla kimchi* . . .

"What are you doing?" I asked.

"Writing it all down so I can transfer it to my diary later."

"What?"

"Miru writes down everything she eats." Myungsuh answered for her.

Everything? Miru ignored my stares and continued writing it all down.

"Why do you do that?" I asked.

"Because then it feels real," she said.

"What does?"

"Being alive."

"Have you written down everything you've ever eaten since you were born?" I asked.

"Of course not!" Miru chuckled.

"Then why? What's the motivation?" I couldn't help but laugh, too. With all of my questions, I felt like I was interviewing her.

We picked up our spoons and began our first meal together. The cat curled up at Miru's feet. Myungsuh stuck a huge spoonful of rice in his mouth and slurped down the soup. Miru did not touch her rice but ate small spoonfuls of the soup. I mixed half of my rice into my soup. She had seasoned it well. The green mallow leaves were tender. The pink of the shrimp complemented the green of the mallow. I still couldn't believe we were eating together. I picked up a perilla leaf and placed it on Miru's rice. It was something my mother used to do for me. When did my mother get to eat? I had more memories of her feeding us than of her eating. She used to beam with pride over how heartily my father ate, and she encouraged me to eat like him. The way he ate, it was almost as if he were eating something different and tastier. Seeing him eat made me want to hurry up and eat, too. He really was a hearty eater, before she became sick. After my mother died and it was just the two of us, we could still feel her sitting between us at the table, though neither of us ever talked about it. Those may have been my loneliest moments while living back at home. My mother loved to watch my father eat, and she was forever pushing the side dishes closer to us and placing bites of meat and vegetables on top of our rice: *Eat it while it's still warm, while it's still flavorful, while the seasoning's just right* . . . Did I ever return the gesture? I would think about her and find myself unconsciously reaching over to push the side dishes closer to my father. He in turn would unconsciously place pieces of dried seaweed on the spoonful of rice I was raising to my mouth. Maybe that was why we still felt her there. After she passed away, my father no longer feasted on squash, or picked a fish clean of meat, or slurped down soup like it was water, or asked for sesame oil to drizzle on his *bibimbap*. Half of his rice was always left untouched.

Miru wrapped the perilla leaf around a big spoonful of rice, stuffed it in her mouth, and smiled with her cheeks full. I smiled, too. I would never have guessed that I would be sitting here in my room with the two of them, sharing a meal and laughing. My mother would have liked watching Miru eat. To my surprise, she ate heartily, like my father. My mother would have patted her on the back and been all smiles, and she would have said that Miru's way of eating brought luck. No matter what the situation, my mother expressed everything through food. If something bad happened, she said it was on account of being a picky eater, and if something good happened, she said it was a reward for eating every meal like it was a feast.

"You're a hearty eater," I said.

"Me?"

"Yes."

Miru looked like no one had ever told her that before.

"My mother would have enjoyed watching you eat," I said. "She used to say that people had to know how to enjoy their food. She said that was how you could be sure to always get your share, no matter where you went. People who know how to enjoy food know the value of it."

My mother's words still rang in my ears. She was fond of Dahn because of his appetite. Whenever he came over, she would set out extra silverware and made sure he ate with us. And just like she did for my father and me, she would push the side dishes closer to him and even place food on his rice.

"Let's visit your mother someday," Miru said.

If only we could. If only I could take them to see her someday.

"My mother is dead."

It was the first time I had ever said those words to someone. Myungsuh and Miru looked up at me. The fact of my mother's death hit me again, the same way it had when Myungsuh appeared before me like a beacon of light in the center of the riot-swept city. *My mother is dead.* The words echoed in my ears. A chill ran over me, but the feeling soon passed. Maybe I had already come to terms with her death while typing up the poems in *We Are Breathing*. Miru placed a perilla leaf in my bowl. I wrapped it around the rice, put it in my mouth, and chewed. I could hear my mother saying, *Our little Yoon is such a good eater.* As soon as I swallowed, Myungsuh put another leaf in my bowl. I put a leaf in his bowl as well. Then he put one in Miru's bowl. We picked up the leaves, wrapped them around the rice, and stuffed them in our mouths at the same time, giggling as we chewed.

I picked up a piece of brisket and held it out to the cat, but Miru stopped me.

"She can't eat anything with salt or onions."

"Why not?" I put the brisket in my own mouth instead.

"Cats can't digest salt."

"Then what should we feed her? She must be hungry."

"She won't eat anything anyway. She's very vain. She never eats between meals."

"Really?"

"Yes."

Miru looked at the cat as if to say, *Isn't that so?* The cat sat there and showed no interest in the meat, even though she must have smelled it when I held it in front of her. Miru was right. I realized again how little I knew about cats.

"I wonder why they can't digest salt. That's where all the flavor comes from."

It's what my mother used to say.

"That's true. Come to think of it, I did once hear about a cat that lived near a salt lake."

"Salt lake?"

"Yes. Where was it? Turkey? Greece? The path to the lake is crusted with salt. At night, the moonlight reflects off it, and it glows white. The description of the path is so amazing that I can still picture it in my head. People who are ill and at their life's end go to that lake to soak in the saltwater, and the cat walks with them along the path and listens to their life story. The cat enjoys their stories and waits at the entrance for people to show up. Whenever someone shows up looking ill, the cat guides them to the lake."

"Where did you hear that?" I asked.

"I read it in a book."

"What's the title?"

"I can't remember. Do you remember the title of that book my sister had?" she asked Myungsuh. He cocked his head as if trying to remember.

"I thought the path sounded so beautiful that I was obsessed with trying to picture the lake, but my silly sister was worried about the cat because she said salt makes them sick."

"I guess she knew everything there is to know about cats."

"She wasn't always like that. I remember when she first brought the cat home. Her friend's cat had five kittens, and this one was the runt. The stronger kittens pushed her away when they fed, so she couldn't get enough to eat. When my sister saw that she couldn't eat and kept getting her tail bitten, she brought her home. She was so small. It was easy to lose her. She could hide inside a manila envelope, and you would never find her. She looked like a ball of white string rolling along the floor. But despite her small size, she had sharp claws. I was fascinated by them. She scratched up all the furniture. My mother and Mirae used to fight about it all the time."

Myungsuh placed another perilla leaf on Miru's rice. She looked down at it quietly and said my name. I looked at her. Her dark eyes locked on mine.

"Can I have more rice?" she asked.

"More? Really?" Myungsuh sounded shocked.

We each had another bowl of rice and another bowl of soup. When we ran out of side dishes, Myungsuh took the containers out of the refrigerator again and heaped more food onto the serving dishes. He kept glancing at Miru as she ate.

Stuffed, we left the messy table as it was and collapsed on the floor. The cat tiptoed languidly between us and leapt up onto my desk. She tucked her front paws together, arched her back, and huddled over to look down at us. She looked like a pile of fresh snow that had fallen only on that one spot. My cousin had told me that cats were independent and kept their distance from people. But Miru's cat did not seem to mind when Myungsuh held her or when she was placed in my arms. Cats were also supposed to be sensitive and react to even the slightest touch, but Miru's cat seemed to be unperturbed by anything. She had an elegant way of lifting her feet and arching her neck. Without quite realizing it, all three of us were staring at the cat.

"She's deaf," Miru said.

I looked at her in surprise.

"She can't hear anything."

"Really?"

"That's why she's so quiet."

Finally, I understood why the cat barely moved and made so little noise.

"They say ninety percent of that breed are deaf."

"What kind is it?" I asked.

"Turkish Angora."

It was hard to believe that those lovely little ears could not hear a thing. I had thought, *What a regal cat, too noble to be hanging out with someone like me, who sits in the street with no shoes on.* When Miru told me it was deaf, I started to warm up to it. If I were sitting closer, I might have even reached out to stroke its ears.

"How did you figure out it was deaf?" I asked.

"She didn't seem to recognize her name, no matter how much my sister and I called to her. At first we thought all cats were like that. But then we realized that no cat could sleep that deeply. We would see her sleeping under a chair when we left in the morning, but when we came home at night, she would still be asleep in the same spot. She slept anywhere and everywhere. As a kitten, she slept under cushions and inside plastic bags. When she got a little older, she slept on top of the bookshelf and behind curtains . . . She would sleep inside boxes . . . She would sleep and sleep. She was more like a lump of sleep than a cat . . ."

When Miru said that, I pictured an animal called sleep.

"When she finally started sleeping less, she started staring at everything that moved."

"Like what?"

"Leaves shaking in the wind, bells dangling in the air, drops of rain sliding down the window, a ball of yarn rolling around, broken laces, glass beads, that sort of thing . . . She would stare at them. When they moved this way, she turned her head this way, and when they moved that way, she turned her head that way."

"I see."

"One time, she was sitting in the window with her back to us. When we went to take a look, the first snow of the year was falling. The cat was watching the snowflakes dance in the wind. All day long, she moved her head in time with those whirling snowflakes. We took turns calling her name, but she never turned to look at us. That was when my sister realized something was wrong. The cat was deaf. I hadn't even considered that possibility, but when I started watching her more carefully, I realized she wasn't reacting to sound but to the air—the vibration of a door opening, the drumming of footsteps. I snuck up behind the cat once when it was gazing out the window and clapped my hands right next to its ears. But she just kept looking out the window. We took her to a dog hospital and had her examined. Sure enough, she really was deaf."

"Why did you take a cat to a dog hospital?"

"We couldn't find any veterinarians that treated cats."

"What do you call her?" I had finally gotten around to asking the cat's name.

Myungsuh answered before Miru could.

"Emily Dickinson," he said.

"What?" I was shocked.

"Emily Dickinson," Miru said. "My sister picked the name."

Dahn's face flashed through my mind. She named the cat Emily Dickinson? I got up and went to the desk and took out the very first book I had ever bought in this city—the collection of her poems. I pointed at the picture of Emily Dickinson on the cover and looked at Miru as if to say, *You mean this Emily?* Miru nodded. It seemed Emily had been with us even before we met. We were connected to each other through her, even though we hadn't grown up together. Dahn had read her poems and then given them to me; meanwhile, Miru's sister was naming the cat after her.

"Ms. Dickinson probably wouldn't be too happy about it, would she?" Miru said.

"What do you mean?"

"That we named a deaf cat after her."

I hadn't considered that. I looked at the cat and called out, "Emily Dickinson!"

"Just call her Emily. That's what my sister did."

It was just the three of us, but Miru brought up her sister so often—my sister did this, my sister said that—it felt like there were four of us in that room. Myungsuh opened the book of poems and read one out loud.

> I stepped from plank to plank
> So slow and cautiously;
> The stars about my head I felt,
> About my feet the sea.
>
> I knew not but the next
> Would be my final inch,—
> This gave me that precarious gait
> Some call experience.

When he got to "About my feet the sea," Miru joined in. It seemed they had read poetry out loud together before. Their voices harmonized. As I listened, I remembered Professor Yoon's book and opened my bag. I took out the copies of *We*

Are Breathing and gave one to each of them. I felt like the purpose of my long, unexpected pilgrimage across the city had been to deliver these books. I let out a sigh as if I had completed some arduous task. While Myungsuh and Miru opened their copies, I looked at the cat on top of the desk, the cat that could not hear a single sound in this world, and called out, "Emily—."

When the lecture ended, I slipped out of the classroom before Yoon could turn and see me. She sat in the very front. I was staring so hard at her all through class that I didn't even hear the professor's voice, but I couldn't stop myself from dashing out of there as soon as class was over. Then I saw her in the middle of a deserted street that had just been stormed by protesters. I thought I was seeing things. She was standing among the tall buildings downtown with her back to me, her hair disheveled, nothing in her hands, barefoot. I called out her name, and she turned to face me. It was her. I remembered the first time I saw her, in the early morning fog next to the river in Ilyeong. It was hard to believe they were the same: that face dripping with tears like she had just washed it in the river and this lone pair of eyes floating in the middle of a city swept by demonstrations. But that's what it's like to live in this city—these things happen all the time, like it's nothing.

| | |

I read about the Genovese murder in the book I stole. It took place on March 13, 1964, before I was born. A woman named

Catherine "Kitty" Genovese had finished a night shift and was returning to her New York apartment at three-fifteen in the morning when she ran into a suspicious-looking man who attacked her with a knife. Thirty-eight of her neighbors heard or saw her dying, but no one came to her aid. When Genovese yelled for help, the lights all went on in the apartment building, but no one opened their door or came down the stairs. One person yelled from their window, "Let that girl alone!" and the assailant ran away. Bleeding profusely, Genovese collapsed on the sidewalk. Nobody came outside to help her. The lights in the apartments went out, and the street grew quiet. The attacker, who had been hurrying back to his car, returned and stabbed Genovese again. She screamed again, and the lights went back on. The attacker ran away again. While Genovese struggled to crawl into the building, the lights went off. The attacker, who had only been hiding, came out once more and finished what he started. Genovese died after being stabbed in three attacks over thirty minutes. Each time she called for help, the lights went on and the attack stopped; when the lights went off again, the attack resumed. It was documented that thirty-eight people watched through their windows as Genovese was stabbed to death. Is this what it means to be human? I felt like putting the book back where I'd found it.

| | |

Miru laughs more now because of Yoon. They're like sisters. Since Yoon gave us our copies of We Are Breathing, Miru has been carrying it in her bag everywhere she goes. The three of us sit together in the professor's class. Sometimes we stop by his office afterward. It's the first time I've ever seen Miru pay attention in class. He even calls her name when he gets to the end of the attendance sheet.

Some of the people in class turn and look at her when he does this. Yoon looks, too, and smiles. Sometimes, in the middle of class, the professor will walk over to us and pat Miru on the back. I wonder if he and Yoon realize—aside from me, they are the only two people that Miru allows to see her scars.

| | |

I met Yoon today, and we walked along the old fortress wall that used to encircle the city. She walks everywhere, even to school. It's hard to picture her not walking. I've been following her and making my own new discoveries. As we walked along the wall, I told her about the Genovese murder. She listened intently.

"She probably would have survived if only one person heard her screams, rather than thirty-eight," she said.

"You think so?" I asked.

"That's what psychologists say," she said, and explained. "They say that's how people's minds work. If one person witnesses someone in danger, they won't hesitate to help. But if there is a group of witnesses, each person will unconsciously wait and do nothing."

I asked her if that was because they all shifted the responsibility to one another, but she said it was not a transfer but a diffusion of responsibility.

"According to psychologists," she said, "the more witnesses there are, the smaller the sense of individual responsibility."

I asked if she was studying psychology, and she said it was one of her electives. Then her face turned gloomy.

"But can human beings really be explained through psychology and psychoanalysis?"

I stared at her. I don't think she was expecting an answer, because she grabbed my hand and mumbled to herself:

"How frightened she must have been each time the lights went out . . . Her terror was probably worse than the pain of being stabbed to death."

—Brown Notebook 4

CHAPTER 5

City Walls

I used to take walks alone, but Myungsuh and Miru started joining me.

We would walk side-by-side until the road narrowed, and then we would fall into single file—Myungsuh in the lead, Miru in the middle, and me in the back. When the narrow road ended, we walked side-by-side again. Walking with them was different from walking alone. I thought I would not be able to see the city in detail the way I did when I was alone, since being a threesome meant we would be paying more attention to one another, but because there were three of us, there seemed to be more to see. If one of us pointed at something and said "Look at that," we would all come together and look as one. I saw things I would have missed on my own. Miru mostly pointed at things in the sky: dark clouds, white clouds, a blazing sunset, the crescent moon hanging primly in the night sky, a halo around the moon at midnight, birds traversing the dark. I started paying more attention to the clouds at night thanks to her. I even looked for constellations like I did when

I was little—first locating the Big Dipper and then using it to find Cassiopeia and Andromeda. Myungsuh mostly pointed out people: ruddy-faced manual laborers working hard to make ends meet; a middle-aged woman diligently turning hairtail fish as they roasted to a golden brown over a brazier set at the entrance to the market street; a grandmother with her back bent forward at a ninety-degree angle, walking so slowly that each step seemed to take a full minute as she carried vegetables to market; red-cheeked children, who looked as if they were growing taller as they played, charging after a bouncing ball; a drunken man perched precariously on an overpass with a cigarette dangling from his mouth.

We made a game out of fixing things that had fallen over or were hanging crookedly. Signs knocked down or hanging askew, shoes dragged outside a door—whenever we spotted something, the three of us would run over together and right it. Miru became especially immersed in the game. Even when we weren't playing, she was obsessed with correcting anything that was out of place. She returned trashcans that had been pulled out into the alley, and she even replanted flowers that had been planted for decoration. Once, while passing a fruit stand, she stopped to line up the apples in even rows. But when the owner came out, she hid her scarred hands in her pockets, and he thought she was stealing. We fixated on silly, pointless things sometimes to fight off our anxiety and loneliness. If Myungsuh saw two lovers walking hand in hand, he would try to step between them to force them to let go. Miru and I stopped him at first, but later we joined in the fun, trying to see how many couples we could separate within a certain distance. After a while, we started looking forward to doing it. Once, we saw an especially affectionate-looking couple, so Miru and I stood back and watched to see if he could actually separate them. When he succeeded, he flashed us a victory sign with his fingers, and we all grinned at one another. But then he pointed back at the couple, and we turned to see that they were walking closer together than before and holding each other's hands more tightly.

Our walks together colored my days even when I was alone. While at home, watching the stars twinkle down at me from an indigo sky, I would catch myself murmuring, "Look at that!" It was as if they were beside me. I would think, *Is that the Milky Way?* and Miru's name would slip out of my mouth. I thought of Myungsuh whenever I watched the ruddy-faced man at the bun shop downstairs pull back the big cast-iron lid to take out a freshly steamed bun, because I knew that Myungsuh would have pointed him out.

On the streets of this city, we often laughed over nothing at all. We would laugh for a bit, and then the mood would turn strange, and our laughter would die out. I had never laughed so hard before. Was it okay to laugh like that? The question seeped into my thoughts now and then. All summer long and through most of the fall, Miru wore that flared skirt every day. I had never seen her wear anything else. Around the city, just as in school, that skirt stuck out like a sore thumb. Even when I was laughing my heart out, if my gaze came to rest on her skirt, I would feel anxious and my laughter would fade.

Sometimes we were joined by a fourth: the boy named Nak Sujang, whom Myungsuh had told me about the day I bumped into him downtown after getting caught in the demonstration. The boy in the joke was a real person who went to the same school as us; he was an aspiring architect who preferred to be called Nak Sujang rather than by his real name, Chaesu. I didn't find out until then that Naksujang, or "Fallingwater" as it was called in English, was the name of the legendary Frank Lloyd Wright house built over a waterfall. I also found out upon meeting him why he had chosen that as his nickname. The house—which he said was not just a house but a work of art—was built above a waterfall on Bear Run in the Pennsylvania mountains as a weekend home for a department store president. Chaesu's face filled with longing as he talked about how surprised visitors were when Fallingwater was completed. It was built without removing a single tree. The Bear Run stream ran below the house, and the living room and four bedrooms floated unsupported above the water. You heard the water before you saw it. The terrace, which was larger than the interior of the house, was positioned to allow entrance into the house from a bridge over the falls. Chaesu added that the house was proof that even architecture has a soul. He preferred to be called Nak Sujang. He had never left the city, having been born and raised there. We tried telling Miru the joke about Nak Sujang and the girl, but she didn't laugh. She looked sad instead. She sighed and leaned against a telephone pole.

"You're supposed to laugh!" we said.

"Sounds like a sad story to me," she said.

She continued to look glum. Feeling sheepish, I leaned against the pole with her. "I should take a picture," Myung-suh said as he tried to lift the mood by making a frame with his fingers and pretending to take a picture of the two of us. But then he, too, joined us in leaning against the pole. The three of us stood there for a long time and watched as people walked by.

Nak Sujang knew everything there was to know about the city. He took us to Bukchon, where old tiled-roofed houses stood with their eaves touching, and to Tongui-dong to see a six-hundred-year-old white lacebark pine tree.

"It's almost as old as this city you're so curious about," he said to me.

I walked around the pine tree again, marveling at how long it had survived.

"They say it stopped growing during the Japanese occupation," he added.

We sneered at him, but he laughed and said, "I don't believe it, either, but I *want* to believe it!"

One day, we were walking along Cheonggyecheon Stream toward Dongdaemun Market. I often walked that way to visit the used-book stores on that street. But the road Nak Sujang took us to had much more than just bookstores. It was after dark when he guided us to a market street. There, people who slept by day and worked at night were rushing about. The market stalls stood shoulder to shoulder, divided by building and block, and I could not tell one place from another. The market was so dense with stalls that I could never have memorized all of their names. Dongdaemun Market, Gwangjang Market to the north, a wholesale market that sold only shoes, Dongdaemun Jonghap Market . . . The market stalls, all with "Dongdaemun" in their names, looked like a maze, but Nak

Sujang guided us forth easily like an explorer. We made our pilgrimage through Pyeonghwa Market, Shin Pyeonghwa Market, Dong Pyeonghwa Market, and Cheong Pyeonghwa Market, and then followed the stream until we emerged on either the north or south end and continued on to the Dongil mall, the Tongil mall, Donghwa Market, Heungin Market, Nam Pyeonghwa Market, the Susanmul fish market . . . Nak Sujang was like a walking map of the city. I understood why Myungsuh included him in our travels. He told us that Baeogae Road was named after Baeogae Market, which was what Dongdaemun Market was called during the Joseon Dynasty. He also told us Gwangjang Market was the very first market to be built in the modern era. He said it was created at the urging of the people of Joseon after the Japan-Korea Protectorate Treaty. After the signing of that treaty, which paved the way for Japan to colonize Korea, Japanese capital was used to take over Namdaemun Market. When he told us all of this, he sounded like a professor of modern Korean history. As I watched him speak, I found it hard to believe that he was the same person who had flubbed a joke so badly because of a cute girl. He seemed to know what I was thinking because he added, "And that was in the year 1905!" and grinned at me.

On the days that we walked with Nak Sujang, I left my maps at home. Later, our excursions turned into a club. No one formally proposed that we start a club, like the people who had proposed Gwangjang Market in 1905, but gradually, more and more of our friends began to surreptitiously follow us until, one day, I found myself walking near my own neighborhood of Dongsung-dong with Nak Sujang and nine other people. He told us that Marronnier Park was once a college campus, that there were streetcars and music halls and a coffeehouse where students used to go to drink tea, listen to music, and discuss literature and politics. I looked where he was pointing, and there was the sign for the Hakrim Dabang coffeehouse. I had walked past it all the time without realizing how old the coffeehouse was. To me, Marronnier Park had never been anything more than what it was at that moment.

Someone suggested to Nak Sujang that we invite Professor Yoon on a tour of the old fortress wall in the mountains overlooking the city.

"You can't see it all in one day. You have to choose a section," Nak Sujang said.

"Even if you packed a lunch and spent the whole day at it? What about a three-day, two-night tour?"

Everyone laughed at the suggestion.

"It's not that easy. The Seoul Fortress Wall is really beautiful. It doesn't look that long when it's right in front of you, but it's broken up into different sections. You have to hike down and back up again to reach the next section, and the path is long and winding. Not even three days and two nights will be enough to see all of it. Besides, we have to make sure we have time to hang out and have fun while we're there."

"Nak Sujang! Whence came your knowledge?" someone joked.

"'Tis a dream of mine to be an architect!" Nak Sujang followed suit.

"But what does all this have to do with architecture?"

"Architects have to know everything there is to know about a space. You have to know its past and its present. That way you can build its future."

"Then you should be majoring in architecture!"

"I already told you I didn't get into the architecture program. Anyway, I'll be an architect someday. Just you wait and see! I was born in this city. I want to spend the rest of my life here, designing new spaces and preserving old ones. If you want to see the wall, we can get to it from here. Shall we? We just have to get to the top of Naksan Mountain."

We followed Nak Sujang out of Marronnier Park and headed for the mountain, which I had seen only from my window. With all the walking we were doing, I was turned around and confused about exactly where we were. Someone exclaimed, "I can't believe there's a place like this in the city!" Others doubted whether those narrow alleyways were really leading to the fortress wall. Nak Sujang told us about the mountain, that it was solid granite and shaped like a camel's back. Meanwhile, I looked down and caught sight of the roof of my building. I pictured myself down there as if I was watching someone else: there I was, watering the table palm, tying my shoelaces before leaving for school, coming out to the rooftop late at night and drawing hopscotch lines, tossing a pebble and hopping on one foot, grabbing the pebble and hopping back to the first square, just as I used to do in the courtyard of my childhood home.

I was trailing behind the group, still gazing down at my building, when Myungsuh walked up next to me. He came close and whispered in my ear.

"I'm in love with you, Jung Yoon."

Startled at his confession, I could not take my eyes off of the building below. Without meaning to, I blurted out, "More than Miru?"

He looked down at my building with me and said, "So much that I think of you when I picture where I want to be in ten years."

"But more than Miru?" I looked over at her. She was walking beside Hyuntae, who had earned the nickname Sunflower because he sat in the very front row of Professor Yoon's poetry class and swiveled his head back and forth to follow Professor Yoon's gaze. Miru's skirt blocked the granite of Naksan Mountain for a moment before moving away again.

"When I was little," Myungsuh began, "my older brothers and I went to our grandparents' house. My brothers snuck out of the house after dark to hunt for sparrows with one of our older cousins. I went with them. That was how I found out that sparrows live inside the roofs of thatched cottages. There were so many of them. They shivered every time we shined the flashlight on them. My brothers started grabbing them with both hands. One grabbed five birds at once. The birds were helpless. We were soon short of hands. My brother pulled a baby bird out of the straw, put it in my hands, and told me to hold on to it. The baby bird was too frightened to flap its wings and just cowered in my hand. It was so warm and soft. I was afraid it would fly away, so I put it in my pocket. I couldn't stop petting it. I think it was the first time I ever touched something that young. My small pocket was squirming with life. It felt like I held the entire world in it. I

don't remember how old I was, but I remember the joy I felt.
I love you as much as the joy I felt."

As much as the joy I felt—each word was like a drop of rain.
I trailed my hand along the fortress wall and stared at Miru's
skirt moving ahead of us.

"More than Miru?" I asked again.

"My brothers were still catching sparrows when my cousin
told me to give him the baby bird. I didn't want to, but I took
the squirming bird out of my pocket anyway. I wanted another
look at it. It was so small. I don't think it could fly yet. My cousin
plucked the bird from my palm and went off with it. I should
never have taken it out of my pocket. When he returned, the
birds were all burnt to a crisp. Their bones were popping out
of their skin. I couldn't even tell which of the birds was mine. I
looked at their burnt feathers and blackened skin and burst into
tears. I cried for him to give me back my bird, but it was too
late. My yelling must have irritated him, because he grabbed the
smallest one and shoved it in my face, and said, 'Here it is.' When
I took that charred baby bird from him, I felt the world crash
down on me. It was the first time I had ever held something that
had died. I love you as much as the sorrow I felt."

As much as the sorrow I felt—those drops of rain continued
to fall. In order to avoid his eyes, I asked again: "More than
Miru?"

Though I had meant it as a joke at first, my words sounded
more serious, and I felt strange. I wasn't sure what I was really
asking him.

"After I moved to the city, I met up one night with some
old high school friends. It was March, but it was snowing hard

that day. Seven or eight of us met up in front of the university, and we wandered around the city until late. When we got to Namdaemun Market, it was the middle of the night. Inside one of the covered food carts was a row of grilled sparrows. As we shivered in the cold, we pooled the last of our drinking money and were deciding on drinks and snacks when someone suggested grilled sparrow. Everyone got excited. I was the only one who hadn't had it before. While I stared sourly at the birds, my friends argued over whether grilled sparrows were better when brushed with sesame oil or sprinkled with salt or grilled over a real charcoal fire, and whether you should catch them with a net or use a shotgun. One guy even said to soak uncooked grains of rice in liquor and sprinkle them around the birds' nests, wait an hour for the birds to get drunk and fall asleep, and then collect them. It seemed like the whole world was divided into those who had eaten grilled sparrow and those who had not. Meanwhile, the sparrows were brushed with oil and roasted over the grill and then placed before us. The feathers were plucked and intestines removed, so the bodies were flat, but the heads were still attached. It was such an uncomfortable feeling. Everyone grabbed a bird and started eating. The bird in front of me had a crack running down its tiny skull. All I could do was stare at it, so the guys goaded me to eat it. They said, 'You're not getting philosophical on us, are you?' They started berating me for not joining in. They all stared at me as they ate. They seemed to be saying, *We'll see how long you can hold out.* There on that noisy market street with the snow falling around us, I picked up the sparrow with the cracked skull. I don't know what made me do it. I could have said no. I bit into the bird's head. The sound of the skull crunching between my teeth echoed loudly in my ears . . . I love you as much as the despair I felt."

As much as the despair I felt—his voice seeped into me and sent ripples through my heart. Why couldn't liking someone simply be joyful? Why must it also contain sorrow and despair? I took my hand off of the fortress wall and hurried to join the rest of the group. When he called to me from behind, I already knew what he was going to say. I turned to look at him.

"Let's remember this day forever, right? Is that what you were going to say?" I said.

He raised his eyebrows, and the corners of his mouth lifted into a bashful smile. He walked up to me and took my hand. I squeezed his back. His voice had sounded melancholy. It was suffused with the loneliness of one who knows he is bound for loss. Ten years later, twenty years later . . . Where would we be in that time? I felt confused and squeezed his hand again. He squeezed back even tighter.

"Miru is in love with someone else," he said.

"Who?"

His face darkened.

"The guy who disappeared?" I asked.

"Professor Yoon."

"Who?" I was sure I'd misheard him.

"Professor Yoon."

Miru was in love with our professor? I suddenly felt sorry for her. It was like seeing a green apple lying on the dusty ground of an orchard, overcome by the summer rains before it could ripen. I pulled my hand out of his and looked ahead at Miru. Though the path was steep, Miru was walking with both hands in her pockets and her head down. If she had been within reach, I would have shook her by the shoulders and yelled, "Miru, no!" I ran toward her. The houses at the base of Naksan Mountain rushed past, and the rays of the setting sun pierced my eyes. As I ran, panting for air, everyone turned to look at me. They must have thought I had something urgent to say, because all eyes were on my face when I stopped next to Miru. I let out a deep breath. She stared at me wide-eyed. I put my hand in her pocket and clasped her scarred hand. It squirmed inside of mine. I squeezed it even tighter than I had squeezed Myungsuh's hand. When I did so, the ache that had swept through me subsided somewhat. Miru's hand stopped squirming. We stayed that way until Myungsuh caught up to us. The whole time, I was staring at the rays of sunlight shining on Miru's skirt. When the others, who all assumed I had something to say from the way I'd run to them out of breath, saw that I was only standing there with my hand in Miru's pocket, they shrugged and continued on their way. Myungsuh caught up to Nak Sujang and fell in beside him.

"What's wrong?" Miru asked when it was just the two of us.

Miru always had her copy of *We Are Breathing* with her. She must have had it all but memorized. She also carried a notebook with her that she used to record everything she ate. If she ate noodles in clear broth, she would not just write *noodles* but would record the dish in minute detail, describing the white noodles in anchovy broth, the spring onion and shiitake mushroom garnish, the five pieces of sweet pickled radish, and even the size of the diced white radish kimchi. Eating with her meant having to first watch her record everything in her notebook. It was as strange as when I found out that Dahn was afraid of spiders, and I would catch myself staring at her scarred hands. She looked very serious when she made those entries, as if she were carrying out a ritual.

The three of us used the same notebook when we took turns writing stories. We would go to the library or to a café, and she would open to a clean page in that notebook filled with lists of food organized by date. One of us would begin by writing down a sentence. The next person would write the next sentence, and so on. It would begin with random thoughts, but after a while we would get more serious about what we were writing. Once, Miru wrote, *Hands are my favorite part of a person.* I followed that with *Pitiful, gracious hands that never have a moment's rest.* Myungsuh wrote, *You can tell a person's life from their hands.* Watching our sentences accumulate one line after another felt like watering a bean and waiting for the sprout to appear. I thought about how Miru would rest her left hand on top of her copy of *We Are Breathing* whenever the three of us continued one another's sentences.

"What's wrong?" Miru asked me again.

This time, she was the one who looked worried. Her eyes were fixed on me. The slender fold in her left eyelid looked deeper than the one on the right. I had never looked this closely at her eyes before, my own having always been drawn to her scarred hands first. Her glossy black hair blew in the wind and covered her smooth forehead. Was everything Miru had written about hands that day not fiction after all? After

Myungsuh wrote, *I bow my head in respect to all hands rough with labor,* Miru had added a very long passage: *To hold someone's hand, you must first know when to let go. If you miss the chance to let go of a hand that you have carelessly grabbed, the moment will pass and turn awkward. I had gotten off the bus and was coming out of the underpass in front of the school when I bumped into him. I meant to say hello but grabbed his hand instead. His thin hand rested in mine. His strong bones. The skin felt rough. He smiled with his eyes and squeezed my hand back. I should have let go then, but we started walking together hand in hand. The pleasantness vanished and was replaced with an uncomfortable silence. Since we had missed the chance to let go naturally, I became more and more aware of my hand. It would have been too awkward to drop his, but I couldn't keep holding it either. He must have felt the same. We didn't say a word but continued walking to school, awkwardly holding hands. Sweat was dripping from mine, I was so intent on figuring out when I should let go. On pins and needles I walked and, after a while, I started to calm down. I wanted to stay that way forever, walking hand in hand with him. We passed a hotel. We passed a bookstore and a clothing store. When we crossed the street and reached that spot across from the auditorium, the campus was noisy. There were students sitting on every bench and standing around every pay phone and bulletin board. He looked at me and asked, "Can I have my hand back now?" He sounded like he was asking for my permission. I finally let go. He patted me on the shoulder and strode on ahead of me.* Was the hand that belonged to "him" in Miru's story that day Professor Yoon's hand?

"Ouch! Let go of my hand!"

I loosened my grip.

"Do you hold Myungsuh's hand that tightly, too?"

"What?"

"You squeeze too tight!"

We looked at each other and started laughing. Miru tried to wiggle her hand free, but I held on. Suddenly she asked me to meet her in front of the Dongsung Bathhouse at three on Saturday afternoon. It was a neighborhood bathhouse. From my room, I could see the redbrick chimney rising up between the old houses and the white letters that spelled out "Dongsung Bathhouse," but I had never been inside.

"Are you asking me to go to the public bath with you?" I asked.

"Yes."

It was the first time she had invited me somewhere alone—and to a public bath, of all places, not the movies or a café? I looked at Nak Sujang. He was standing on top of the fortress wall and pointing east, as if his body were a compass, showing the others where Samseon-dong and Changsin-dong were. He explained that we had climbed up the western slope of Naksan Mountain, and down there was Dongsung-dong, and over there was Ihwa-dong, and over there was Changshin-dong. Myungsuh looked back at Miru and me. The setting sun bathed him in its light.

Natsume Sōseki was an esteemed Japanese writer from the Meiji period who traveled to England on a Japanese government scholarship. His experience in England was so upsetting that he temporarily suffered a nervous breakdown. After becoming a writer, he quit his post as professor at Tokyo Imperial University, which was an honorable position to have held, in order to concentrate on writing novels. Writing seemed to be the only way for him to accept and overcome the shock of modernity that had so scarred him mentally. They said that in his later years he spent his mornings studying English literature and writing the modern fiction that he had mastered, and his afternoons composing Chinese poetry. You could say that he split his day in half in order to travel between East and West. Some say that it shows how refined he was, but I see it as a mental struggle to not be sucked under by either side.

| | |

Today, I was over at Yoon's, sitting on the wooden deck outside, when she showed me something in Miru's notebook. It had been a while since we last wrote stories together, and we were getting *ready to start a new round of sentences. Miru had gone inside to wash her hands first. Listed in Miru's notebook were the names of people who had disappeared for suspicious reasons and the details of their cases.*

"Do you think she'll ever find out what happened to her sister's boyfriend?" she asked.

As we continued searching for him, all we found were other missing people who had died gruesome deaths—we never found any trace of Mirae's boyfriend. While Yoon was poring over the notebook, I pushed her hair back and peered at her face. Her dark, questioning eyes met mine.

"If Miru ever asks you to help her look, say no!" I said.

I sounded crazy, but she just looked at me.

"Promise me," I said. "You won't be helping her if you do."

She asked me what on earth was wrong and looked back down at Miru's notebook.

"Don't let her leave," I said.

She looked back and forth between me and the notebook and then suddenly kissed me on the lips.

—Brown Notebook 5

CHAPTER 6

Empty House

On Saturday, I was just about to leave when he called.

"What are you up to?" he asked.

"I'm heading out the door to meet Miru."

"You're meeting Miru?"

I could have just said yes and left it at that, but I hesitated. It was the first time she and I would be hanging out without him.

"Where?" he asked.

"We're going to the public bath."

"Dongsung Bathhouse?"

"How did you know?"

He let out a long sigh. I felt bad for leaving him out. But he couldn't exactly go to the public bath with us. Neither of us said anything for a moment. I looked down at my shower basket filled with a towel, a comb, shampoo, and other bath items.

"It's good," he said finally.

I wasn't sure what he meant by that exactly, so I kept listening.

"It's good that Miru has you."

He hung up without saying goodbye. His voice was so flat that I was caught off guard by how distant he seemed. It felt like very long ago that we had walked around the city together and watched Miru straighten crooked signs and line up scattered flowerpots, or drank coffee and went to the Twelve Young Artists Exhibit, or wrote stories together, or went to Professor Yoon's class. I stood there with the phone in my hand long after he had hung up

My father had brought the telephone the last time he and my cousin came to visit. He had applied for a phone number and installed it for me. The whole time he was visiting, he fretted over the fact that I lived on top of such a steep hill. He always called early in the morning or late at night. The phone would ring, and I would know at once that it was him. I was never wrong. My father and cousin called the most often, followed by Myungsuh. I had written my phone number on his and Miru's palms. Miru called me exactly once to say, "So this is the right number," and hung up.

When I stepped outside, I saw the mailman putting a letter in my mailbox. Since I had never received any mail at that address, I was going to just leave it there, but the handwriting on the envelope sticking out of the mailbox looked familiar. I bent down and peeked inside to discover it was from Dahn. I opened it immediately.

October 9
Yoon,
I'm heading up to the city. I'll call you in a few days before
I get on the train. I got your address and phone number
from your father.
Dahn

Dahn's letter, written in his energetic handwriting, was so brief that it could have been sent by telegram. He didn't ask how I was or say how he was doing. I had not told Dahn that I had moved back to the city. I hadn't even sent him my contact information. It must have hurt his feelings, but he never mentioned it. I put Dahn's letter in my pocket with my mother's ring and walked down the alley. A cold breeze blew down the back of my neck. As I walked in silence with my head down on the way to meet Miru, I kept touching the letter in my pocket. I realized that this was the longest I had ever gone without talking to him. I saw Myungsuh and Miru every day, but I had not told Dahn how to find me. The truth was that I couldn't bring myself to. Each time I thought of him, I was reminded of the way he had said, "You don't love me."

As soon as I saw the public bath, Miru's skirt caught my eye. She stood out everywhere she went because of that skirt. Even more so when the seasons changed. She stood out in the summer because the pattern clashed with everything around her, and the rest of the year, she stood out because the fabric was meant for warm weather. Miru was holding the tickets for the public bath—she had already paid for us to get in. When

I walked up to her, she handed me a locker key. We went in and stood in front of locker numbers sixty-one and sixty-two. I took my clothes off and started folding them. I glanced over at Miru, who was unhooking her skirt.

"Why do you always wear that?" I asked.

Miru hesitated. Then she folded the skirt and put it in the locker without answering. She took off her shirt as well, folded it, and put it inside. Even when we were alone together, Miru was often so lost in thought that I felt compelled to ask what she was thinking. She slipped off her underwear and placed it on top of her clothes. Everything—her bra, her underwear, and even the shirt she wore with the skirt—was white.

Though it was a Saturday, there weren't many other women. In one corner, a young mother was shampooing her daughter's hair. The girl looked like she was around four years old. There were two women in the tub: one who looked old enough to be a grandmother and a middle-aged woman who looked like her daughter-in-law. Miru and I rinsed off first under the standing showers.

"We had a public bath like this close to where we grew up. My sister and I went there all the time. Our mother would buy us a month's worth of bath tickets at a time. We would get up in the morning and head straight there to wash our faces, shampoo our hair, and play in the water . . ." With her face covered in water droplets, Miru smiled as if she had just remembered something. Her cheeks were red from the heat.

"The owner of the bath had four sons. He used to get drunk and line them up out front and recite their business motto. Passersby would stop and watch. All four of the boys were very handsome, not to mention good students, good athletes, and well behaved. The other boys were constantly being compared with them. 'They get good grades, so why can't you?' 'They're tall, so why are you so short?' I think the owner did that so he could show them off. He had a big smile on his face each time. My sister and I used to go there just to hear him. After a while, everyone in the neighborhood had all but memorized the bathhouse's business motto."

I asked her what it was and, with a solemn look on her face, she recited it for me line by line: "You all have to clean up sometime. It's just a matter of time. And if we do our job right, we'll clean up, too."

We laughed at the pun. The woman washing her daughter's hair must have been listening because she also started giggling. Even the grandmother soaking in the tub had a smile on her face.

"One of those boys was Myungsuh!" Miru said.

"What?"

I plopped down on the floor under the shower and burst out laughing. The more I tried to stop, the harder I laughed until I was almost in tears. I could see Miru's body clearly, even through the cloud of steam. Her legs, which were always covered up by the skirt, were long and her back was straight. Her hair was pinned up with a gold barrette, baring the line of her neck where it curved gently into her shoulders. While we were showering, the tub emptied. I climbed in first, and Miru followed. We leaned against the tiled wall side by side, stretched our legs out, and sank into the water. My cousin used to invite me to the public bath with her, but I always avoided it, saying, "Who goes bathing together?" She would counter by saying, "We can scrub each other's backs." But I would retreat into my room. What would she have said if she saw Miru and me in the public bath together? The only person I had ever gone to a public bath with was my mother. I pictured the way my mother used to bathe me at home when I was little: boiling water on the stove, pouring it into a big tub, adding cold water, and testing the temperature with her elbow. She was so young back then. I remembered copying her and dipping my little elbow into the water. She used to pluck peach blossoms when they were in bloom and float them in the bathwater. "To whiten our little Yoon's skin," she would say. She also used to clip the irises that bloomed all along the alley outside our gate and boil them in a large pot of water to add to my bath. I remembered dozing off in the water as she scrubbed my back and washed my face, the soft, delicate scent of blossoms tickling my nose.

I felt sad suddenly, so I poked Miru's foot with my own under the water. She tapped mine back in response. I kicked her again, a little harder than before. She followed suit. Our little game started off quietly but soon turned to splashing. The middle-aged woman, who was washing the grandmother's hair, looked over at us. Embarrassed, I rolled over onto my stomach and rested my arms against the edge of the tub; Miru copied me. The scars on her hands shimmered in the water.

"She used to sit in the water and wonder what the weather was like outside," Miru said.

"Who?"

"My sister," she said. "Do you wonder what the weather's like outside, too?"

"Sometimes," I said. "When you're in here, it feels like another world. Sometimes I do wonder, is it raining out there? Or maybe snowing?"

"My sister used to say that, too."

"What's she like?"

Miru dipped her face in the water. Drops of water hung from her eyelashes.

"She wore the same clothes every summer for four years. But the next summer, she took them out to discover that they were threadbare and unwearable. The sleeves were frayed. She took them to a seamstress and asked her to make her a new set in the exact same style from the exact same fabric. The tailor examined the frayed clothes and said she could make the same style but the fabric was no longer available. So my sister left. I told her the tailor could make her something better, but she said there was no point if it wasn't the same fabric . . . That's what she was like."

I began to wonder about Miru's older sister.

"She also had a sweater our mother knitted for her in elementary school that she wore until middle school. She grew and grew, but she kept putting it on even when it rode up in the back. The year she started middle school, she grew fourteen centimeters. The sweater didn't fit anymore. She asked our mother to knit her the exact same sweater as a birthday present. Our mother had stopped knitting by then, but my sister badgered her until she started re-knitting it with new yarn in the same color. She even learned a new knitting technique and added a pocket, which the first sweater did not have. When she gave my sister the sweater, my sister said it was different from the old one and refused to wear it. That's what she was like."

Miru's face suddenly darkened. "To tell the truth, I don't really know. What kind of person she was, I mean. We were only a year apart in age, but she was born twelve years after our parents got married. They said they thought they couldn't have a baby and had given up when my sister suddenly came along. Our mother became pregnant with me just two months after my sister was born. I guess that's why I felt like I had been keeping an eye on her ever since I was in our mother's belly. I must have been really attached to her. When we were little, I did everything she did. If she bobbed her hair, I got mine bobbed, and when she started learning piano, I started learning piano. When we played hide-and-go-seek with the other kids, they only had to look for my sister to find me. I was always right there beside her. It wasn't because she was older than me. I just didn't feel like myself unless I was with her. Do you know what I mean?"

I was an only child, so it was hard for me to understand.

"When she was nine, my sister announced that she wanted to become a ballerina. I still remember the look on her face when she said it. She was enrolled in elementary school first, of course, but I went to school right along with her. When she moved up to the second grade, I stayed behind in the first grade. So I was in second grade and she was in third grade when she said she was going to be a ballerina when she grew up. Up until then, I had assumed she had no secrets from me, but I had no idea what ballet was. I felt like ballet was pushing us apart for the first time. Maybe it would have been better if we had grown apart then . . ."

Water dripped from the ceiling onto Miru's shoulder.

"I decided that I had to do whatever it took to become a ballerina like my sister. We started taking lessons every day after school. One of the girls in our class had been studying ballet since she was six. My sister burst into tears when she heard that. She thought she couldn't compete with the girl and complained that she would "never get that time back." She wept hysterically. She was only nine, but she already knew what it felt like to have her heart broken. Because she came along so late, my sister was very special to our parents. To console her, they not only had her take lessons at the academy but they even installed a barre in the house so she could practice. They invited the ballet teacher over to give her private lessons. I followed along beside her. I heard the ballet teacher whisper to her that she had the right body type for ballet, but the teacher just looked at me apologetically. I didn't care. She was right. I wasn't as flexible as my sister, and I didn't enjoy it the way she did. I just followed along because she was doing it."

The water dripping from the ceiling must have tickled because she wiped the drops off with her palm and laughed.

"Flexible, ha! I was as stiff as a board. I definitely did not take after her in that respect."

I smiled.

"I couldn't even do something as basic as the splits. The classes centered on my sister. By the time she was doing arabesques, I was still figuring out how to stand in first position.

But it didn't matter. I was happy to watch her grow more beautiful and more talented by the day. Since I had no interest in comparing myself to her or surpassing her, I had no complaints. Those were our happiest times. Our parents looked happy, too. They expected great things from my sister."

The other women in the bathhouse slowly trickled out until we were the only ones left.

"You have to have an ear for music to do ballet. I was less interested in doing ballet myself than in watching my sister's movements grow deeper, subtler, and more sophisticated with each day. But most of all, I liked listening to music with her. My sister understood ballet intuitively. She mastered complicated movements quickly and would lose herself in them. It was like she was born to be a ballerina. When she wasn't practicing, she read books on ballet. She sounded like a teacher when she talked about the history of ballet, the costumes, the ballerinas and ballerinos. Her cheeks would turn red with excitement whenever she told me something new she had learned. I learned the names of legendary ballet dancers from her—Ulanova, Pavlova, Nijinsky, Nureyev. If the moon was out on a night when she was telling me about ballet, she would go outside and dance under the moonlight. Her dream was to dance the role of the Dying Swan. She really did look like a swan in the moonlight."

"I've never heard anyone talk about their older sister the way you do."

"What kinds of things do other people say?"

"Most just talk about the fights they have."

"Fights?"

"I think most sisters push and shove each other and argue about which one should get the better room, or wear an outfit they like first, or read a book first, or get to use the hairdryer first. But you put your sister before yourself."

"That's because she was better than me." She sounded pained. "Do you think we're unusual?"

I didn't answer.

"Well?" she asked again.

"You don't seem like normal sisters."

"We don't?"

"Do you really have to ask?"

Miru sighed. The water had cooled. I reached over and turned on the faucet to add more hot water. Miru dipped her face. She seemed to be holding her breath. She stayed under so long that I was about to yell her name when she lifted her face and exhaled deeply.

"Yoon," she said, "will you go with me to my old house?"

"When?"

"After we're done bathing."

She looked sad, so I agreed. After hearing my answer, she stuck her face back underwater.

The house was up a very steep hill. Miru lifted a rock beside the green front gate to retrieve a hidden key. Inside the gate was a small yard overgrown with weeds. A sunflower, heavy with seeds, hung its head. It was apparent that no one had been by in a long time. A small deck, the wood faded, sat in the middle of the yard as if someone had discarded it there, and a rusted drying rack lay flat beside it. The thick weeds looked as if they would barge in through the front door at any moment.

"The house is vacant?" I asked.

"For now," Miru said, her voice trailing off.

I saw something poking up from among the weeds like stalks of green onions. Small white flowers hung from the tips. As I was looking at them, Miru told me they were called white rain lilies. I crouched down in front of them and stared at the white blossoms. The petals looked even paler in contrast to the dismal surroundings. Miru walked up the steps to the front door, the keys in her hand, but then she hesitated and turned back.

"I can't do it," she said.

"What's wrong?"

"Let's just go."

Miru's face was pale.

"I thought I could go inside if you were with me," she said. "But I can't."

Her voice was trembling. She was already at the front gate, so I grabbed my basket and joined her. She locked it and put the key back under the rock. Carrying our shower baskets, we made our way down the hill. The sun was still out when we left the public bath, but now dusk was falling. Halfway down the hill, I glanced back. The lights had already gone on in the other houses; Miru's old house seemed to be watching us from between them. Was that really where the three of them had lived together? Miru was once again walking with her head down like she was staring at her own heart.

As if reading my mind, she suddenly said, "It is."

"What?"

"That house—it's where Myungsuh, my sister, and I used to live."

"Why don't you live there anymore?"

"Because she's gone," she said. "Without her, it wouldn't look right for me to live in the house alone with Myungsuh, even if he and I did grow up together. I didn't think anything of it when my sister was around, but afterward we naturally parted ways. He moved in with his relatives in Jongam-dong, and I went to Myeongnyun-dong. I think the house has been empty too long. It looks abandoned. Our parents rented it for us at first, but later they bought it and put it in my sister's name."

"Hmm."

"I know what you're thinking," she said.

"You do?"

"Yes."

"What am I thinking?"

"That our parents were rich . . . Am I right?"

When she said it out loud, it seemed I had been thinking that. Night was falling over both of us. We walked through Dongsung-dong and Hyehwa-dong toward Myeongnyun-dong. We didn't speak the whole way. Passersby stole curious glances at our shower baskets. Miru's skirt fluttered in the evening breeze.

There was a demonstration in front of Myeongdong Cathedral today to support laid-off factory workers who are on a hunger strike. I was there with Nak Sujang. Yoon found out somehow and came to find us. Even amid all those hundreds of people, she immediately caught my eye. I must have caught her eye, too, because she came right over to where we were sitting and shouting protest slogans. She sat down next to me. We tried to head farther into Myeongdong, but the riot police came after us and chased us around until we ducked into a small bookstore. The store was packed with people like us. All of the other shops had shut their doors, but the bookstore owner seemed to have kept his open to help the protesters. It wasn't until we made it inside that I realized Nak Sujang was no longer with us. Yoon and I leaned against the wall, our eyes red from tear gas. When I asked her why she came, she said she wasn't necessarily trying to find me. She said, "I'm just here because you are." She picked up a book of poetry from one of the displays and opened it. It had been lying face down, as if someone was in the middle of reading it. Yoon read the copyright date and opened to the first page. She liked to know when a book had first come out. I looked at the price tag: 350 won. In a quiet voice, she read the preface: "I make my way forward like a donkey with its head down, groaning beneath its heavy burden and enduring the taunts of mischief makers." She whispered the last line, as if it were meant for my ears only. "Whenever you want me, wherever you want me to be, I will be there." Through bloodshot eyes, she read the poet's name last: Francis Jammes.

| | |

Lǔ Xùn was one of the greatest writers of modern China. He was respected by Nationalists and Communists alike, despite having gone to Imperial Japan for his education. I asked the professor about Japan's victory in the Russo-Japanese War. Did people in other parts of Asia share in the sense of victory, since it was the first time an Asian country beat a European country, rather than criticizing Japan as an aggressor nation? After mulling it over for a moment, the professor said that Lǔ Xùn was critical of Japan's aggression toward China, but after the Russo-Japanese War, people from all over Asia wanted to learn from Japan. So it was a natural choice for Lǔ Xùn to go there to learn advanced Western medical science. The professor also said that when Lǔ Xùn was a student in Japan, he had a Japanese teacher who took all of his students, including Lǔ Xùn, to a Confucian shrine in Ochanomizu. Lǔ Xùn had left China in order to distance himself from premodern things that symbolized Confucianism, so this must have been a great shock to him. What went through his mind when his teacher, whom he had met in a far-off land that he had traveled to in order to learn new ways, presented him with the very thing he had been trying to discard and made him bow down before it?

What the professor said gave me a lot to think about.

| | |

Yesterday I went back to the bookstore where we'd found the collection of poems by Francis Jammes so I could buy it for Yoon. But the owner said it wasn't for sale. He said it was a private copy given to him years ago by his first love. I walked out of the store feeling disappointed, but he ran out after me and handed me the book. I offered to pay, but he patted me on the shoulder. "What would you pay me for it? 350 won? I think it's more meaningful if I just give it to you. Later on, if someone wants a book that only you own, you can return the favor." I watched him walk back into the store. I thought about what the professor had said: everyone has his or her own means of defining value.

| | |

I'm trying to think about what I can do. But instead all that comes to mind are the things I can't do. How do we judge truth and goodness? Where are justice and righteousness hiding? A society that is violent or corrupt prohibits mutual communication. A society that fears communication is unable to solve any problem. It looks for someone to shift the responsibility to and turns even more violent.

| | |

I want us all, starting with me, to be confident and stand on our own two feet. I want relationships that are honest and free of secrets and abuse.

—*Brown Notebook 6*

CHAPTER 7

Bottom of the Stairs

Miru stopped in front of a house and swung open the waist-high wooden gate. The gate seemed to be shared by several households. The yard was much bigger than it looked from outside. Miru led me away from the yard toward a staircase just a few steps away from the gate.

"Watch your step," she said.

The stairs led way, way down. Each time I thought we had surely reached the bottom, we turned the corner to find another set of steps. It felt like we were climbing back down the hill we had just come up. Miru's small studio was at the bottom of the stairs. She took a key from her pocket and fit it into the lock. The door opened, and she reached inside, flipped on the light, and called out, "Emily!" I glanced back at the stairs. It felt like we were cut off from the surface of the earth. Her room was much darker than the abandoned house she had taken me to after the bathhouse. She probably had to keep the light on even during the day.

"Come in," she said.

Miru stepped inside first and slipped off her shoes. I did not see any other shoes except for the sneakers she once loaned me. I thought about how she tied the laces for me that day. Later, I had crouched down in front of the faucet outside my studio and washed them. Those shoes, which I had set out to dry on the sunniest part of the waist-high concrete wall that ran around the edge of the roof, only to accidentally drop them and have to run downstairs to retrieve them and wash them all over again, were the same ones I had worn on the day we went from the riot-swept streets to my place to eat together—the same day that I had grabbed her hand in Professor Yoon's office. Her fingers had trembled in mine. They would have been slender and pale if not for the scars. Later still, I had grabbed her hand again as she lay on her stomach in my room and leafed through her copy of *We Are Breathing*. My cousin used to do the same thing to me. If she saw me staring mindlessly at my own hands, she would grab them and say, "You're lonely." She thought people tended to look at their hands when they felt lonely. I had never thought of it that way, but later I thought of what she'd said whenever I caught myself staring at my hands. I guess it's true that people's habits rub off on each other when they live together. After I touched Miru's hands for the first time, she stopped hiding them from me.

Miru quietly called out the cat's name.

"Jung Yoon," she said, "come look."

I took off my shoes and set them beside Miru's. I set my shower basket beside hers as well. Then I joined her.

"Look how she's sleeping."

Emily was asleep in a small box below the window. She was lying on her back with her mouth open, belly exposed, and all four limbs in the air. I couldn't help but giggle. The cat was oblivious to our presence. It was the first time I had ever seen a sleeping cat this close up. Her nose and ears, and even the spaces between her tiny claws, were pink.

"Is that how cats normally sleep?" I asked.

"No. Sometimes she sleeps curled in a ball or sprawled out flat like a puddle. Sometimes she even sleeps standing up with her eyes closed, or with her face resting on her front legs. She's so flexible that she can sleep with her lower half stretched out flat and her upper body facing the other way. That's my favorite. She looks so peaceful when she sleeps that way."

The cat did look peaceful. Her pose suggested that she did not care who might walk in. It was very different from when she strutted around elegantly with her tail in the air. There was a green smudge on one of her white cheeks.

"Where did that come from?" I asked.

Miru pointed at the window. Level with the base of the window was the yard we had passed on our way in. Long green stalks were peeking into her room. Emily must have been lying on the windowsill.

"Hungry?" Miru asked.

"A little."

"I should have bought something on the way home. I just realized there's nothing to eat here. What should we do?"

"It's okay. I'm not that hungry. I'll eat at home later."

I looked down at Emily asleep in the box and then went to the window. Because of the long staircase, I had assumed that Miru's room would be completely underground, so it was a surprise to see all that greenery. It looked like it would fill the room the moment the window was opened. I assumed she left it unlocked even when she was out, because the window slid open with just a slight push. As I had pictured, the tall green stalks unfurled their limbs and spilled into the room.

"Those are lilies," Miru said.

"Lilies?"

"This room is built into the side of a hill. It's underground on one side and aboveground on the other. If you stand over here, you can see out. Myungsuh didn't want me to move here. He said it doesn't get enough sunlight. I do feel bad for Emily, but I like it because of the stairs. Myungsuh asked me why I wanted to live in an underground cave. But I insisted, and on the day I moved in, he planted those flowers. He said lilies don't need a lot of sunlight to grow. He planted so many of them that I had to move some when they started sprouting. Last spring, each stem had two or three flowers, and the whole place smelled like lilies. When they bloom, they hang their heads down like they're staring at the ground. One day, Emily disappeared, and when I went to look for her, I found her curled up in a ball, sleeping beneath the lilies."

I ran my hand over one of the lily stems that Myungsuh had planted. The bulbs were buried underground like potatoes. They must have been very strong to bloom so fiercely between spring and summer, only to spend the rest of the year waiting. While the stalks withered above, the bulbs rode out the winter below, and when spring returned, they pushed out fresh shoots that bloomed white and filled her room with their fragrance. I nudged the stalks out of the way to close the window and then looked around Miru's room. A wooden ladder the same color as the flooring led up to a loft bed. Underneath was Miru's desk. The twenty books that Professor Yoon had recommended to us were sitting on top. She must have been reading them or planning to read them. I stared closely at a small poster taped to the wall above her desk. Were those cypress trees? A single small boat was approaching an island floating in a black sea. The caption read "Arnold Böcklin's *Isle of the Dead.*" In the boat, a man dressed in white stood over a coffin draped in white fabric with his back to the viewer. I could just make out an oarsman behind him. The island looked tranquil, but heavy, barren-looking cliff walls encircled it like wings. Inside the walls, a cluster of cypress trees stood as dark as the sea and rose straight up as if to push aside the shrouded sky. They looked like a portal into the island. The small boat rode a bruised wave into the shore, sailing straight for the black water beneath those trees. I was so absorbed in the painting that I did not notice Miru had come over and was standing beside me.

"The artist painted it after having the same dream over and over," she said. "He made five different versions."

It was my first time seeing this painting.

"They say the original title was *A Quiet Place.*"

It did indeed look like a quiet place. I wasn't sure if it was because of the cliff walls or the black cypress trees or the dark water, but the boat did not look like it would be going any farther.

"We should go to Basel someday," Miru said.

"You mean in Switzerland?"

"This painting is in a museum there."

"That island doesn't look like it's a part of this world."

"They say there's an island cemetery in Venice that resembles it. We should go there, too."

I wasn't sure why, but when Miru said we should go to Basel and Venice, I had the feeling that she was not really saying it to me. As the black seawater seemed to spill out of the painting and rise around our ankles, I grabbed Miru's hand. I heard Emily rustle in her box, and then her face poked out and she looked over at us. She jumped out of the box and arched her back, pushing her haunches high to stretch her spine, belly nearly grazing the floor. She tapped me with her tail as she sauntered past.

Though Miru had said there was nothing to eat, she managed to find an apple. She peeled it with a fruit knife and arranged the slices on a plate. My hunger made the apple taste even sweeter. Miru took out her notebook and wrote: *Apple, four slices.* I stole a peek at her notebook. She had even made a note for the day the three of us had gone to eat ramen noodles together.

"Too bad you don't have a camera," I said.

"What do you mean?"

"If you took a photo, you could see what you'd eaten without having to write it all down."

"I prefer writing," Miru said.

Miru filled a mug with water and poured it into Emily's stainless steel bowl. Beside it was another bowl filled with cat food. I took a closer look and saw that next to the food bowl was a flowerpot planted with sprouts. Miru saw me looking and explained that they were rye sprouts. I had never seen anyone grow rye sprouts in their room before.

"Cats swallow a little hair each time they groom themselves. It collects in their stomach and blocks their intestines. The rye sprouts help them cough up the hairballs. That over there is her scratching post."

Emily was clawing at a small upright post wound with rope. Miru picked up something next to it that looked like a fishing pole and dangled it over Emily's head. The cat stopped scratching and leapt at it. Miru's face brightened. Each time Emily got close, Miru held the pole a little higher and shook it.

"It's fun for her, but it also gives her exercise," she said.

After a while, she set the pole down and returned to the table. The cat followed. I reached down to scratch the cat's ear. Emily stretched leisurely and licked her paw, then tucked her feet together and lay flat. She looked like a pile of melting snow.

"Would you like to spend the night?" Miru asked me.

The look in her eyes made it hard to say no. I swallowed, the taste of apple still on my tongue, and said okay.

We did not go to bed until after midnight. I fell asleep while reading a book on the floor. Suddenly she was shaking me awake. She sounded worried. I opened my eyes to find her looking anxiously at me. As soon as our eyes met, she looked relieved.

"Do you want to come up to the bed?" she asked.

Miru climbed the ladder first, as if to show me how, and looked down at me. I stood up and climbed the ladder just as she had. Books were scattered all over the mattress. It looked like she fell asleep reading every night. She pushed aside the books to make room for me. One of the books was turned facedown, as if she had been reading it the night before.

"Do you want the inside?" she asked.

Attached to the ladder was a railing that ran around the outside of the bed. I moved closer to the wall. Miru turned on the desk lamp and turned off the fluorescent ceiling light. The green lily stalks outside the window cast their shadows on the glass. I reached my hand up and touched the ceiling.

"Are you uncomfortable?" she asked.

"No."

It was not so much uncomfortable as unfamiliar. It was the first time I had ever climbed a ladder to go to bed. I imagined Miru climbing the ladder every night, and I felt a little sorry for her. If she wasn't careful, she could knock her head against the ceiling. Miru lay beside me and closed her eyes.

"When I was little," she said, "I always thought it was weird to see people sleeping. It scared me to see them with their eyes closed. Like they might never wake up again. I used to watch my parents or sister when they were asleep and fret over when they would wake up. Even now, sometimes, when I'm about to fall asleep, I think, 'What if I don't wake up this time?' How can people sleep so fearlessly and so bravely?"

"Is that why you woke me up earlier?"

"You looked like you weren't going to wake up."

"Yoon Miru . . ." I turned her face toward me. "My mother used to say if I was angry at someone, I should look at them when they're asleep. She said that a person's face when they're asleep is their true face and that if you look at someone when they're sleeping, you can't stay angry at them. Whenever I feel angry or stressed, I take a nap. Don't you feel more relaxed when you wake up? Try thinking of sleep as a kind of rebirth."

She didn't say anything. I assumed she disagreed with me. Emily hopped up the ladder and curled up next to us. Miru reached out to stroke the cat's neck.

"I just thought of the title of that book," she said.

"Which book?"

"The book about the cat that goes to the salt lake."

"What was it?"

"When Your Journey Ends, Tell It to a Stranger."

I thought about the story she had told me of people who bathed in a salt lake and told their final words to a cat. Was the cat their "stranger"? I wanted to read that book.

"Do you have a copy?" I asked her.

"My sister took it with her when she left. She wanted to give it to her boyfriend."

Miru sat up, lit a candle at the head of the bed, and turned off the lamp. The candle flickered and sent our shadows drifting across the walls and ceiling.

"The world is too quiet, isn't it?"

When she said that, I realized that I had forgotten all about the world outside her room. Where was Myungsuh, and what was he doing? He used to call me on Saturday mornings to ask if he could come over. We would meet in the morning and hang out well into the evening. But since I had started going to the public bath with Miru every weekend, he and I had stopped spending our Saturdays together. Suddenly I wondered what he did without me on those days. Miru sat up, reached over, and turned on a small radio.

"Eight minutes and one second," she said.

"What?"

"The second movement of the Emperor Concerto is eight minutes and one second long."

"Beethoven?"

"Yes."

The piano concerto wrapped around us and seemed to lead us to some far-off place.

"Whenever I can't sleep, I put this on and tell myself I have to fall asleep in eight minutes and one second . . . It's like a spell."

"Does it work?"

"Sometimes. Other times I think about the fact that no one knows I'm sleeping here. No one would know if I didn't wake up. Listening to this makes me feel better. And sometimes I fall asleep without trying."

Her words shook me. I'd had the same thought sometimes while going to sleep in my rooftop room. On those nights, I would open the window and look down at the darkened city. I would stare for a long time at the tower on Namsan Mountain. On rainy nights, I enjoyed watching the lights of the tower slowly reemerge from its thick shroud of fog. Other times, I would go out onto the roof and play hopscotch by myself. I suppose while I was doing that, Miru was listening to music underground. Some of those moments probably overlapped. Spending the night with someone in their room made it easier to imagine what he or she was doing when you were not around. After that night, I would be able to picture Miru's nights in this city.

"Miru." I think it was the first time I had ever called her by just her first name. "The next time you can't sleep, call me. And I'll do the same."

"Why?"

"We live close to each other. We could meet in the middle. Or you could go to my place and sleep, or I could come here. What do you think?"

"Yoon," she whispered. "What if we moved into that house together instead?"

Emily climbed onto Miru's stomach. Her shadow grew large and wavered in the candlelight. I was caught off guard by Miru's proposal. I reached out to stroke Emily's fur. I could hear Miru breathing as she waited anxiously for me to answer. The shadows of the lilies outside that had seemed ready to barge in at any moment were now leaning back like sentries at rest. What was on Myungsuh's mind as he planted them beneath the window? The fragrance of lilies must have filled her room for nights on end. The stalks would wilt with the first frost; only the bulbs buried underground could survive the winter. The minutes kept passing as I thought about the lilies. I knew I had to give Miru an answer, but I kept getting distracted. I pictured the white rain lilies in front of the abandoned house, the overgrown weeds in the yard. What were their lives like when they were living there? I could not begin to imagine it.

"If you don't mind, Myungsuh, too."

She spoke as if we didn't need to ask him for his opinion. I wondered if he was the type of person to do something just because Miru suggested it. I was speechless. Was she trying to re-create what she'd had with her sister? The minutes ticked by. I felt like our friendship might sour if I didn't answer right away. But it was also as if Miru's older sister, whom I had never met, had suddenly dropped in.

"I need more time," I said.

"Don't overthink it," she said. "The house is sitting empty. And right now, we're each paying rent on separate places. Myungsuh is living at a relative's house. We could combine our resources."

If living together were that simple, I would never have moved out of my cousin's apartment. Emily came over to me. Miru tried to call her back, but the cat ignored her and pressed her paws against my stomach, shifting her weight from one paw to the other.

"See," Miru said. "Emily wants to live with you, too."

"What are you talking about?"

"When a cat kneads you like that, it's a kind of gift. It means she loves you. Myungsuh has always been sweet to her, but she's never done that to him. I think he feels like she's snubbing him. Emily must like you."

I stroked the back of Emily's neck, and she purred.

"She makes that sound when she's really happy. I bet if we lived together, Emily would be closest to you."

Our shadows wavered over the bed. The piano concerto had already played three times in a row. The melody was beautiful, haunting, and as soft as Emily's fur.

"Jung Yoon." She called me by my full name again. "I surprised you, didn't I?"

"Yes, to be honest."

"Of course. It's one thing to be friends and another thing to live together. You don't know that much about me, and I'm just starting to get to know you. So it's not fair of me to ask you that yet. I understand. Take your time. But will you promise me you won't take too long to decide?"

"Don't worry. I won't."

"When I moved into this place, I thought I was going to spend the rest of my life here. I never imagined I would want to move out . . . I want to go back to school."

Emily stopped kneading me and hopped back down the ladder. I watched her leap onto the windowsill. She sat and watched the lilies swaying in the wind, occasionally lifting a paw to swat at their shadows. The room was still except for the piano music and the flickering candlelight. I could hear Miru's quiet breathing. I felt mean for not giving her the answer she wanted.

"Miru." I could not take the silence any longer. "I wanted to get to know you better, too."

"You did?"

"I don't know if this will make sense to you, but ever since I moved out of my parents' house, I've preferred being alone to being with other people. I got used to it. I'll think some more about your offer. But it's not because of you. It's because of me."

"I guess we were thinking the same thing."

"What's that?"

"I prefer being alone, too. I tried not to get close to you because I was afraid of hurting you. If I ever do anything to hurt you, please don't hate me for it."

I didn't say anything.

Then to my surprise, she said, "If I do ever hurt you, forget all about me. Erase me from your memory."

"Why are you saying that?" I asked, surprised.

"Never mind . . . Yoon, you have to remember me. Don't forget me."

Her voice shook. I rolled over to face her and reached out for her hand. Her scar-covered hand felt warm. If only we could have met each other sooner. We had led such poor and fragile lives, each alone. Maybe I did know what was going on in Myungsuh's mind when he planted the lilies beneath her window. I squeezed her hand a little tighter.

"Let's remember this forever," I said.

I was surprised to realize I was echoing Myungsuh. Is this what he felt when he said it to me? Was the grief that I was feeling for Miru, who seemed so inscrutable and enigmatic, what he felt toward me? Maybe that was all there was to say when no words could offer solace, when there seemed to be no way forward.

"My sister used to say that," Miru said.

"Oh?"

"She used to say it all the time when the three of us were living together: 'Let's remember this day forever . . .'"

Between the notes of the second movement of the Emperor Concerto, I heard the faint ringing of a telephone. It was coming from the desk beneath the bed. Miru made no move to answer it. She seemed to know who was calling.

"That summer . . ." She took a long pause. "If it weren't for that summer, my sister could be a prima ballerina right now, just like she wanted."

"What happened?"

"My sister and I went to our grandmother's house. Back then, our parents were fighting all the time, so our mother told us to go spend a few days at her mother's house in the country. It was a last-minute decision. She tried calling her, but there was no answer. Our mother said she would call again after we'd left to tell her we were on the way. Our grandmother lived down south in Sancheong. When the Korean War started, she fled to the south on her own with our infant mother on her back. She moved to a remote part of Sancheong and built a house just like the one she had lived in as a child. My sister and I loved that house. She had all kinds of interesting things there. Our mother told the driver to take us all the way to our grandmother's house, but my sister sent the driver away instead. She suggested we take the bus by ourselves. She thought it would be fun. We took an intercity bus and walked from the stop to our grandmother's house. It felt like we were going on a picnic. I remember how my sister's hair flew around in the wind that blew in the bus window and tickled my face. And the way she kept whispering, 'Look at that!' while pointing out trees and flowers and the sky as we walked down the back roads.

"It was late afternoon by the time we got to our grandmother's house. We called out for her as we went in the gate, but the house was empty. The trees, which were like family to my grandmother, stood in a friendly congregation, casting shadows over the wall, and colorful summer flowers planted near the front door were in full bloom. The only way in was through the front door, but it was padlocked. My sister and I sat on the veranda in the shade of the trees and waited for her to come home. Since our mother said she would call her, we assumed she would be there already. We had gone to visit her before without calling first, but she had always been home. She was usually working in the courtyard or the vegetable garden, wearing a hat and baggy pants and carrying a hoe, but the moment we would step in through the gate and call out to her, she would drop what she was doing and rush to welcome us. She called us her 'puppies.' I would always run to her and give her a big hug. I loved the smell of her sweat.

"It was strange and a little frightening to see the house without her in it. I kept praying for her to appear. I have no idea how long we waited. I kept thinking, 'She'll be here any minute.' But the shadows of the sunflowers planted along the wall were getting longer and longer and still she hadn't come. We were getting hungry, too. One of our stomachs grumbled loudly. Since I was the younger one, I kept whining that I was hungry, even though there was nothing my sister could have done about it. She tried to make me feel better by saying our grandmother would be home soon, but her stomach was also growling. She must have been more anxious than I was for our grandmother to appear. She stopped staring at the front gate and got up and went to the locked front door. Even though we knew no one was inside, she banged on the door and yelled, 'Grandma!' I went to her side and yelled with her. When we got tired of that, we leaned against the door and started ticking off the things we would ask our grandmother to do when she finally showed up. Our grandmother had a lot of expensive brass dishes. She told us that in the village in the North where she grew up, whenever important guests came to visit, food was served in brass bowls with brass spoons and chopsticks. It was a sign of respect. Our favorite food was the *pyeonsu* she would make for us."

"What's *pyeonsu*?"

"That's what they call dumplings where she grew up. They cook them in beef broth. My sister and I sat there and listed all the things we wanted her to cook for us. Not just *pyeonsu* but also steamed pork with kimchi, soup made with gourd-shaped rice cakes, stew made with bean paste and dumplings—all of the things she usually made when we visited her over winter vacation. We must have listed fifty different foods and still she hadn't come. I could not stop whining about how hungry I was. The more I whined, the hungrier I got. There was nothing my sister could do but keep reassuring me that she would be there any minute. I said, 'What if she never comes home?' My sister said, 'Why wouldn't she come home? It'll just be a little longer.' Then I really got worried and said, 'She could have gone on a trip,' and I listed all the reasons our grandmother might not return that day. My sister kept knocking on the door. I kept thinking that if only we could get inside, we would have plenty to eat, and that thought made me even more eager to get in. The longer the door stayed closed, the more convinced I was that our grandmother was never coming back. I had never seen it padlocked like that before. Finally I asked, 'What if she went somewhere far away and won't be back for several days?' My sister stood up.

"She searched all over for something to pick the padlock with—anything long and thin and strong enough to fit inside the lock. But nothing worked. The sun was setting and we were hungry, so we were starting to panic. We forgot all about waiting for our grandmother and became fixated on picking the lock. We racked our brains trying to find something that would fit in the keyhole. The persimmon, plum, and cherry trees in the yard kept watch as we ran around frantically. We must have trampled all over the cockscomb in our frenzy to find something sharp. My sister found a wooden toolbox in the shed and carried it to the front door, groaning from the weight. By then, the sun was on the horizon. We crouched in front of the door and stuck every pointed object we found in the toolbox into the lock. But nothing fit. It was as if the locked door expected some kind of sacrifice first. We stared at the toolbox in disappointment. Our grandmother's neatly organized tools were jumbled together and strewn everywhere.

"My sister said she had to pee and went behind the plum tree. Even though she loved our grandmother's house, she hated using the outhouse. Whenever she had to go, she would make one of us wait outside. She would call out to us to make sure we were standing right outside. I would say, 'I'm right here!' And she would say, 'Stay there and don't move.' I thought it was funny that my big sister preferred to pee behind a tree than use the outhouse, just because the house was empty, and I said to myself, '*Unni* is a chicken.' As she lifted her skirt and squatted behind the tree, I took the awl out of the toolbox and fitted it into the keyhole. I was hoping to impress her by getting the lock open before she came back. I started chanting, 'Open, open, open . . .' But if she couldn't pick the lock, why would I be able to? I struggled with it for a while, and then got mad and threw the awl down as hard as I could. My sister called to me. She was standing in front of the tree, the hem of her white skirt in her hand, one foot raised high into the air. Her hand was resting on a low branch like it was a ballet barre. She began moving to invisible music.

"She called out my name again and asked, 'What did Fokine say to Pavlova?' Fokine was the one who choreographed the Dying Swan solo for Pavlova. My sister used to share everything she had learned about ballet with me. She would read me the stories from her ballet books and then quiz me on them later. She asked me questions like 'Who was it who said that any song can be made into a ballet?' I rarely knew the answer. But every now and then, the answer would come to me. 'George Balanchine!' I would say, and she would stroke my head. That was how we talked about ballet. You know how, before a performance starts, the soloists come onstage to give the audience a brief preview of what's coming? My sister was doing turns like that. She wasn't wearing her toe shoes, but she managed a few light turns and called to me again. 'Miru! I asked you what Fokine said to Pavlova!' I answered: 'You are a swan.' That was her favorite quote. When I answered correctly, she collapsed forward, gently and quietly. She was mimicking the way a swan folds its wings as it dies. I couldn't take my eyes off her. She really did look like a dying swan. Once, we had watched some very old footage of Pavlova dancing the Dying Swan solo. It was from long before my sister and I were born. The film quality was quite bad, and the lines on the film made my eyes hurt, but my sister couldn't stop crying as she watched it. Later that night, I woke to find my sister on the floor next to our bed—she was curled up like a swan with its wings folded over its head. When I saw her lying under the plum tree, I burst into tears. She looked like she really was dying. It was just so beautiful. She was surprised to hear me cry and folded back her swan wings and flew to where I sat in front of the door. She kept asking me what was wrong. The darkness was rolling in behind her. 'Why are you crying?' she asked, but I couldn't answer her. I couldn't stop crying, either. Maybe I sensed it— that it was the last time my sister would ever dance. Something was bothering me. But I couldn't explain why I felt so scared and sad. Since I wouldn't stop crying, my sister went back to the door to try again to unlock it. She grabbed the padlock and dropped to her knees. Suddenly her sharp scream pierced my eardrums. I felt like I had jumped off a cliff. I immediately stopped crying and ran to her. She was clutching her knee. The awl that I had hurled away in anger had gotten lodged between two floorboards and was sticking straight up. It was embedded in her knee. She leaned forward and fell flat.

"After that day, my sister never danced again."

I sat up and looked at Miru. She was scratching Emily's neck with one hand and resting the other on her forehead. I grabbed her hand. Her scarred, winkled skin felt warm.

"It's hard to listen to, isn't it?" she asked.

I could not get the words out to tell her it was okay. "Miru."

She looked at me.

"Finish the story," I said. "Don't hold it all inside."

"Are you sure?"

"We'll get through it together."

Would sharing her story help heal her wounds? She couldn't forget what had happened, but I wanted her to start putting it behind her. I wanted her to overcome her faded scars and move on.

"My sister's accident has been stamped in my memory ever since. Maybe if she had hated me for it, I would have gotten over it. But we never said a word about it. Not once after that day. While she was in the hospital, I watched as my parents took down her ballet barre. And then it was like everyone forgot. No one said another word about it—not my grandmother, not my parents, not my sister, and not me. I don't remember anymore why my grandmother wasn't home that day or what time she finally showed up. All I remember is that she took one look at my sister lying on the ground and ran to the nearest village, which was on the other side of a hill. I also remember going with her to the hospital with a young man from the village who put my sister in the back of a tractor with the awl still lodged in her knee . . . When my grandmother passed away, she left the house to me. She said she wanted me to look after it. There are traces of my grandmother all over that house. She planted the same trees that grew in her hometown up north. If only the accident had never happened, I could have loved that house. My grandmother made all her own blankets and coverlets on her sewing machine, and she planted the courtyard so that different flowers bloomed every season. Some of the flowers resembled the wildflowers that she had seen up north when she was young, so there were always unfamiliar flowers blooming and fading and then blooming again in her garden. Now there's no one to keep the place up, so it's probably falling apart."

"We should go there someday." I said it with the same intonation with which Miru had said we should go to Basel someday. I could feel the word *someday* making its way back to me. After my mother died, I had stopped saying the word, but before then, I used to say it to myself all the time. Back then, it was the only word that could comfort me. When my mother learned that she was dying, the first thing she did was to send me to live with my cousin in the city. I didn't want to leave her. I wanted to be with her as badly as she did not want me to see her suffer. But I had to obey her. She had already spent more time persuading me to leave than getting treatment for herself. I had to leave in order for her to start getting proper care. The day I left, I said, "Someday, Mama." Those words would repeat themselves in my mind countless times. When she did not have a single strand of hair left on her head, all I could say to her even then was "Someday, Mama." What I most longed for—to see my mother regain her health and go back to her old self—never came true. When I lost my mother, I threw out the word *someday*. The word became meaningless, a phantom word with no power to change anything. After I stopped using it, my habits of swallowing a bitter laugh, biting my lip, furrowing my forehead, and walking alone to console myself returned intact.

"Do you mean it?" Miru asked.

"Mean what?"

"That we should go to my grandmother's house someday?"

"Yes . . . someday." I felt a sudden urgent desire to keep that promise.

"Will that day ever come?" she asked. It was as if she were reading my mind.

"As long as we don't forget," I said.

"If we don't forget?"

I felt sad so I sat up beside her and said, "Let's take Emily, too."

"And Myungsuh," added Miru. Then she closed her eyes and said in a monotone, "And Professor Yoon, too."

We were both quiet for a moment. Had she and Professor Yoon become so close that she could propose taking him with us? As if to dispel the silence between us, Miru added, "And Nak Sujang, too." I laughed. We started listing every single person we knew. I added Dahn's name, though Miru had never met him before.

"Who's Dahn?" she asked.

"We grew up together."

"I want to meet him."

"You will."

"Yoon, I want to live in that house someday. I want to till the land with my own hands, like my grandmother did. Plant seeds in the spring and harvest the fruit in the fall. Plant vegetables in the garden, live off the land, and write. My grandmother must have left the house to me and not my sister because she knew that's what I wanted. Even though I never went back after that summer, she knew. The house is vacant right now, but I plan to return and open it up again. After my sister's accident, that house became a forbidden place that we never spoke of, even though no one had told us not to. Even when my grandmother left it to me, my sister didn't say a word. It's not that things were bad between us. We were as close as any other sisters. But we never spoke of the accident or that house again. The only time my sister mentioned it to me was when she wanted to hide him there."

"Him?"

"The man she loved as much as ballet," she replied. "When my sister started college, she took Emily and moved to the city. By the time Myungsuh and I joined her the following year, she was like a different person. The dark cloud that had hung over her after she stopped doing ballet was gone. Even her voice returned to normal. She had a way of saying, 'Miru! Look at this!' whenever she saw something that she liked or that surprised her or that she wanted to brag about. She didn't come home often, so I had seen very little of her that year. She was always busy, and I was preparing for the college entrance exam. After a year apart, my sister's black hair shone and her cheeks glowed. Her steps seemed lighter, too. She'd returned to who she was before the accident. It was all thanks to the new man in her life. Her days revolved around him rather than around school. Words like 'socialism' and 'the labor theory of value' and 'human rights' seemed to fall naturally from her lips. And that wasn't the only thing that had changed. Books I had never heard of before were sitting on her desk. They had titles like *Western Economic History* and *Capital*. There were books by Frantz

Fanon. *A Stone's Cry* and *How the Steel Was Tempered*. *The Communist Manifesto*. *Pedagogy*. *History and Class Consciousness*. I would wake up in the morning to find my sister sitting at the table, reading books like *The White Rose* the way she used to read books on ballet in the old days. She would be so absorbed in reading that I could walk right up to her without her realizing it. I became more and more curious about this man who was making my sister read *Liberation Theology*. But all I knew of him was what she had told me. He had yet to appear before us. Then, one day, my sister told me he was coming to dinner. She asked me if it would be okay, but all I could think was that I was finally going to meet him. I will never forget that day. Not because of him, but because of how my sister acted. She got up at dawn and took Myungsuh to the Noryangjin Fish Market to buy a load of blue crabs. She said they were his favorite. Blue crabs? I was surprised. They didn't seem to go with the type of person who could make my sister read *A Critical Biography of Che Guevara*. But she and Myungsuh bought the crabs and released them into the kitchen sink.

"The crabs went all over the place, their claws snapping. They were so full of life that it took all three of us to catch them. And she hadn't stopped at crabs. My sister had bought a little of everything that comes from the ocean. She seemed determined to move the entire fish market to our house. Abalone, scallops, sea squirts, sea cucumbers . . . She must have spent half of the allowance our parents sent us—money we were supposed to live on for the month. The kitchen was a disaster area. Those crabs were so strong. I remember how she stared at them with a helpless look on her face and asked Myungsuh what she was supposed to do with them. He said, 'Maybe they'll die if you remove their shells?' She tried to pull the shell off a live crab with her bare hand. She almost got her hand pinched in its claws. I would never have imagined it. When we lived in Busan, my sister couldn't stand the smell of low tide, so she wouldn't even go down to the harbor. By sunset the crabs had stopped moving, as if they'd finally died of exhaustion. She steamed several pots of crabs and stacked them on a tray. We tried to help her, but she did it all on her own. My curiosity about her boyfriend kept building—what kind of person could transform my sister so completely? Myungsuh apparently had never seen crabs being cooked before. He said he thought they were always red. He was so fascinated by the way they turned red while steaming that he kept lifting the lid to peek at them in disbelief. I complained, 'Why blue crabs, of all things?' They're difficult to eat, especially in front of someone you've just met for the first time. You have to smash them open and dig out the meat . . . I couldn't imagine digging out crabmeat in front of someone I didn't know. I thought, *How can one person eat this many blue crabs, even if they love them?* It was strange to watch my sister cook, but at the same time, I felt surprised and happy. It was the first time I'd ever seen her cook. She lived in a boardinghouse when she first moved to the city, and when we lived together, Myungsuh and I did most of the cooking. It wasn't that I wanted her to. I never really expected anything from her. And yet, there she was, making flounder-and-mugwort soup with mugwort that she had cleaned and trimmed herself."

"Did it taste good?"

"I have no idea. No one got to eat any of it. That page is blank in my notebook."

"What happened?"

"He never showed up."

Miru mumbled the words, her voice as faint as if it had sunk to the deepest reaches.

"He called while my sister was boiling the crabs. I heard her say that he didn't need to bring anything, so I figured he had asked if he should buy something on the way. He must have kept asking because then I heard her say, 'Miru likes lilies. But only get one . . .' I looked at her, and she crinkled her eyes at me. He seemed to know where we lived. I don't think he asked for directions. But two hours went by, the crabs got cold, and he never showed. After a while, it got dark. My sister looked so worried that I said, 'Something must have come up. We can just eat together another time.' She mumbled to herself and then said, 'Of course we can eat another time.' She added, 'It's not the dinner that's worrying me. Let's pray that nothing happened to him.' I didn't understand what she was talking about. She asked if we wanted to go ahead and eat. But no one was in the mood, and she looked too worried. She went to the phone and made a few short calls. Then she pulled on her shoes and dashed out of the house. Emily followed her to the door, but she left without so much as a glance back. Myungsuh was worried and decided to follow her. Her behavior was so erratic. When we got to the bottom of the hill, she was standing on the curb. It was dark, and the street was lined on both sides with trees. She stepped down into the road and was about to run across. A bus sped by just in front of her, and a taxi pulled up. The driver stuck his head out and started cursing at her. Myungsuh guided her back onto the sidewalk, but she kept trying to run out into the road. We stood close and kept an eye on her. She wouldn't listen to us, but she looked so anxious that we couldn't leave her alone, either. Finally, I told Myungsuh we should drag her back to the house, but she jumped into a cab that had just pulled up the curb and vanished before our eyes. We stood there staring after the cab for a long time before finally trudging back up the hill. It was late at night. Myungsuh covered up the boiled crabs and put away the food that was on the table. With my sister gone, we couldn't imagine touching any of it."

The phone rang again, drowning out the sound of the concerto that had started over. The ringing stopped and started again. I was so distracted by the phone that I missed some of what Miru said. She didn't react at all. In fact, she was so oblivious that I couldn't bring myself to ask why she didn't answer it. The ringing of the phone threaded into the line of piano music and then faded back out.

"My sister didn't come home that night or the next day. We went to her school and checked every classroom where she might have been, but we couldn't find her. She was gone for two days. I had no idea where she'd been or what she'd been doing, but she returned looking haggard. Her eyes were bloodshot, like she hadn't slept a wink. I asked her what happened, but she just looked at me wide-eyed and passed out on the bed. Myungsuh and I had to throw out all of the seafood that she'd bought. The crab had spoiled and smelled terrible.

We cleaned and swept the kitchen to get rid of the stench. Each time I opened her bedroom door to check on her, she was still asleep.

"Emily sat on her pillow and kept watch over her. Myung-suh wiped her face with a damp washcloth. I cleaned her hands and feet. She was so exhausted that she slept through all of it. After sleeping like the dead for maybe a dozen hours, she bolted awake as if someone had startled her and started making more calls. She grew paler with each phone call. Finally she hung up and held her face in her hands for a long time, and then she grabbed her bag. I asked her where she was going, but she didn't answer. I couldn't let her leave again. I yelled, 'What about us? You can't leave us in the dark like this! You have to tell us something before you go!' It was the first time since the accident at our grandmother's house that I had yelled at her. She plopped down on the floor and looked at me through bloodshot eyes. She said, 'Miru, he's missing.' I didn't know what she meant at first. How could I have known? How I wish I could have seen what was coming, if only just a little. If I had, I would never have let her leave. She said, 'I have to find him.' But she looked calm, not like how she was when she was making those phone calls or collapsing on the floor in front of me.

"She asked if it was okay to send him to our grandmother's house if she found him. It was the first time since we were kids that we had ever talked about that house. I pressed the key into the palm of her hand. Yoon, I had no idea why he disappeared, but I genuinely hoped he would find sanctuary at our grandmother's house. If he had to go into hiding, then I wanted him to hide there. I didn't know if he was a good person or a bad person or what he had done. But my sister looked so exhausted because of him that I hoped he was somewhere she could reach him. I never thought I could feel that way toward a person I'd never met. I followed my sister to the front door and asked her to call me every day at the same time. She said she would call at midnight. At first, she kept her promise. I would ask her if everything was okay, and she would answer brightly that it was. But her voice would trail off when I started asking more questions. Her calls became infrequent, from once every three days to once every five days, and then the phone stopped ringing altogether. Every now and then she would show up in person, looking terrible, and sleep like the dead until she got her energy back. Then she would grab some cash and leave again. Sometimes she would pet Emily, a vacant look in her eyes, as if she'd only come to see the cat. The days that she came home to sleep off her fatigue seemed to be the days that she got really bad news about her missing boyfriend. After she had stumbled home and slept it off, she would suddenly start talking about him. She told me that the day he was supposed to come over for dinner, some men came looking for him. Judging by the time, it must have been right before he would have left for our place. 'Who were they, and why did he go with them instead of coming over here?' She kept asking me questions I could not answer. She looked worse and worse each time she came home. 'Someone saw him get in a cab with those men, but then he jumped out and ran away. What happened in the cab that made him run away?' She would mumble to herself. One day, she told me his real name was Minho. I assumed she had met his family. I think she and his older brother were looking for him together. She seemed hopeful and said his brother might be able to find him, and that his brother looked just like him. 'He calls him Minho.' She kept mumbling his name to herself. Another time, she came home and said someone had seen him escaping into the woods in front of a police checkpoint, but she looked disappointed and said that it turned out it wasn't him. Then she said, 'No, no, that's good. What would he be doing hiding in the woods?' I could only tell where she had been by the things she blurted out. Someone told her they saw his body floating under a bridge in the Cheongna Reservoir, but when she went to Cheongna, there was no one there, let alone anyone she could ask. Another day, she mumbled, 'Miru, why would he have gotten on that train?' She would come home, say things I didn't understand, sleep like the dead, and leave again. Each time, I got another unfulfilled promise that she would call me once a day. It was ridiculous how powerless I was. Even though it made her grimace, the only thing I could say to her was, 'If you don't promise to call me every day, then I won't let you leave!' What I learned from her searches was that countless numbers of people had gone missing—not just her boyfriend. While she searched for him, I started to notice how many people there were wandering around in search of loved ones, friends, coworkers, and sons who had abruptly vanished. How could something like that happen?"

Miru stopped talking for a moment. I sensed that she was torn between needing to continue and knowing she should stop. She looked tortured by the words she could not swallow, as if there were a giant thorn in her throat. I placed my hand on top of hers.

"If it's too much," I said, "you can stop. We can finish the story later."

"No, I want to talk about it. But only if you're okay."

The telephone rang again. Miru continued.

"I got a phone call from my sister early one morning. She said she was back and needed a bath. She asked me to meet her at the bathhouse. I thought she meant she was back for good. I packed a change of clothes for her. Underwear, a toothbrush, a towel . . . and this skirt."

She pushed my hand away and pointed to the floral skirt she was still wearing.

"It was your sister's?"

"Yes. She always wore it around the house.

"I packed up her shower basket and went to that public bath where you and I went last time. She was already inside. We bathed together like we used to when we were kids. We scrubbed each other's backs and rinsed each other off. My sister's face, which had looked so anxious ever since her boyfriend disappeared, looked peaceful that day. I thought maybe she had found him. She offered to wash my hair for me. She used to do that sometimes when we were younger. I loved it when she would wash my hair. She squeezed shampoo into the palm of her hand and gently scrubbed my scalp with her fingers. She washed away the suds and rinsed my hair over and over until the water ran clear. Then she combed my hair straight, rolled it up into curls, and pinned them in place. She stroked the back of my neck and asked me how school was. My eyes stung with tears. I thought the fact that she was asking me about school meant that she had come back to her senses. We stayed in the bathhouse for a long time. When we went back into the locker room, our toes were swollen and wrinkled from the water. My sister dried me off with a towel. She even took her time drying my hair. Then she put lotion on my back. She dressed herself in the clothes I had brought for her, but when she saw the skirt, she said she would wear it at home. I thought her jeans were too dirty to wear again, but I didn't think much of it. We came out of the bathhouse, and she retrieved her bag from the counter. It was a big backpack that I had never seen before, the kind you use to go camping in the woods or trekking cross-country. It looked heavy, so I suggested that she take it off so we could carry it together. She said it wasn't as heavy as it looked. She suggested we get something to eat even though it wasn't lunchtime, so I figured she was hungry and followed her without a word. She led me to a new sushi restaurant on the main street that I had been wanting to go to. She didn't like sushi. I had mentioned that it looked good, but we had never gone. We ordered a combination plate and some udon noodles. To my surprise, she seemed to enjoy the food, even though she kept saying, 'I've never had this before.' Her forehead was sweating, and she didn't leave a single piece of sushi uneaten. After we were done, she took a wrinkled manila envelope out of her backpack and asked me to hold on to it. I asked if she was coming home, and she said she had to return the backpack. She told me to go home first and said she would join me later. She sounded like she meant it. On the way out of the restaurant, she told me to hurry home. I said, 'Promise you'll come back?' She nodded. As she walked away from me, I said once more, 'Promise?' She said yes. Then she told me to hurry up and go home. I said I would wait until she got into a cab, but she told me to leave and gave me a little push. There was nothing I could do, so I turned to go. But then she called me back and gave me a hug. She smelled like the soap we had shared in the bathhouse. 'Miru, I'm sorry. I'm sorry.' She said it twice. I told her, 'It's okay, as long as you come home.' She let go of me and told me to hurry off again. I said, 'See you soon, *Unni*,' and started walking toward home. When I glanced back, she was standing there watching me. Then she quickly turned and left. I don't know what it was, but something didn't seem right. I sensed that I shouldn't let her get away. I ran after her. I saw her cross the street, carrying that heavy backpack, and flag down a taxi. I hurried across as well and jumped into another cab. I pointed out the cab she was in and asked the driver to follow her."

The phone rang again. This time, Miru stopped talking and listened to it ring. Who on earth could be calling her so persistently at this hour?

"Can you stand to hear a little more, Yoon?"

"Keep going."

"You might regret it. Ever having known me, that is."

"It's okay. Talk."

Miru took my hand in her own scarred ones.

"If it's hard to listen to it, tell me to stop. Just say, *that's enough*. Understand?"

". . . Yes."

"My sister's taxi was heading toward her boyfriend's college. When we got close to the school, the traffic was all backed up. The cars weren't moving. My sister got out of the cab, so I got out, too. The street leading to the school was packed with people. I think they were holding a rally to protest his disappearance. I saw a banner waving in the wind with his name and face on it. She stopped and looked up at his picture. I thought she was going to the rally, so I decided to head back home. I was still carrying our shower baskets, after all. But my sister crossed the street instead of joining the group of people. She stopped in front of a ten-story building and stared up at the roof. I stared up at it, too, wondering if she had spotted something up there, but I couldn't tell what she was looking at. *What is she doing?* I thought, and continued to follow her. She looked all around the building with that huge backpack on her back. Suddenly, she disappeared from view. I hurried over with the baskets in my hands to the front of the building where she had vanished and searched everywhere for her. It was strange. There were no cafés or restaurants inside. It was just a phone company building. Over where I thought she might have disappeared was a stairwell. I climbed up. Second floor, third floor, fourth floor, and then finally the ninth and tenth floors. After that was the roof. I wondered why on earth my sister would be on the roof of a phone company building for no reason, and I started to turn back. But just then, through a crack in the door that led to the roof, I caught a glimpse of her. She was standing at the edge of the roof and looking down at the street where the demonstrators and riot police were standing off against each other. She looked so desperate. Up until that moment, I still had no idea what she was planning to do. How could I have known that she was planning something so extreme and so horrible? She looked down at the people below and then set her backpack down. She opened it and looked inside for a while, as if steeling herself. Even when she took a white plastic jug out of the bag, I stood there staring, clueless as to what she was doing. She pulled the stopper out of the jug and struggled to lift it overhead; she doused herself from head to toe with the contents of the jug. *What is she doing?* I wondered, and swung the door open. And then the smell hit me. *No*, I thought. I knew at once. It was the smell of gasoline. I ran toward her and tried to shout. But no sound came out. My tongue had lost all feeling and was floundering in my mouth like it had forgotten how to speak. When I finally managed to squeak out the words, *Unni, Unni*, she turned to look at me. Her face was white with fear. The tops of our heads were blazing in the hot sun. All of the noise and shouting in the street below seemed to stop all at once; everything went silent. It was like we were in a vacuum, just the two of us. 'Miru, don't come any closer. Get out of here. Go home.' She pleaded with me to leave. But she never raised her voice. 'Go on. Get out of here. Miru, please go.' I covered my ears with my hands and screamed, 'Are you insane? Please don't do this! He's not worth it . . .' The seconds ticked by like eternity. We stood there on the roof, staring at each other, begging, *Please. Don't.* Then it seemed she couldn't wait any longer. She bent over and rummaged through the backpack, gasoline dripping off her, and pulled something out. I ran forward and grabbed the backpack, but she pushed me. I fell backward. She tried to flick the lighter, but her hands were too slippery. Then she took out a matchbook and struck a match. I screamed and jumped up. When that tiny flame from the match leapt onto her skin, I grabbed her hands. The flames seared my palms. It felt like thousands, tens of thousands, of flaming hot needles pierced my hands all at once. I saw the blaze catch the hem of her shirt and instantly swallow her face and hair. All I could do was panic. All I remember is black smoke, the sounds of the crowd below who had finally noticed us, anguished screams . . . Finally, my sister shook off my hands . . . Her body went over the railing and I saw her float in midair for a moment. Her arms were stretched out toward the sky. I fell to my knees as though hammered down. I couldn't move. I thought I heard a thunderclap and saw lightning coming from the sky, but it was a hallucination. The sky was so blue that day. People rushed onto the roof, and I was taken to the hospital."

Yoon, who suddenly became far less talkative after spending the night at Miru's place, asked me, "Where were you when Miru's sister died?" We had just finished eating some noodle soup that I made in Yoon's kitchen and were standing on the roof, gazing out at Namsan Tower shining in the distance. Yoon had asked me to make the soup when we were walking back to her place from school. It was something I made for her from time to time. The table palm on Yoon's desk was growing. Yoon sat at the pullout table in the kitchen with her chin in her hand and watched as I filled a pot with water and placed it on the stove. Cooking for her reminded me of living with Miru and her sister, Mirae. But when I served the finished soup, Yoon barely touched it. She kept transferring noodles from her bowl to mine. "You said you wanted noodles?" I asked. In a dead voice, she said, "Not anymore." I ate almost all of her noodles along with my own. She waited until we were outside on the roof and looking down at the lights of the city to ask me where I was when Miru's sister died. My heart sank. For some stupid reason, I blurted out, "So now you know?" She said,

"I didn't realize Miru's sister was that Yoon Mirae." I couldn't bring myself to ask whether she also knew that the scars on Miru's hands came from grabbing her sister. But Yoon seemed to guess what I was thinking, because she brought it up before I could. Neither of us spoke for a moment. I felt a lump in my throat and reached out for Yoon's hand, but she pulled it away. That was the moment I realized I'd been secretly hoping the two of them would never become friends. The city lights flickered over Yoon's face. She said, "How could something like that happen?" Her face hardened. It looked as if Miru's pain had transferred to her. "How could that happen?" I had asked myself the same thing countless times. Mirae's boyfriend, who disappeared the night we were all supposed to have dinner together, is probably already dead. Inside the envelope that Mirae handed to Miru were detailed notes of everything she had learned while searching for him. She must have figured out that he was never coming back. Maybe she did what she did because she had finally faced the truth. She said that on the night he was supposed to join us for dinner he was seen boarding a train with some strange men who had come looking for him at the school. After her sister died, Miru took up the search for her sister's boyfriend, and I joined her. That was how I found out that there were so many people who had gone missing. Some of the disappeared were later found dead in crashed cars, or with their skulls cracked open from accidental falls, or with their stomachs swollen with water in reservoirs where they had no business being. Yoon said she didn't know what to say or do for Miru. "Hearing about it was painful enough," she said, "so how can she . . ." Yoon didn't say another word until I left. After midnight, I left her place and was walking down the hill when she called out to me and came running. When I turned,

she threw herself into my arms and told me not to go. I could feel her chest rising and falling against mine. Her tears were wetting the neck of my shirt. We stood in that dark alley as if rooted in place.

| | |

Miru asked me if we could all move in together.

"Like we did before. But this time with Yoon?" she asked.

After their sleepover, they were no longer Yoon Miru and Jung Yoon to each other but just Miru and Yoon. Miru's face had brightened, while Yoon's had turned dark. I asked Miru if that was really what she wanted. She said yes.

"Did Yoon agree to this?" I asked.

She said she was waiting for her answer.

"In the same house as before?" I asked again.

She nodded.

"If you promise to stop looking for him," I told her, "I'll move back in with you."

She mumbled something under her breath. I was afraid of what she might say next.

"Yoon said she would help me look," she said finally.

She refused to look me in the eye. I felt like she was asking me if I had already forgotten about Mirae? The whole time she and I had been looking for him, I figured he was already dead. Miru must have, too. How could she not have felt what I was feeling? Her sister had poured gasoline over herself and set herself on fire in order to send a message to everyone about her boyfriend's suspicious disappearance and unexplained death. Just thinking about it made my whole body ache. Like I was the one on fire. If this is how I feel, and I wasn't even there, then how much worse was it for Miru, who watched her sister burn to death right before her eyes?

Mirae must burn at the center of Miru's mind all the time. I felt so angry and resentful toward Mirae. Was there no other way to get her message out? Though I sympathized with what she must have felt, she shouldn't have done it. I asked Miru if she wanted Yoon to suffer like us.

"What do you mean, 'like us'?" she said.

I raised my voice at her.

"Look at us! Do you think we're normal? Look at you. You're throwing your life away!"

My words weren't just aimed at her but also at myself. After her sister died, Miru and I let everything fall apart. What would have happened to us if it weren't for Yoon? The thought of life without her makes me feel like I'm trapped inside a cave.

| | |

With each passing day, Mirae's pain is becoming my own. She must have learned about the deaths of others who had disappeared, too, while searching in vain for her disappeared boyfriend, just as Miru and I did in our own search. Why did he get on that train with those strange men, when he was supposed to be eating dinner with us? When he had planned a retreat with the other leaders of his organization? Someone said his body had been found on an island. But it turned out it wasn't him. Mirae probably went to that island, too. She must have known it wasn't him, but maybe she couldn't erase the image of the person's body drifting in the ocean—the one who had slipped and cracked his skull. The bodies of the disappeared that had been found in reservoirs were discovered to have plankton in their lungs, kidneys, and spleens. And in their hearts and livers, as well.

| | |

Nak Sujang has taken over our walking tours of the city. On the first day of our overnight tour of the fortress wall with Nak Sujang and Professor Yoon, Yoon showed up with a friend. She told me they grew up together and that he'd taken an overnight train without telling her first, so she had to bring him along. His name was Dahn. Dahn listened quietly as she introduced him to the group.

"I'm going into the army in a week," he said. "So I came up to the city to see Yoon first."

I don't think Yoon knew he was starting his military service. Her eyes widened with surprise. We decided to tease him a little.

"Did you buy a gun?"

"A gun?" he asked.

"Yes, an M16. Wait, you mean to say that you're joining the military and you haven't bought your gun yet?"

"Am I supposed to?"

Dahn sounded so serious that even the professor and Miru burst into laughter. Yoon was the only one not laughing.

"You have to have a gun."

"You'd better get out of here and go buy one right away."

"I know a place where you can buy one. Want directions?"

Everyone started jumping in. They told him what type of gun he had to buy and which stationery store sold them for cheap.

Even Professor Yoon added, "Be sure to add live ammo to your lunchbox."

Dahn was eating it up, staring at us in shock, saying, "Really? Really?" But when he finally realized we were joking, his face relaxed and he laughed.

"Don't worry," he said. "I'll find a good one. Ten-hut!"

As we walked, I kept glancing back at Yoon and Dahn. Even Miru, who kept tagging after Professor Yoon, turned to look at them now and then. It looked like Yoon was doing all of the talking and Dahn was doing all of the listening. I heard her ask him, "How are you going to make it through training? What if you run into spiders in the middle of an exercise?" She sounded worried. But why spiders? I was curious to hear more, but their voices grew faint. I marveled at the fact that she had someone she could speak so freely with.

It made me a little nervous, too.

—Brown Notebook 7

CHAPTER 8

A Single Small Boat

Y*oon.*

*   I thought I was not going to write to anyone on the outside until I got out of the army. But here I am writing to you, so I guess it was a pointless resolution. On a blank piece of paper, I wrote your full name, "Jung Yoon," then just your first name, "Yoon," and then back and forth between the two ten more times. Just now I wrote "Yoon" again, put a period after it, and sat and stared at your name for a long time. Why did I resist writing letters? I feel less like a soldier at war and more like a man at battle with his desire to write. My sister wrote to say that you asked for my address. I've been waiting every day since then to get a letter from you. Not a response sent to a letter I wrote, but a letter sent first by you.*

*   We call everyone outside the military "civilians." In other words, you are a civilian, and I am a soldier. You'll probably laugh when I tell you that I decided not to write to anyone on the outside because I want to live as a true soldier. But as long as I'm in the service, that's all I want to do. This place is my escape. I want to forget about the soft "me" that lived out there in society and become*

strong and armed through discipline and training. I went to see you before coming to the army because I was determined not to write to you or even to see your face until I was done. But my will is weak.

Took me nearly a year to realize that my feelings for you are not something I can control. I fear I might ask you in this letter to come visit me. But if by chance I do write those words, you must not come. I even forbade my family members to visit me. I don't want to see any civilians in this place. I mean it. I threatened my mom and my older sister that I would go AWOL if they tried to come with me on my first day or if they tried to visit me when I took my first leave. I said that in exchange I would do well at target practice and earn a reward leave, and then I would visit them myself. But I didn't get to keep that promise. Some other guy got the award, so he shared the rice cakes he got from his mother with the rest of us. I bet you're thinking, They send you on vacation if you're a good shot? You'd probably laugh and tell me to stop joking. But Yoon, I've found myself here. As it turns out, I am an excellent marksman.

Yoon.
Once again, I write your name and stare at it for a long time. I often think about the friends of yours that I met when I visited you. It made me quite happy to see that you have friends like that by your side. I also never thought I would get to meet Professor Yoon, whom I knew only from books. You all looked so beautiful. He seemed strict, but warm at the same time. I envy you for having him as a professor. Maybe the reason I ran away to the army was that I didn't have friends like yours where I was. I felt I'd become part of a "we" when I was with you all. The hours we spent walking with

your friends along the fortress wall were like a dream. I wait for no one, Yoon, but I do wish I could relive the night we all spent camping overnight in a tent pitched fearlessly—and illegally!—next to the fortress wall. That memory will stay with me until I leave the army. Also, sleeping in that house and eating dinner with you and Miru and Myungsuh—that memory will stay with me for the rest of my life. Whose guitar was that? Those songs we sang together. To think that I spent several days living with people I'd just met. Why was that house sitting empty? I remember the look in Myungsuh's and Miru's eyes when they saw that we had pulled all of the weeds in the yard the next morning. Sometimes I wonder if any of all that happened was real. Even though I've only been to the house once, I am certain I will be able to find my way back without ever getting lost. So that must mean it wasn't a dream. I was so glad I could spend that time with you. I can't believe I am only telling you this now.

I wonder if Miru still writes down everything she eats. I teased her that if she keeps hunching over when she walks, she'll be a hunchback by the time she's old. Does she still walk like that? One night, when we were staying at the house, I woke up and went to get some water. Miru's diary was sitting on the table, so I stole a peek. I've never seen a diary like that before. I've never met anyone who takes such pains to write down every single thing they eat. That night, as I flipped through those entries listing everything she had eaten every single day, a strange feeling came over me. After a while, those simple lists started to sound like poems. Like she was shouting, I am what I eat and what I have eaten . . . Every once in a while, there was an entry where she went on a binge. It pained me each time I came across one of those. I also read the parts between her food entries where the three of you wrote stories together. It gave me a glimpse into how the three of you spent your time together. Miru came into the kitchen and caught me reading her diary. She took it in stride, while I was the one surprised. She even asked me indifferently which of you I thought was the better writer? But I wasn't thinking about the quality of the writing when I was reading it. What I was marveling over was the fact that three different sets of handwriting could harmonize so nicely. Does it sound strange to say that I found something comforting about those jumbled stories? I told her I wanted to add illustrations in the margins, but she asked me to do it later, when we all meet again someday. Sometimes I think about that promise she and I made to each other. That day will come. Someday, I mean. Someday, when we meet again, I'll illustrate the stories the three of you wrote.

Yoon.
How could I have ever imagined that you would show up in the waiting area at the training center, holding a book of poems by Emily Dickinson? When you called out to me from afar, I thought I was seeing things. And you didn't come alone but also brought Myungsuh and Miru and even Emily the cat. There you were, right before my eyes, when I'd been so exhausted and depressed about stopping my mom and sister from visiting. I used to hate the idea of someone watching me walk away. I even hated sticking my hand out of a car window or door and waving. I waited to get my hair cut until I was on my way to the first day of training, so you were the first ones to see me with a buzz cut. Embarrassing. I keep picturing Myungsuh's face when I asked why you'd come and he said, "It was my idea!" The face of a hyeong, a man's older brother.

Thank you, too, for bringing Emily and giving me a chance to hold her. I felt bad because I avoided her each time she came near me when we were staying in that house. I'd never held a cat before. It felt warm. So warm that I can still recall that heat. If I'd known cats were that warm and soft, I would have held her the whole time I was there. I regret that. And then there was you. You insisting I take the book of poems anyway, after I said I wasn't allowed to have it inside the compound. You telling me to sneak it in somehow. Don't be surprised. That book is right here on my lap. I've been using it as a smooth surface on which to write this letter. After I leave the army, I'll tell you how I was able to hold on to it all this time. My army discharge gift to you.

Yoon.

It feels like so long ago that I gave you this book. You told me that a guy you went to school with, the one nicknamed Pedal, took the book I gave you and vanished, but somehow you found a new copy. These Dickinson poems that have found their way back to me are my patron saint in here. Whenever the cravings for homemade kimchi get too strong, or when I come across a spider, I recite this poem from memory:

> *That Love is all there is,*
> *Is all we know of Love;*
> *It is enough, the freight should be*
> *Proportioned to the groove.*

I repeat "it is enough" to myself two or three times. That's the line where I can feel my arachnophobia subside. Starting tomorrow,

*we're doing night drills for three weeks. I hope I don't fall out of
rank.*

Take care.

From GI Dahn to Civilian Yoon

Dahn sent me the first letter a year after he joined the military and was selected for the special forces. It was more than
five pages long. He didn't mention anywhere in it that he was
in a special forces unit. I unfolded the letter and put it on
my desk. *From GI Dahn to Civilian Yoon* . . . I stared at those
words for a long time. It pained me to realize that I had never
written him back. I filled a fountain pen with ink, took out
a new notebook, and wrote his name at the top of the page.

Dahn.

Dahn as a baby, Dahn as a child, Dahn as a seventeen-
year-old, eighteen-year-old, nineteen-year-old, then a college
student, then a soldier. Right after he joined the army, I didn't
hear from him for some time. I called his sister to get his address, and she told me he had been assigned to a special unit.
She said they had nonstop drills every day, and that sometimes he had to survive in the mountains for half a week with
only a canteen and a bayonet. *You know how on Armed Forces
Day,* she said, *the soldiers parachute in formation? His unit is
one of those.* But why Dahn? She told me he had the right phy-
sique for the special forces. But they must do aptitude testing
as well? I pestered his sister with questions, but it made no
difference. I wrote his name in my notebook again. I could

not picture Dahn parachuting out of an airplane. How did he survive on his own for days in the mountains? In the space between the words *civilian* and *soldier* rested the sense of distance that prevented me from picturing him doing a road march or maritime training. I imagined his unit must spend so much time in the mountains that, after being discharged from active duty, the mere mention of mountains would make them turn their heads in disgust. To think that was where he was. Dahn the arachnophobe in the special forces having to survive for days on his own in the wild? Even after I had his address, I kept starting letters and abandoning them because I could not begin to imagine what he was going through. Then his letter arrived first.

Dahn.
I got your letter. I hope the night drills went okay.

Unsure of what to write next, I closed my notebook. How many times during those three weeks of hard training did Dahn have to recite Dickinson to himself so he could face down a spider? I started to put Dahn's letter back in the drawer but paused and stared for a moment at the other letters stacked inside. I took them all out and placed them on top of the desk. They included lettercards and even ordinary postcards. I could not believe I had never written back to him, despite the many times he had written me. A scrap of paper mixed in with the letters caught my eye, and I pulled it out.

Start reading again.
Write down new words and their definitions.
Memorize one poem a week.
Do not go to Mom's grave before the Chuseok holiday.
Walk around the city for at least two hours every day.

The first time Myungsuh and Miru came over, I made them wait outside while I went in and pulled that piece of paper off the wall. It must have gotten mixed in with Dahn's letters. I flattened it out and stacked the letters on top of it.

The image of Dahn at the waiting area flickered before my eyes. We had arrived at the training center two hours early and were waiting for him. Since we hadn't arranged to meet, we thought there might be too many people and that we might not get to see him. There were only a few others at first, but it soon grew into a crowd. Most were friends of the new recruits. If we had not been standing in front of a military training center, it would have looked like we were waiting for a concert to begin. Myungsuh spotted Dahn before I could. While I was staring way off into the distance, he tapped me on the shoulder and pointed to him. He even called out to Dahn before I did. Dahn was shocked to see us. It was so strange to see him with a buzz cut that I could not stop staring. His scalp, and even the underside of his chin, looked blue from where it had been closely shaved. He stared at me for a moment and then took the cat from Miru. I guess saying goodbye makes us reach out for those we would ordinarily ignore. Maybe we care about them more, too, when it is time to part. He cradled the cat in his arms and looked around at us. He had stayed away from Emily when the four of us were staying in the old house, but now it felt like she'd been his from the start.

Dahn did not put her down the whole time. Not even when we went to a coffee shop, which took forever for us to find, and not even when I handed him the book of poems and told him to sneak it on base somehow. Finally, just before returning to the training center, he handed Emily back to Miru. Then he walked away without once looking back. I caught myself chanting the words, *Turn around!* Myungsuh mumbled, "That's cold." I ran. Dahn was walking straight ahead in the crowd of blue-skinned heads when I caught up to him.

"I'll write to you," I told him. "I'll come visit you, too."

Dahn told me not to worry about it and smiled. Later, sitting in the bathroom at a rest stop on the way back to the city, I pictured Dahn disappearing into the crowd without looking back and had to close my eyes from the pain. Then, back on the bus, I thought about that time very long ago when a night train chugged past right in front of us, and I had to squeeze my eyes shut even tighter.

I picked up his letters at random and read them.

Yoon.

I have a new address. This letter I'm writing now will not be sent through the military mail service. I asked a friend of mine in the Civil Defense Corps to mail it to you from the post office in town. That way I can write to you without worrying about the censors.

So much has happened to me. The special forces are quite tough. The training is bad enough, but life in the barracks is awful. Though they're very strict about rank, many of the guys were in gangs before they joined the army, and they get into fights at the drop of a hat. They throw field shovels at each other in the squad room, and in the middle of evening call, one guy will knock the soldier next to him over with a jumping side kick. Once or twice a week, they muster us up to remind us that such misconduct is forbidden. We're woken up in the middle of the night and forced to bend over in our briefs, balancing for as long as we can on the tips of our toes and the top of our heads with our hands behind our backs. The sergeants beat the corporals who beat the privates first class who beat the privates who beat everyone else. Officially, they're not allowed to beat us. The only corporal punishment that's permitted is physical endurance punishments. But they secretly do it all the time and justify it as maintaining military discipline. Among the senior conscripts, the softhearted ones can't bring themselves to beat us, so they get drunk together first and then do it.

One day, they had us mustered at midnight, but the club they brought broke so they brought out the handle of a pickax instead. While I was getting beaten, the club landed on my lower back instead of my butt. The pain was so intense that I thought I was dying. I screamed and fell to the ground, but the senior members cussed at me, called me a crybaby, and kicked me. At that moment, I really, truly thought I was going to die. When I came to, I was in the infirmary. While the medic was checking my spine, I heard him cluck his tongue and say, "Those bastards!" If the higher-ups found out about it, everyone, including the commanding officer, would have had hell to pay, and several people might *have even been thrown in the brig for it. The first sergeant saw to it that I was exempted from further drills and sent me to a clinic outside the compound to get acupuncture. A soldier who was the same rank as me carried me there every day on his back. After more than a month of treatment, when I was able to move around on my own, the first sergeant told me that I wasn't cut out for the special forces and sent me to this base as a kind of temporary duty. This place isn't much better, but compared with the last one, I may as well be on vacation.*

I am stationed on the west coast, close to the front line. My new assignment is coastal guard duty. I sleep in the squad room during the day, wake late in the afternoon, and am deployed at dusk to one of the observation points staggered along the beach. I stay up all night with the sea in front and barbed wire behind. Since I'm not doing drills like I did in the special forces unit, it's not as taxing. But the tradeoff is that you don't get any leave when you're stationed at the coast. Nor do they allow overnight passes. In this remote exile, I aim my rifle at an invisible enemy who could invade at any moment.

I think I nursed a certain misunderstanding and fantasy about military life before I joined. I thought that, while it might be demanding physically, becoming part of an organization would help free me of the inertia that has always plagued me. But on my first day of basic, I saw how foolish that assumption was. I was ordered around and pushed around by the drill sergeant and other officers, and I realized just how deluded I had been. (My ears are still ringing from when the officers treated us like animals and screamed, "There are soldiers and there are human beings! You are

not human beings!") Then there was the individual combat training, and running—or sometimes crawling—from the fallback area
to the firing line. At first, it was bewildering; later, infuriating. But
my anger soon made up for the resignation, the depression, and
the disillusionment. After surviving as a "conscript" and again as
a member of the special forces, suffering through cold, sleep depri-
vation, and hunger, I started to feel like I really wasn't a human
being. I never guessed that I would feel as lost here as I did in
college, where I struggled to fit in. I can handle the tyranny of the
older soldiers and the physical exhaustion. But realizing the belief
that I am me—the idea that I am worth something—is just dust,
nothing more than wind with no substance, fills me with the bit-
terest of agonies that gnaws at my insides. Here, in the army, I am
learning all over again that human beings are nothing more than
rats in a maze with no exit, running in circles forever. So maybe
that's why I feel this way. Every time I stand on guard duty in the
dark of night, facing those empty mudflats as the searchlights play
over them and the sea crouching just beyond, I feel like I am facing
my own darkness within.

*Faces float to mind like salvation. Laughing faces that shine like
stars. Loving voices, bright smiles, sometimes even a sulk . . . Each
time that frigid ocean breeze hits me, I call out the names of my
far-off loved ones one after the other as if saying the Lord's Prayer.*

Yoon.
  After I get to my observation point around six in the evening
and set up the guns around the bunker, there is usually a little
time left before the sun goes down completely. I use this time to

jot down my thoughts, including letters to send to you, and draw sketches of the ocean and mountains in pencil. A soldier who is in the same formation as me sits at a distance smoking a cigarette. This moment, when there are no higher-ranking soldiers or officers to worry about, belongs entirely to me. I think these—when I am surrounded by waves and wind and am writing to you—are the happiest moments in my life right now.

A few days ago, at dawn, right before finishing our shifts and retreating from the coast, we scooped up the straw that was spread on the floor of the bunkers during the winter and burned it. On the other side of the sand dunes, where the tide had pulled out, I saw fishermen and their wives on their way to work. The discolored straw wouldn't burn at first, but the flame soon caught and burst into heat and acrid smoke. I stood with five or six other soldiers and stared into the glowing fire for a long time. In an instant, the flames collapsed into black ash, and I felt the fortress walls that had claimed their space inside of me also slowly collapse.

I woke up late this morning to find that it was foggy and drizzly out. I stood outside for a while, enjoying the sweet feeling of those thin drops of rain brushing over my skin. Even by afternoon, the fog was still so thick that the water's edge was just a faint outline between the pine trees. Both sea and sky were sunk beneath a depressing gray. I had nothing to do and nothing to read, so I spent the whole day thinking about you. Do I get this sentimental each time it rains because I am still stuck in puberty, psychologically speaking? Back in college, whenever it rained, I would wander around the city all day. There was a café I used to go to where a DJ took song requests. I would go in, drenched with rain, and ask for some low, quiet song, like "Seems So Long Ago, Nancy" by Leonard Cohen or "Old Records Never Die" by Ian Hunter or "Private Investigation" by Dire Straits. Now that's all just a distant memory. There was another song I used to listen to a lot. I can't remember the singer's name, but the song was called "Time in a Bottle." Yoon, how I wish I really could save time in a bottle and take it out as I needed it.

Last night I was on border patrol when the battalion commander pulled up in a jeep. Luckily I wasn't dozing off, so I was able to salute him properly. He did an inspection, gave me a few encouraging remarks, and was about to get back in the jeep when he turned around suddenly and asked, "Hey, Corporal, you got a girlfriend?" It's an unspoken rule in the army that if a senior officer or anyone who's been in the service longer than you asks if you have a girlfriend, you say yes regardless of whether it's true or not. I thought of you and said, "Sir, yes, sir! I do, sir!" Then the commander asked, "You think she's faithful?" I hesitated, and then barked, "Sir, she'll wait for me, sir!" He stared at me for a moment, like he was going to say something, but then he called me a dumb fuck and hopped back in the jeep. I stood and watched until the taillights of the jeep disappeared into the darkness, and I thought about what he'd said. Why did he ask me something so childish and trite and then call me a dumb fuck? Did it just pop out as he was trying to think of something comforting to say? One thing I am sure of is that our brief conversation in the dark showed him who I really am. I am a dumb fuck.

Yesterday, one of the guys on KP duty caught four snakes by our unit. The snakes, which are called rock mamushi or red-banded snake, had yellow venom on their tails. They said snakes crawl all the way into the squad barracks in the summer. Imagine that. Lifting your blanket and seeing a snake crawl out. When I came back from the beach this morning, they told me the platoon leader and some of the older guys roasted the snakes and ate them with soju. I wasn't disgusted by that. I did worse things in the special forces. If I told you what people resort to in order to survive in the mountains, you would probably never want to see me again. People eating live snakes still squirming after their skin is pulled off like a sock and their guts scraped out . . . I've seen and done so many bizarre things since I joined the army.

Whenever I look down at the ocean through night vision goggles, I feel like a nocturnal animal. Rifle slippery in my hands. Waves breaking against the shore and exploding into shards. Even now, in my dreams, I march around and around the training ground in formation until someone barks Ten-hut! and I wake.

Compared with how desolate it is at night, the beach is beautiful in the daylight. Yesterday, the entire squad stripped down to our government-issue briefs and ran double-time to the shore and dove into the ocean. The water was so achingly cold at first, but as we shouted and crashed into one another, it felt almost lukewarm. It occurred to me that maybe if things keep going this way just a little longer, I, too, could become a simple, well-adjusted being, one who fits the label of soldier or enlisted man, and be able to return to society. I no longer feel as anxious as I did when I first started. I love to recite this clichéd line of poetry: "Should this life sometime deceive you, Don't be sad or mad at it!" All the while wondering if perhaps it is not life deceiving me, but me deceiving life.

Yoon.

   The sky is very overcast today. I grabbed a raincoat, just in case, along with my notebook, and patrolled the ceasefire line, huffing and puffing my way to the top of the bluffs. My face was red and hot by the time I got there. I sat at the edge of the cliff and looked down at the murky sea. Sketched a single small boat in the distance that looked like it was penciling a line across the water with its wake. I like the sketch, so I am sending it to you.

Dahn seemed to be braving his time on the coastal border patrol by writing to me. One of the letters asked me to come visit. He had changed so much. I stared at the letter for a long time. I couldn't believe this was the same person who had refused to receive any letters or visits. He sounded lonely and overwhelmed and most of all worn down. That was the sense I got.

Yoon.

   Lately, the military has been on constant alert, so everyone is under great stress. At least once a day we get orders to increase our vigilance. Everyone below the rank of company commander is particularly nervous about next month's full military inspection. Originally, our company was supposed to pull off the coast and regroup with the main force while another was sent in to replace us, but it keeps getting pushed back. As a result, we have not had even our regular days off.

Yoon.

Is there any chance you could come see me someday next week? Of course, since we have to deploy to our observation points on the beach every night, we are not officially allowed to have visitors. But if you can come, I'll try to sneak out for a day. I'll have to grovel to this one guy who's younger than me but has been here longer. But I would be willing to degrade myself if it meant I would get to see your face, even if only for a few seconds. The mountains are dark behind me, and in front of me, the surface of the water glimmers like scales in the moonlight. I carry a loaded rifle, keep watch over the night, and think of you.

I put my face down on the desk. I remembered that night with Dahn so vividly. I had debated for several days whether or not to go. He had avoided contacting me, even when he was on furlough, because he didn't want me to see him with a shaved head. To get to where Dahn was, I had to take a train and two different intercity buses. At the last stop, I met a civilian defense soldier who was on his way to night duty at the unit on the coast where Dahn was on patrol. He took me all the way to the unit where Dahn was stationed. Dahn rushed out, his rifle slung over his shoulder, hand grenades and bayonet on his army belt.

Armed to the teeth, Dahn and I walked along a forest path lined with dry pinecones. There was no one else around. We came down a path along the bluffs and followed the coastal ceasefire line until we had left his patrol route. We walked forever down that dark path along the waterfront. I had no idea where we were. We seemed to be moving away from the water, because the sound of lapping waves grew faint. The stars gazed down at us, shimmering as if they might spill down at any moment. Dahn walked beside me in silence. I didn't say anything, either. For me, there was nothing stranger than seeing Dahn dressed as if he could be sent into battle at any moment. I could not think of what to say to the Dahn who was no longer Dahn the individual that I knew but Dahn the nameless soldier in khaki combat fatigues. We walked on and on but never came across another person. Suddenly Dahn asked, "Want to hear something scary?"

"Seeing you armed like that is scary enough."

He laughed.

"I deserted my post," he said.

"What do you mean?"

"If they find out I'm with you, I'll be court-martialed."

"Is it that bad?"

Dahn laughed again at how serious I sounded.

"Don't worry. When you do coastal duty long enough, you realize that everyone does what they have to in order to see their family or girlfriends. We all look the other way. The company commander and first sergeant probably know about it. No one believed me when I said I had a girlfriend, so they made a bet."

"On me?"

"Sorry."

"What was the bet?"

"They said if you showed up, they'd let me stay out overnight."

"This is too dangerous. I don't want something bad to happen to you because of me."

"Bad? What are you talking about? I'm so happy right now. I can't believe you're here beside me."

I was nervous, but talking to Dahn made me feel better.

"What was the scary story? More spiders?"

"I'm not afraid of spiders anymore."

This was not the same Dahn who had worn a headlamp to accompany me to my mother's grave, the Dahn who trembled in fear of stepping on a spider. He told me that his fear of spiders went away while he was in the special forces. He said that after all of that daily hiking, crawling, jumping, and soaring up in the mountains, he found himself grabbing spiders with his bare hands.

"Really? So there is some benefit to joining the army!"

Dahn's laugh sounded hollow.

"So what's your scary story?" I asked again.

Dahn pointed to some spot in the dark, to where the sound of the waves was coming from.

"There's a guard shack down there, between the bunkers, where the soldiers take turns napping during their patrols. They say a soldier fell in love with a girl from one of the villages nearby. The girl would come by from time to time and spend the night with him in the shack. Whenever she came to see him, she always brought a pot of ramen for him as a midnight snack. But after the guy got out of the service, he took off without giving her his phone number or even so much as a glance back. She was so heartbroken that she hanged herself from the ceiling of the shack where they had been sleeping together. Turned out she was several months pregnant. After a while, rumors started to circulate. Whenever a new arrival fell asleep in the shack, he dreamed that a pretty young woman opened the door, smiled, and came inside. Carrying a tray with a steaming pot . . ."

". . . And?"

"The soldier would take the tray and open the lid to find the pot filled with ramen. Bright red ramen boiling in blood."

I shrieked and grabbed his arm.

"Is it true?" I asked. "Did you see her, too?"

"Of course not! It's just a legend that's been passed down in our unit. The Legend of the Blood Ramen Ghost . . . Soldiers probably made it up to tell their girlfriends when they visited, like you. The girls get scared, just like you did, and grab their boyfriends' hands or leap into their arms."

"What?!"

So he had been trying to scare me, too. I tried to shake off his arm, but he pulled me closer and said, "I'm so glad you're here!" With the sound of the waves coming to us through the darkness, we passed a cornfield and walked single file along a ridge between two pepper fields until we came to a house. We decided to ask if we could stay there, since we couldn't keep walking all night. The woman who lived there must have been used to overnight visitors from the base, because she immediately led us to a tiny corner room with a porch. Dahn asked if there was anything to eat. She was surprised that we had not eaten yet and told us to wait a moment. Soon she came back with a tray filled with battered and pan-fried slices of squash, steamed and seasoned eggplant, kimchi, rice, and soup. She set the tray down on the porch. As she turned to go back to the kitchen, Dahn asked if there was any soju. She started to say there was none, but then she asked if we wanted her husband's half-empty bottle. Dahn thanked her. She came back right away with the soju, two shot glasses, and a small dish of pan-fried tofu. She told Dahn to take off his helmet and rifle. "Doesn't that scare your girlfriend?" she joked, and looked at me as she laughed. She told us the room would warm up in a moment and turned to leave. We ate on the porch. The plates were old, but the eggplant smelled savory and aromatic, like it had been freshly seasoned with sesame oil. Dahn filled his own glass with soju and looked at me. As I shook my head to say I didn't want any, I spotted a spiderweb dangling above the porch.

"Spider!"

Dahn took a look and stood up. With his bare fingers, he plucked the spider as it crawled down its web, trembling in the light, and tossed it into the yard.

"I'm not afraid of them anymore," he said.

Dahn sat down again and drank his soju. He looked at the kimchi and tofu but didn't touch any of it. I had a few bites of eggplant and then set my chopsticks down. I was hungry but couldn't eat any more than that. While Dahn drank, I stared at his combat boots and my sneakers where we had left them in front of the porch. I stuck my feet out and slid them into his boots. They were loose. I got down from the porch and staggered around. Dahn laughed out loud. "How on earth do you wear these heavy things?" I asked. I took off the boots and opened the door to the room. On the yellow linoleum floor were two blankets and a flat pillow. It must have been past midnight by the time we went inside and spread out the bedding. Dahn's helmet sat on the floor next to us. We lay side by side, Dahn still dressed in fatigues and me still dressed in my street clothes. When we were little, we used to go over to each other's houses to play and wind up falling asleep. Either his sister or my mother would come find us and carry us home on their backs. The sound of the waves surged in through the small window and lapped the rim of my ear.

"The ocean must be right outside," I said.

"Just the beach. The water's farther off. How are Miru and Myungsuh? Are they good?"

"Miru started looking again for the guy who disappeared, and Myungsuh is almost always at Myeongdong Cathedral, protesting the government."

"Who is Miru looking for?"

What was I supposed to tell him? Though I had brought it up, I did not have the heart to tell him the story when he was already looking so low.

"You know the house where we all stayed for a few days? Miru's parents sold it to someone else."

"So now we can't go back?"

"No . . . It's not her house anymore."

Brokenhearted over losing the house, Miru had started looking for her sister's boyfriend again. She would show up at my place looking disappointed and weary, stay for a few days, then set out again. I had gone looking for her, to see if she wanted to go with me to visit Dahn, but she was gone.

"How are you doing?" Belatedly, I asked Dahn about his own life.

"Like I'm trapped in a spider web."

"I thought you weren't afraid of spiders anymore."

"I'm not. Not of the spiders that live in the mountains. But I think I've found a much bigger spider."

He sounded sad. I felt him move toward me, and suddenly his face was directly over mine.

"I hate the sound of rifles. And the feeling of my finger on the trigger."

The smell of the soju on Dahn's breath filled my nose. He stared deep into my eyes. They wavered, and then his lips were against mine. His uniform pressed against my street clothes, and his hand slid inside my shirt and over my breast. When his breathing grew rough, I pushed him away from me. I could feel the strength in his hands when he grabbed my wrists.

"Dahn, please." I felt his breath against my skin. "Don't."

I tried to push him away, but he wouldn't stop. As I struggled, my hand brushed his cheek and I felt his hot tears. His lips pressed against mine again, and he tried to unbutton my shirt.

"You're the only exit I have left," he said.

The next thing I knew, my shirt was pushed halfway up my chest, and Dahn was trying to unzip my pants. I twisted away from him, but he climbed on top of me and held me down. I do not know if it was because of his tears on my fingertips, but I felt confused and lost all strength in my body. I realized that the whole time I had been debating how to respond to Dahn's invitation, I had known deep down that this would happen.

"You don't love me," Dahn said finally, and rolled away from me. "It's because of him, isn't it?" he asked. I knew who he was referring to.

Embarrassed by what had happened, the two of us probably got no sleep all night. I reached out and felt for Dahn's hand, but he did not move. At some point, it started to rain. If the sound of rain could be counted, I probably would have counted the drops. In the morning, our eyes met as we were folding the blankets up. His eyes were bloodshot. We took the same path we had taken the night before. I felt indescribably sad. We walked over the pinecones wet from last night's rain, made our way along the deserted forest path, and stood at the edge of the cliff and looked down at the sea. Below the dazzling sun sitting just over the horizon, barges were rocking in the waves. The sun seemed to shine even brighter after the rain. A tractor made its way around the driftwood and fishing nets scattered along the beach. What was a tractor doing on the mudflats? It was an unusual sight for me, as I was more accustomed to seeing cultivators moving back and forth between rice paddies. Each time the wind blew, the water wrinkled and grazed the sandbanks, one fold after another. The distant sound of engines sounded like something in a dream. A flock of seagulls wheeled through the morning sky and called out to one another.

"About last night," Dahn started to say, a glum look on his face. I quickly cut him off.

"Don't worry about it. I'm fine. We'll forget all about it in a few days."

"Okay." He nodded gravely.

"So, have you caught a spy yet?" The question popped out before I could stop myself.

"No one in my unit has, but they say someone caught a whale a few years ago."

"A whale?"

"Yes. We don't normally get whales in the West Sea. But once in a while, one gets lost and crosses the South Sea to this side of the peninsula. They say that when whales swim toward the coastline in the dark, they sound like North Korean spy submarines infiltrating. The soldier on duty followed procedure and fired off a flare, then remote detonated a claymore and opened fire with a machine gun. After the sun rose and they went in for a closer look, they discovered that it wasn't a spy, after all, but an enormous whale floating belly up and ripped to shreds."

"Poor whale."

"The colonel gave the soldier a commendation and rewarded him with a seven-day pass because he performed his guard duty properly without dozing off."

After the story of the whale mistaken for a spy, we didn't have anything else to say. It was the first time we had ever felt awkward around each other. We walked back between the cornfield and pepper field that we had passed the night before and arrived at Dahn's unit. I told him I would be on my way and turned to leave. After a few steps, I glanced back to see that he was still standing there, glued to the spot, watching me go. After a few more steps, I glanced back again, and he was still there. I gestured at him to go on in, but he did not move. I got farther away and looked back again. His head was hanging down.

Yoon.

Right now, the rain is falling. A heavy bluish mist hangs over the pine forest and the sea. I keep picturing the way you glanced back at me the day you left. When I'm lying under my blanket, your breath and your voice tickle my ear. I wonder what you're doing right now. Are you also looking out the window at the falling rain?

After that visit, I stopped answering his letters.

I lowered my head until my chin was nearly grazing the paper and started to write to him.

Dear Dahn,

The places I have visited the most in this city are Gyeongbokgung Palace and the museum on Sejong Street. At first, it took me about an hour and ten minutes to get there from my neighborhood. Now I can get there in fifty minutes. I'm not walking any faster, I just know the streets better. But I don't always go inside once I get there. If I'm on my way to school, I just pass by. Also, sometimes I like to walk around the outside wall of the palace rather than going in. I walk all the way to Samcheong-dong and then head home from there. I only go inside the museum or pay for a ticket into Gyeongbokgung Palace on days when the things I don't want to think about have built up inside of me and filled my head with noise. It's strange, but entering the palace is like entering another world. The moment I step through the gate and walk onto the palace grounds, the hustle and bustle of the world outside, the speeding cars, and the sky-high buildings all vanish. I guess that's why I go there. When I am inside the palace, I forget about who I am outside the palace. The first time I went there, everything felt so fresh and new. I felt stupid for never having realized how close I lived to a royal palace. Did I tell you about my plan to walk around the city for a couple of hours every day? I started doing this so I could learn about the city, and so far it has helped me to discover these places. All of these city dwellers live beneath the sheltering wings of this palace, so why don't they visit it more often? It's strange to me. Considering that I had always thought of Gwanghwamun Gate as just another intersection and not as the front gate of Gyeongbokgung Palace, I never even took a good look at the gate itself until after I had gone inside. Of course, it has only occurred to me that those are my two favorite places now that I am writing you this letter.

Last Sunday, it started drizzling in the middle of the night. I got up very early and walked to Gyeongbokgung Palace. Carrying an umbrella seemed like too much of a bother, so I wore a hooded jacket. The drizzle was very light. By the time I got there, my hair and clothes were damp. The palace is usually crowded on Sundays, but there was hardly anyone there that day, probably on account of the weather. I hadn't planned on going inside, but I changed my mind because there were no lines at the ticket booth, and the palace looked abandoned and alone. I had been inside numerous times, so I thought I knew it really well. But the old buildings looked completely different in the rain than they did on sunny days. Even Bugaksan

Mountain, which I could see from Geunjeongjeon Hall, looked like an entirely different mountain. The hexagonal Hyangwonjeong Pavilion on the island in the middle of the wide lotus pond where I went all the time also looked new to me. And that's not all. Gyeonghoeru Pavilion looked so mysterious in the rain. It was only a little rain, and yet everything looked so different. As I walked through the palace, I came across something new. Every time I go there, I make a point of going to Gyeonghoeru Pavilion, so I know the area around it really well. But this time, I spotted a wooden staircase that I had never noticed before. The stairs led up to the second floor. There was a "no trespassing" sign, but I went up there anyway. The pavilion was open on all sides. I was stunned by all that open space. It was even more overwhelming because I had only ever paid attention to the outside of the octagonal roof, which looks like it could take to the air at any second, or the decorative tiles shaped from wet clay to look like open-mouthed birds before they were baked and affixed to the ends of the roof ridge. The bottom floor had stone pillars, so I guess it never occurred to me that the second-floor pillars would be made of wood.

Do you remember how we used to go sledding over the ice in the winter? I mean the icy road next to the levee where the water parsley sprouts up fast and green in the spring. We would throw a rock at the ice before getting on the sleds. We did that to see if it was thick enough to support our weight. Do you remember the time we threw a rock and the thin ice cracked? As I was climbing up to the second floor of the pavilion, I thought I could hear that keerack! in my head. I raced up the rest of the stairs but managed to calm down once I got to the top. My forehead was sweaty, but it immediately cooled. I stood there in a daze. My eyes ached from *all that beauty. The floor was lined with planks of wood of varying heights. I felt like I had uncovered one of the city's secrets. I was so thrilled at my triumph that I couldn't stop smiling. Now I know that anytime you see a "no trespassing" sign, it means you've got to go in and take a look. Maybe that sign was the reason I had never noticed the wooden stairs, despite the many times I walked around the outside of the pavilion or sat gazing at it from a wooden bench.*

I stood there for a long time and then tiptoed carefully onto the wooden floor. I walked as lightly as I could, creeping forward one step at a time. The lotus pond looked amazing from above. The floating water hyacinth waved in the breeze, and the raindrops sent ripples, big ones and little ones, skidding across the water. On very clear days, you can probably see the pavilion's reflection in the pond. I've seen all the way to Inwangsan, Bugaksan, and Namsan Mountains before. The soil that was dug up when the lotus pond was built had been used to create Amisan Garden, behind the queen's living quarters. I could see that, too, right before my eyes.

I carefully sat down. The moment I did, all the nervousness I felt about trespassing vanished, and I relaxed. I'd been feeling angry at myself for not keeping the promise I made to Miru to help her look for him, and now she's gone off on her own again. But as I sat on the wooden floor of the pavilion, even that anger seemed to loosen its grip just a little. The floorboards seemed to speak—their words, muted for a hundred years, pierced through a deep silence and rose into the air.

Dear Dahn,

Remember how both of our houses where we grew up had narrow wooden verandas that ran around the sides of the building?

My mother always kept the wood polished. She told me my father built it himself using trees from the mountain behind our house that had fallen during a typhoon. She said the wood would last a long time if you took good care of it and kept it swept and cleaned and lacquered. Do you remember how we used to lie on our stomachs reading books on the veranda, and how we would fall asleep facedown on the wooden floor while doing our home-work or playing?

Don't laugh.

That day, I woke up on the second floor of Gyeonghoeru Pavil-ion to find someone shaking me. It was the groundskeeper. I must have been asleep there for forty minutes. After you get out of the army, I'll tell you how I managed to get away from him. It'll be my discharge gift to you.

Dear Dahn,

Someday, Dahn. Someday. I'll take you there.

I stopped writing. With my face nearly grazing the paper and the fountain pen clenched in my hand, I stared at the sentences I had just written.

The tiny letters in the word *someday* grew bigger and bigger until they were all I could see.

How I wish I could take Dahn up to the second floor of Gyeonghoeru Pavilion someday. If the day were ever to come when we could go there together, I would tell him the rest of the story. I would tell him that when the groundskeeper shook me, I bolted upright from where I had fallen asleep facedown on the wooden floor. That the first thing on my mind was not

"What am I doing here?" but rather "Where on earth am I?" That I then remembered walking around the lotus pond in the falling rain, seeing the "no trespassing" sign, and climbing the stairs to the second floor. I would tell him how the rain kept falling. How the dirt ground of Gyeongbokgung Palace was wet, and how Inwangsan Mountain was covered in mist. I would tell him that the groundskeeper gave me a hard look and scolded me and asked what I thought I was doing sleeping in a restricted area. That I immediately dropped to my knees and swore to the groundskeeper that I would scrub and polish the floorboards myself. I would come every day and polish them until they shone. The groundskeeper stared at my sleep-addled face and let out a hearty laugh. He said that I couldn't polish the floor, since visitors were not supposed to be up there without permission, but that I should never forget my promise. "If the day ever comes that people can come and go up here as they please, you'll keep your promise then, right?" He asked the question again, but with a softer look this time. Before I could even answer, he said, "As long as you never forget your promise, as long as you mean it when you say you would scrub this floor everyday, then I'll let you go this time."

So many forgotten promises. Broken promises that have long since vanished from memory.

I placed the tip of the fountain pen beneath the words *Someday, Dahn. Someday. I'll take you there*, and prepared to write the last line, but instead I sat there without moving. All I had meant to write was *Sincerely* or some other closing word, but I felt like I had driven myself into a corner. Like someone stammering for words because they have reached a dead end but have to say something, I wrote, *Take care*, and then crossed it out. I wrote, *Stay strong*, and crossed that out. Then I wrote, *I'll write to you again*, and crossed that out, too. My last image of Dahn standing there with his head hanging down flickered over the blacked-out letters of my final farewell to him. The blue of his shaved head spread in my mind like ink. I bit my lip and crossed out the words *Someday, Dahn. Someday. I'll take you there.* I wrote them again. I erased them again. Wrote them, erased them, rewrote them.

The page was one giant smudge.

"Yoon!"

I had fallen asleep at my desk when I heard someone calling me. I lifted my head from the smudged notebook and listened carefully to the sound coming from outside the door.

"Yoon!"

It was my cousin. I got up and opened the door. My pregnant cousin's freckled face looked happy to see me. She was carrying a container of kimchi.

"Why didn't you answer the phone?" she asked.

The phone had rung? She set the kimchi down in the kitchen and looked at me.

"Your father said he tried to call this morning," she said.

He had?

Early one morning six months ago, my father had called to tell me about Dahn. He said he thought it was better for me to hear the news from him rather than through someone else. I think he still walks to my mother's grave every day at sunrise and sunset. When the days grow cold, he wraps straw around the base of my mother's crepe-myrtle tree to insulate it, and when spring returns, the very first thing he does is remove the straw. The branches grew out wide over my mother's grave, like an umbrella on rainy days and a parasol on sunny days. It didn't look like it had been uprooted and replanted but rather like it had always been there.

"He asked me to come check on you because he's been trying to call since the day before yesterday. Do you know what time he called me today?"

I looked at her without answering.

"Six in the morning. He must have been waiting for the sun to come up first. Why didn't you pick up?"

"I didn't hear it ring."

"I tried calling several times as well."

I looked over at the phone. My father had delivered it to me personally so he could check on me in the city.

"Is it unplugged?" she asked as she ran the telephone line through her hand to check. "Looks fine to me. Why didn't you hear it ring?"

After that rainy Sunday when I had walked all the way to Gyeongbokgung Palace and back, I stayed in for several days. Whenever my room got too stuffy, I would go out onto the rooftop and look down at the city. I would stare for a long time at Namsan Tower shining in the same spot as always like some kind of symbol. When was the last time I'd left my room? I suppose it was the day I had put on my sneakers and walked to school, as I always did, and found out about Professor Yoon. I went to look for Myungsuh, who barely showed his face at school anymore since he was busy participating in a hunger strike that had been going on at Myeongdong Cathedral. I told him that Professor Yoon had submitted his letter of resignation to the university. He had resigned voluntarily. The reason he gave was that he could not continue teaching when so many of his cohorts in the university were being fired for political reasons. Myungsuh did not look surprised. Even when I gave him a copy of Professor Yoon's letter—the one that began, *To my students*—Myungsuh just took it calmly and said, "I guess Miru won't be going back to school now." Even when I told him that Professor Yoon was leaving the city and moving to the countryside, all he said was, "That sounds like something he would do." Sure enough, once Professor Yoon's classes were canceled, Miru stopped going to school. After her old house was sold, she would sometimes come by my place and gaze down at it. Once, she muttered, "They're fixing it up," so I assumed she had been by there. After the new tenant moved in and the house was lit up again at night, Miru said, "I hope they're happy there." It was strange to hear those words coming from her, after she had fought so vehemently with her parents about selling the house. I stared at her face as it glimmered in the city lights. She looked sad and asked me how Dahn was doing. I told her, "He's probably fine."

"Yoon, what's wrong?" My cousin asked as I stared at the phone. Her freckles seemed to have taken over her once-white face since the last time I had seen her. My eyes dropped to her enormous belly.

"I'm huge, right?" She smiled and rested her hands on top of her stomach. "They say if you're carrying high, it's a girl."

She moved her hands down to support her stomach. It was the protective instinct of an expectant mother toward her unborn child. I couldn't believe that she had walked up all those stairs to my place, carrying that big container of kimchi, holding her belly, face full of freckles.

"I must have been sound asleep," I said.

"But how could you sleep through all those rings?"

"I walked a lot yesterday."

Actually, I had stayed in the day before, but I didn't know what else to tell her.

"You're still taking those walks?" She looked worried. "You better call your dad."

I did as she told me and called him immediately. I had no memory of hearing the phone ring the night before. I didn't even remember hearing it in the morning, when I had been sleeping at my desk. I picked up the phone, placed it to my ear, and dialed the number with one hand while closing the notebook that held my letter to Dahn with the other. The blacked out lines filled my eyes. His letters had fallen onto the floor. Just as my father answered the telephone, my cousin picked up the letters and set them on the desk. She rested her hands on her belly and gazed down at the letters. She did not take her eyes off them.

"Dad, I'm fine. I must have fallen sound asleep last night and didn't hear the phone. How are you?"

"I'm fine, too."

Those words echoed inside of me like a bell. I would never have thought that such an ordinary phrase, *I'm fine, too*, could hit me so hard. If only I could hear the same words from Miru, who had stopped calling. If only I could hear them from him, who was getting thinner with each passing day. I held the receiver and listened to the sound of my father's breathing. If only I could hear those ordinary words from Dahn.

"Yoon? Are you still there?"

"Yes," I said finally.

"If things are tough, just come home."

I thought about the year I spent at home after my mother died. That year spent hanging around the country house. The quiet dinners with my father. My father's voice as he called to me on his way in the front gate. The silence that would return to the house after I answered him from my room or the kitchen. Though we never did anything for each other besides just being there, perhaps by calling to each other and responding, we had helped each other to slowly accept my mother's absence. When we were children, Dahn used to call my name from the alley before reaching the gate and stepping into the courtyard. Whenever he found a dead bird or saw a snake that had been run over by a train, he would take me with him to look at it. I must have called his name, as well, countless times. Whenever I slipped in the snow or fell in a ditch, his was the name I yelled. Because he was always there, right beside me, or walking ahead.

"That's okay, Dad."

When I hung up, my cousin was staring at me.

"Yoon." She sounded just like my father. She gently picked the letters up from the desk. She looked like she either had something to say or things she wanted to ask. Neither of us spoke for a moment.

"Why don't you come stay with me?" she said. "My husband is flying to Europe."

That meant he would be gone for several days.

"I'll be fine," I said.

She slowly bent down and sat on the floor. She stretched out her legs and leaned against the wall, but in a moment she was sprawled out flat. Her round stomach pointed up at the ceiling. I thought of the book of poetry Dahn had given me the night before I left home the first time. Because of the quote he had written on the first page—*I began to tread softly . . . Poor people shouldn't be disturbed when they're deep in thought*—the very first book I had bought in the city was *The Notebooks of Malte Laurids Brigge*. The first chapter in the book describes a pregnant woman pushing herself along the wall of a hospital. The dedication read: *The most beautiful woman in the world is one who is pregnant with new life.* My cousin's hands kept moving to her belly. Her freckles spread across her cheek and over the cheekbone to her temples. It was not hot, but there were drops of sweat on her forehead. Each time she took a breath, her round belly rose and fell. I went over and lay down beside her. We used to take naps together, back when I lived with her. She smiled, pushing her freckles up toward her ears. She took her left hand off her stomach and reached out to stroke my cheek. Her hand warmed my face.

"Will you promise me one thing?" she asked. I looked at her. "Promise me you will never cover your windows with black paper again."

I didn't say anything.

"I always liked having you live with me. Except for when you covered the windows and wouldn't come out of your room."

"What was I like then?"

"You were a different person. You looked like you were wrestling with something, and if you lost, you would never come out of that room again."

All I had wanted was to see my mother, who sent me away when her illness worsened. All I had ever wanted was to be by her side.

"I hope you're not going to cover up those windows." A worried look crossed her face. "Promise me you won't do that. And then I won't force you to come back home with me."

"I promise, Sis."

As I called her *Sis*, I suddenly felt sleepy.

"You promised!" she crowed.

I nodded. Then I placed my hand gently on her stomach. It rose and fell with the strong kicks of her unborn child. Thoughts filled my mind: *I have to see Professor Yoon. I have to walk my cousin out. I have to go to school. I have to take a coat to Myungsuh.* But I was overcome with drowsiness and could not open my eyes.

Miru has been arguing with her parents every day, ever since find-ing out that her old house was put on the market and posted in the window of every real estate office in the neighborhood. She's been so distraught that Yoon told me she regretted her decision and said if she had known this would happen, she would never have agreed to it. It took her a long time to accept Miru's invitation to move into the house, and she only did so on the condition that Miru stop wearing her sister's flared skirt. My condition was that Miru had to stop searching for her sister's boyfriend. The turn of events left us all dumbstruck. The house had been sitting empty since Mirae died, but it sold just a few days after Yoon agreed to move in.

When Yoon mentioned Miru's skirt, I tensed up. In keeping with tradition, their parents had piled all of Mirae's belongings in the courtyard of their house several months after her funeral and burned them. Miru stubbornly grabbed hold of that skirt and refused to let go. Afterward, she wore it year-round. She never took it off. Nevertheless, she listened to what Yoon had to say, and her face immediately brightened.

"That's it?" she asked. "The day we move in together, I will take it off and never wear it again."

It is a mystery to me how women can grow so close in such a short time.

Miru begged her father not to sell the house, but he was stubborn. He told her he would buy her another one. She said it had to be that house. They both refused to back down. I understand why he did it. That house holds the painful memories Mirae left behind. All it does is remind them of the grief of losing a child. Who could ever make up for that grief? Miru's father called and asked me to try to calm her down. But Miru would not be appeased. She lashed out at her father and yelled at him. He slapped her, but still she refused to give in. It was shocking to see her so fierce. Once the house sold, she cut off all contact with her parents, and after she resumed her search for her sister's boyfriend, she stopped contacting me as well.

| | |

I met Yoon's cousin at Myeongdong Cathedral. She called me at my uncle's house. I didn't realize how far along her pregnancy was—of course, I couldn't tell over the phone. She sounded so young.

"I would like to meet you without Yoon knowing," she said.

I wondered why she wanted to see me. Yoon talked about her cousin every now and then. She told me she had lived with her when she first moved to the city.

"Please don't tell Yoon," she said.

I felt alarmed and quickly asked if something had happened to Yoon. I hadn't seen her in almost ten days.

"Shall we meet at Myeongdong Cathedral?" she asked. "From what I hear, you're there almost daily. I can head over right now."

Now? At this hour? I checked my watch. It was eight in the morning. But though she had phrased it as a question, her tone made it clear that she wasn't really asking. She told me where to find her, the decision already made for me: she would be sitting in the tenth pew from the back in the sanctuary inside the cathedral. Before leaving to meet her, I tried calling Yoon. The phone rang and rang, but she did not pick up. I hung up and left for Myeongdong.

When I opened the sanctuary door, I thought the place was empty. I went to the tenth wooden pew from the back and spotted an enormously pregnant woman sitting at the other end. For some reason I didn't realize she was Yoon's cousin. She was sitting in quiet contemplation but looked up and smiled at me when I sat down. She got up and started moving down the pew, so I hurriedly stood and made my way toward her instead. She sat back down when she saw me coming. I hesitated, so she spoke first.

"Are you Myungsuh?"

"Yes, ma'am."

"You must have been surprised to hear from me. Please sit down. I'm sorry for calling so early. I didn't notice the time."

I couldn't take the suspense and asked her again if something had happened to Yoon. She looked at me for a moment and moved her hands from the back of the pew to her round belly.

"The problem isn't Yoon, it's Dahn."

Dahn. I breathed a sigh of relief to hear that Yoon was okay. But what happened to Dahn? I hadn't heard anything more about him from Yoon after we all visited him at the training center. Whenever I asked about him, she told me he was probably fine. I thought about the time we had spent together in that old house. Yoon used to stare at Miru and me with this inscrutable look on her face and, once, I asked her what she was staring at. She said, "The two of you seem to share something that I can never be a part of." During our time together in that house, I came to realize what she meant. When Yoon and Dahn were deep in conversation while pulling weeds in the courtyard, or lying on the deck reading books or drinking beer, or in the kitchen cooking rice or seasoning greens, Miru and I could not come between them. They were in a world of their own and knew each other inside and out. Once they started reminiscing about their childhood, Miru and I could not keep up. Sometimes I caught myself looking at Yoon and Dahn the same way that Yoon looked at me and Miru. Yoon would ask what I was looking at, and I would give her the same response: The two of you seem to share something that I can never be a part of.

Yoon's cousin looked up at me, and our eyes locked for a moment. Her cheeks were gaunt, which made her eyes look even more deep-set. I noticed that she had freckles. She had a straight nose and clearly defined lips, and her skin was darker than Yoon's, though that might have been because of the freckles. Her mouth barely moved, but the outer corners of her eyes lifted into a smile. Yoon had often mentioned her cousin's eyes when she talked about her. She said they smiled even when she was angry. Her face looked more or less how I had imagined it.

"Yoon has told me a lot about you," she said, using a formal register. "She would probably be surprised to know that I was meeting you like this."

I told her she didn't need to be so formal, but she pointed out that we were meeting for the first time. Though her eyes remained friendly, it was clear from her mouth that it was hard for her to keep smiling. Then she seemed to give up on trying. Her eyes darkened, and she moved her hands farther down her stomach. We never see these things coming: to think that I would find myself sitting in the gloomy sanctuary of Myeongdong Cathedral, which had not seen a single day without demonstrations . . . I figured she did not have good news, so I didn't rush her to speak. I sat looking straight ahead like a man waiting to be sentenced. The long rows of pews filled my eyes.

"We were told that they were stationed on the beach around four in the morning for a live firing drill," she began. "An older soldier who was almost done with his service was on the machine gun, and Dahn was beside him firing an M16, when they said they heard Dahn scream. They're calling it an accidental misfire during a night shooting drill, but it doesn't make sense."

She had her head down and was dashing the words out all at once, as if reciting them.

"Dahn is dead," she said.

I thought I heard the heavy cathedral door blow open and slam shut again with a bang. Something like a black horse seemed to ram me from behind, vault the empty pews, and punch through the ceiling.

"But it doesn't add up. Something's not right."

What went wrong that I now found myself sitting in this cathedral, receiving this news? Was this the price we had to pay for those blissful days spent in that house before Dahn went to the army? Dahn always stayed behind to draw in his sketchbook whenever Miru, Yoon, and I went out. Whenever I saw him absorbed in sketching, I couldn't bring myself to interrupt him. From what I had observed of his powers of concentration, I assumed he would be an artist one day. It was strange to look back on it now: Dahn whipping

up something in the kitchen for us and setting it on the table: tofu
and kimchi, green onion pancakes, kimchi stews that he made from
whatever was in the refrigerator. His easygoing smile, and the way
he said, "I just threw it together," when I teased him by asking what
kind of man cooks that well. Dahn saying, "Just seven more min-
utes!" whenever we complained that we were hungry, and bringing
out noodles or bibimbap. The four of us laughing gaily and eating
every last bite. As much as I had enjoyed spending time alone with
Miru, it was better when Yoon joined us, and better still when Dahn
was around. Had things been too perfect, and we had to suffer for it?

"They aren't certain of the cause of death," Yoon's cousin con-
tinued. "Whether it was suicide or an accident, or if he had been
arguing with his shooting partner . . . The units stationed on the
coast have regular shooting drills. The soldiers do them on their own
without an officer or even a noncommissioned officer present, so they
say it's possible for mistakes to happen due to carelessness. Even a
small mistake can be fatal. Though Dahn was only there on tempo-
rary duty, they say he was a disciplined soldier and got along well
with the others in the barracks, so it did not look like suicide or an
intentional accident. They say it was just bad luck. The battalion
commander, company commander, platoon leader, and other im-
mediate superiors got nothing more than a reprimand for negligence.
But the problem is that the position and angle of the bullet wound
don't match the conditions of an accidental discharge during a live
firing drill. The bullet that hit him came from his own gun."

I didn't know what to say. We looked up at the figure of Christ
nailed to the cross. Two elderly women who looked like friends
walked slowly past us and sat down several pews ahead. They took
out their white chapel veils and placed them on their heads. A ray

of sunlight pierced through the stained glass window and slanted across the cathedral. The tinted light looked like an indelible stain.

"I came to see you because . . ." Yoon's cousin said.

She stared straight ahead and did not look at me.

"Because of Yoon," she said finally. "I was so shocked and saddened to hear about Dahn. I knew him and his family really well. Though I worried about how they were handling it, I still thought of Yoon first. I guess that's selfish of me. It's already been six months since he died. But Yoon seems so calm—strangely so. I was relieved at first, because I thought it meant she got over it quickly. But lately she's been acting strange. As if she is only now realizing that he's gone. Or no—no, she acts like she forgot what happened."

Dahn died six months ago? I rubbed my ears. Yoon's cousin's voice seemed to grow louder, like she was shouting directly into my ear, and then fade into a distant echo, and then buzz so that I could not understand a single word. Yoon had known about this for six months? I stopped rubbing my ears and rubbed my eyes instead. I felt like my eardrums were bursting and my eyeballs bulging out. Every time I asked Yoon about Dahn, she said, "He's probably fine." Even when I asked if we should visit him, she said yes at first but then hesitated and changed her mind. I looked at her as if to say, What kind of an answer is that? And she said, "I don't think Dahn wants any visitors." Another time she told me he didn't want to see any civilians until he was discharged, and still another time she agreed and said we should go see him. I thought she just couldn't make up her mind.

"I dropped in on her a few days ago," her cousin continued. "She was writing a letter to Dahn. I read it while she was sleeping. It was a reply to a letter he sent her a year ago. She wrote that they *should go to Gyeonghoeru Pavilion together someday and go up to the second floor . . . My heart sank when I read that. I know how she feels—she can't accept the fact that he's dead. I saw how close they were, ever since they were kids. Some people are like that."*

I knew what she meant. When Dahn came to see Yoon, and Miru found out that he didn't have anywhere to sleep and dragged us all to that old house, I knew their friendship was just like Miru's and mine.

"I'm due any day now," Yoon's cousin said, and placed her hands on her belly again. "I want to help her, but I don't think she will let me. That's why I came to see you. It wasn't easy finding your number, and I had trouble getting through. That's why it took me so long. As soon as I got through this morning, all I could think about was meeting you as soon as possible. I'm a little older than the two of you . . . so I hope you don't mind my being direct, but I think people suffer the most when they have no one. Yoon and Dahn share a connection that can never be broken, regardless of whether they are physically together or not."

"What should I do?" I asked. I was eager for her advice.

"Don't leave her side," she said.

"Being with her gives me strength."

Her face brightened, and a warm smile spread across her freckled cheeks. Her eyes wandered over my face.

"I'm glad to hear that," she said. "It must have been quite a shock to hear from me this way."

I thanked her for telling me. And I meant it. If she weren't Yoon's cousin, I would have left immediately to run to Yoon's side.

—Brown Notebook 8

Chapter 9

If We Hug
A Hundred Strangers

To my students,

He took the letter that Professor Yoon had written to us before he resigned, read the first line out loud, and handed it to me. Copies of the handwritten letter had been distributed to each of us. It had been a long time since I'd seen Professor Yoon's handwriting, which I had grown so familiar with. I didn't understand why Myungsuh was handing me the letter, so I just looked at him.

"Read it to me," he said.

"You're still carrying that around with you?"

"I take it out and read it whenever I feel anxious," he said, smiling.

"Then you must have it memorized by now . . . Why do you need me to read it out loud?"

"I never get to hear your voice nowadays. Please. Read it out loud for me."

He must have read the first line out loud in order to prompt me to read the rest. I unfolded the sheet of paper and pictured Professor Yoon's eyes, the way they used to shine behind his glasses. "Read it," Myungsuh said as he lay down on the bench. He rested his head on my lap. He was so tall that his legs hung off the edge of the bench and his feet touched the ground. Two quails sitting nearby startled and took to the air. It had taken us two hours to walk up Namsan Mountain to the base of the tower, which I had so far only looked at from my apartment, so he must have been tired. White blossoms from a nearby acacia tree fluttered down and landed on his face.

"Read it," he said again.

His eyebrows rose, and he closed his eyes. I looked down at his black eyebrows for a moment. He reached out his hand and wrapped it around mine as I held the letter up. When was the last time I had read anything out loud? As my heart began to race suddenly, I took a deep breath, but it did not help. Feeling shy, I brushed away the petals that had landed on his face. He opened his eyes briefly to peek up at me and then closed them again. I cleared my throat.

To my students,

No doubt you have all heard by now, but I have decided to resign from my post at this university where I have taught for many years. These suffocating times, and my worsening health, make it difficult for me to continue taking the podium. I have already submitted my letter of resignation to the university president and, after sending a brief separate missive to the board of directors at the foundation, I am now writing to you.

As I leave this post where I have served and that I have regarded as my calling, it is only natural that I should feel a number of conflicting thoughts and emotions. But what weighs on my mind the most at this moment is what you all must think of me. Your gazes press down on me from a different angle than those of my family or colleagues. Your eyes contain your censures, your silent requests that urge me to stand strong, or preferably, to step forward and take action.

For me, a poet who has made it his profession to deal in words and to wrestle with words, our era has been one of continuous trials and tribulations. In this age when words have lost their value, this age that is therefore dominated by violent words, by words swollen and yellowed with starvation, I have lost the will to speak any more of words. My despair over words is not an admittance of defeat in life. Though I step down from the lectern, I will continue to work hard, look after my health, and, most of all, resume writing the poetry that I put on hold for so long. I accept that as my given duty and my calling. But please do not think of me as a fighter throwing in his resignation as a token of resistance to the current state of affairs. Nor am I a recluse who nihilistically spurns worldly values and sets off in search of some lone nobility. Though I leave the school, I will be with you in spirit, and though I may be discouraged by the rough language of this age, I will endeavor to continue creating poetry. I hope that you take my decision to leave the school as a sign of my desire to see you all again someday, in another place, in some other capacity.

In that spirit, I ask you to ruminate one last time on the story I once told you about Saint Christopher crossing the river.

Right now, you and I are crossing a deep, dark river. Every time that enormous weight presses down on us and the waters of

the river rise over our throats and we want to give up and slip be-
neath the surface, remember: as heavy as the load we shoulder is
the world that we tread upon. Earthbound beings unfortunately
cannot break free of gravity. Life demands sacrifice and difficult
decisions from us at every moment. Living does not mean passing
through a void of nothingness but rather through a web of relation-
ships among beings, each with their own weight and volume and
texture. Insofar as everything is always changing, so our sense of
hope shall never die out. Therefore, I leave you all with one final
thought: Live. Until you are down to your final breath, love and
fight and rage and grieve and live.

Warmth radiated from Myungsuh's head onto my lap. I
read the last line out loud again. The wind sent acacia blossoms pinwheeling through the air. We got up and left the
acacia wood. As we walked toward the tower, I murmured
the last sentence of Professor Yoon's letter to myself several
times.

"In the house I grew up in," I started to say, "there was a
well. The water in that well is the very first water I remember."

I brought up the well so abruptly that Myungsuh just
stared at me blankly. We walked beneath more acacia trees.
As we got closer to the tower, acacia blossoms blew toward
us, floated in the air in front of his eyes, and clung to my face.

"We began every morning at that well," I said. "My mother
would rise at dawn and draw water. My father and I would
wash our faces and brush our teeth next to it. Nowadays, the
whole village has converted to tap water, and the well has
been covered up. But whenever I go home, I lift the cover and

peek inside. It's still full of water. It makes me happy each time I see it. It's reassuring to know that the first water I ever tasted has not dried up."

He listened quietly as I spoke.

"I love you as much as looking into that well."

He stopped short at my unexpected confession. Belatedly, he realized that I was echoing his story about the sparrow he had told me at the old fortress wall a long time ago, and he laughed out loud.

"Back when every house was using well water," I said, "drainage pipes were buried beneath the courtyard to draw the runoff away from the house. At all hours of the day or night, you could hear the murmuring of water. The water was channeled out of the houses and into a small ditch that ran outside of the front gates. Because of all that water, yellow flowers that looked like daffodils bloomed in the alleys every spring. Even after the petals dropped, there would be a thick colony of green stalks. All year round, except for winter, the alleys were teeming with yellow flowers and green stalks. Our house was right in the middle of the village. The runoff from our house was the start of that little watercourse. As you followed it, it joined up with the runoff from another house. And if you kept going, all of that water fed into a bigger gully, which flowed into a canal. But don't think that the water was dirty because it came out of all those houses. The well water was mostly drawn and used in the kitchen. Since all we did at the well was wash our faces and rinse vegetables, the water was clean. It may not have looked like much, but it channeled off all of the rainwater during the monsoon season in summer as well. Once, I wondered where the water went and tried to follow it all the way to the end. It led me across fields, over train tracks, and into more fields that continued on without end."

He stopped walking and turned to look at me.

"I love you as much as that endless water."

I used to wonder where the water in the big gully came from and would walk along the embankment to see where it led. It truly was endless. But no matter where I went in the village, I was never alone. Dahn was always by my side. We would walk along the gully until we reached a place that was called the upper waterway. That seemed to be where the water began. When we peered at where the water gushed out, all we could see was a long, dark channel. The water never stopped pouring out of it. We couldn't go any farther and never did find out the source of the water. But the water never stopped flowing, past village after village, past the banks where women washed laundry on the rocks, along the banks of rice paddies, until it reached the canal where it continued on without end. I had a memory of following the water downstream in search of a single sneaker that got swept away only to return home, frustrated and sobbing, because I did not know where the water ended. Though I could hear the water the moment I stepped out of the front gate, I had no way of knowing where it began or where it ended. Only that it flowed without restraint.

Before we realized it, we had reached the base of the tower.

"In spring, after the seeds have been sown in the fields, and the rain comes, farmers are so happy. Have you ever seen their faces then?"

"No," he said, and smiled apologetically.

"Whenever there was a drought in the spring, people used to climb into the mountains, carrying containers of water on both shoulders, to sprinkle it on the hillsides. The source of that water was the spring rain. When the spring rain came, people walked around in it without an umbrella. And they didn't just say it rained, they said the rain *graced* us. Even now, when it rains in the spring, I get an urge to collect the rainwater. That's what we did every year when I was little. Whenever my mother made soy sauce, she would first catch rainwater in a huge clay jar big enough to hold two adults. She would leave the jar open when the weather was good to collect the good energy and shut it tight when the weather was bad to keep out the bad energy. And though it was too early to plant seedlings in the rice paddies, my father would build up the banks around the paddies to flood them with rainwater anyway, as he said the spring rain was too precious to just let it run off. Even the grapevines, which were all dried up and looking dead at that time of year, would grow green shoots when the spring rain touched them. The barley shoots turned green, and even the spinach sprouted up like weeds in the early spring."

"What did you do with the rainwater you collected?"

"There wasn't much, barely enough to wet the tongue of a thirsty dog lying under a porch."

"Let's collect the rainwater that drips off the eaves some-day," he said with a smile.

"Someday?"

"Yes, someday."

On some such day—not a day still to come but a day long past—Dahn and I had placed a washbasin under the eaves to catch the spring rain. I pictured it: Dahn feeding the rainwater that overflowed the basin to the rose bushes and the persimmon tree; the spring rain that brought dead-looking things back to life. Sap rises in spring—Dahn and I soon understood those words. Once, before spring had fully arrived, he and I had stood in front of a tree and gouged out some of the bark so we would know the exact moment the sap began to rise. My face suddenly felt feverish.

"Let's go to the top of the tower," I said, and walked ahead.

Myungsuh called out to me in surprise. His voice sounded faint.

"What's wrong?" he asked me.

Why did Dahn have to die? I stifled the words I felt like shouting. Did anyone have an answer to this question? We stood in front of the railing at the top of the tower and looked down at the city. People kept coming out of the woods and heading for the tower.

"Yoon."

"What is it?"

"I have an idea."

I looked at him, my hands gripping the railing.

"Let's stand here and count the people."

He was not pointing to the forest path below but to the stairs on the other side.

"When we get to ten, twenty, thirty, and so on, let's run over and hug that person."

"Hug them?"

"Yes."

"Hug strangers?"

"Yes."

I didn't understand what he was up to, so I just stared at him.

"They'll think we're crazy, right?" He was saying what I wanted to say.

I looked down at the city and wondered what on earth he was thinking. He wanted to hug a bunch of strangers? At first I was surprised by the suggestion, but then I felt a surge of anger rise up in me. Would doing that bring Dahn back? I felt like thrashing Myungsuh with my fists. Would that bring him back . . . ? I wanted to shake the trees on Namsan Mountain. Claw the faces of those smiling people. Even as my anger flared, a chill deep inside me made me shiver.

"Are you okay?" Myungsuh asked.

I nodded. I pressed my feet hard into the ground to keep from shaking.

Back when I took a break from school and lived at home with my father, I had spent some time in the hospital. My whole body had broken into a fever. Red splotches, like flowers of fire, bloomed on my skin every half hour, and when they subsided, the chills followed. It was harder to bear the rising fever than it was the onset of chills. I couldn't open my eyes; even my fingernails felt heavy. Sweat poured from my forehead, and I drifted in and out of consciousness. When my hands looked like boiled crabs, my father put me on the back of his bicycle over my protests, rode me to the hospital, and had me admitted. The cycle of fever and chills continued in the hospital. I didn't get better right away. Instead, as the fever worsened, I stopped recognizing people. My body felt like a ball of fire, and I was covered in tiny red spots the size of millet seeds. On my second night in the hospital, I was giddy with fever and lost in agony when I felt someone put a hand on my forehead. That hand was as cold and refreshing as ice. It might sound like a lie, but after the hand touched my forehead, the fever that had been raging for days came down at once. I came to and saw my father asleep on a folding chair. In the morning, I asked him if he had touched my forehead in the middle of the night. He said no. I asked the nurse, too, thinking it must have been her. She also said no. I had no idea whose hand it was that had felt so cool against my skin, but after that hand touched me, the fever and the chills died down. If only I could feel that hand on my forehead once more.

"So, shall we begin?" he asked.

"You really want to do this?"

"Yes."

I looked up at him silently.

"Maybe if we hug a hundred strangers," he said, "something will change."

He kept his eyes on the stairs leading up to the tower and started counting the people as they came up—*one, two, three* . . . A breeze blew up from the woods and ruffled his hair. His dark eyebrows rose each time he ticked off another number. After he counted nine, a child came running up the stairs. The child's mother was running after him several steps below. Myungsuh was about to take off and dash over to the boy. Before he could count ten, I threw my arms around him and held on tight.

The phone rings in the middle of the night. It rings and rings, but when I pick it up, it stops. I told Yoon about these nightly phone calls, and her eyes got big.

"I get them, too," she said.

"You do?"

She said it hangs up when she answers. We stared at each other, our moods bleak. We were both quiet, then Yoon asked, "Do you think it's Miru?"

"Why would Miru hang up on us?"

"That's true," she said.

She asked if I had ever been out of contact with Miru for this long before. Never. I tried calling her parents, even though I knew there was no chance Miru would have gone to them. From the way her mother said my name, I could tell she had not heard from her, either, and was hoping for news from me.

| | |

Now we stand before a storm. I take to the streets nearly every day to join the demonstrators. I can't leave Yoon on her own, so she goes with me. We marched on City Hall, locking arms with the other protesters and advancing toward Shinsegae Department Store.

"When we work together like this," Yoon said, "it feels like we can make change happen, and it doesn't feel so weird to hold hands with strangers."

Whenever we get pushed apart and I lose my grip on Yoon's hand, I reach right out and grab hold of it again. I want to define my own values. I want to stop drifting from one phenomenon to another. Right now, my only strength is this feeling of solidarity. When I take to the streets, the fog in my head and even this bottomless despair seems to lift. Let's remember this forever.

| | |

Yoon smells of chocolate. There was a hole in the back fence big enough for a person to slip through, and on the other side was a small store. I didn't feel like studying, so my friends and I ditched school and slipped through the hole. As we were walking past the store, someone yelled, "Chocolate!" A type of candy I had never seen before was on display, each piece in its own little compartment. One piece of the chocolate cost the same as an entire bag of regular candy. We pooled our money, bought a few pieces, split them up among us, and tasted them. We were all very tense and eager because the one who recognized it as chocolate said it would taste amazing. The candy melted smoothly and easily on my tongue. I had no idea anything in the world could taste like that. I thought I would turn to stone right there.

| | |

On the bus, the radio was playing Blue Dragon's "My Only Wish." Blue Dragon was a college band that had won a prize for this song after performing it on one of those music programs they show on TV—Beach Music Fest, or maybe College Music Fest. When Dahn came to the city to visit Yoon, and we were staying together in the old house, the four of us sang this song together, accompanied by Mirae's old guitar. I rested my forehead against the window of the bus and sang along.

My only wish
is to return
to the ocean in the quiet dusk,
to sleep quietly by the forest.
Clear blue sky above the boundless sea,
I've no use for colorful flags,
no need for a splendid house.
All I ask is a bed
woven of young branches.
No one weeps beneath my pillow
and all that whispers across the dry leaves
is the sound of the autumn breeze.

It had sounded so romantic and lyrical when we sang it in the house together. But now, maybe because of what happened to Dahn, it reminded me of death. I couldn't keep singing. To think that beneath that soft, sweet melody lay the cool allure of death. I think you can only sing it so beautifully and languidly if you do not truly know the tragedy of death and have never experienced the threat of death.

| | |

Yoon's cousin had a baby girl. They'll be celebrating her hundredth day soon.

| | |

I woke from a dream.

I don't know where I was, but I was standing next to a river. I had to cross it to get to the other side. The fog was so thick that I couldn't see anything. I was pacing back and forth, unsure of how to get across, when I spotted a house. Tied up between the house and the river was a ferry. I figured the house was where the ferryman lived and I knocked on the door with delight, but no one answered. I called out, but there was no reply. I pushed on the door, and it swung open. I went inside, but still no one appeared. A book that looked as if someone had just been reading it was lying on the floor, so I picked it up and opened it. I know that I read it in my dream, but after I woke up, I had no memory of what it said. I waited a long time, but the owner of the boat never showed up. So I got into the boat. I tried rowing. The water parted, and the boat slid forward. As the boat began to cross, the fog thinned out little by little. It felt like I was pushing the fog away. The fog was so thick that I could barely see an inch ahead of me, but when I was about halfway across the river, it cleared away almost entirely. It was strange. After the fog cleared, the boat refused to budge no matter how hard I rowed. It seemed to be stuck to the surface of the water. Just then, I heard a shout. The voice sounded desperate. I looked all around and saw someone waving at me from the dock. They were calling out to me. It was too far away to make out the person's face, but he or she was yelling for me to please help them get across the river. I was already halfway across and couldn't turn back. If the boat hadn't stopped, I would never have even turned to look. I tried to keep rowing ahead, but the boat still would not budge. Helplessly, I stopped trying to row forward and rowed backward instead to pick the person up. The boat began to move through the current.

| | |

Sometimes I call Miru's parents' house. Eight months have passed without a single phone call or postcard from her. Usually no one answers, but her mother will sometimes pick up. We never talk, though. Before I can even say hello, the line cuts off. There must be something wrong with their phone. I dial again, but it cuts off again. I wait a little while and then call again, but the same thing happens. Once, I let it ring and ring and ring, but no one answered.

| | |

The streets are quiet now. All of that excitement, like we were going to make something happen, has vanished. Our push for change has come to a standstill. Even our solidarity is now just another phenomenon. The people I once marched with have all scattered and dispersed without having changed anything.

| | |

I started working part-time at a magazine where Fallingwater's older brother is the editor-in-chief. The magazine publishes book reviews and information about new books. Sometimes I take my camera and go to the bookstore to photograph the book covers. The building is far from my uncle's house, so I keep a sleeping bag in the corner of the office. Fallingwater's brother asked if I was planning to sleep there. When I nodded, he looked at me as if to say, we'll see how long you keep it up, and patted me on the shoulder.

| | |

Today, I passed by City Hall and sat with Yoon for a while on the plaza.

Yoon pointed to a long drainpipe bolted to the wall of City Hall and asked, "Do you remember that guy who climbed up the pipe?" I did. When the demonstrators reached City Hall, the doors were locked. I have no idea who that guy was. In the newspaper the next day I saw a photo of him climbing the pipe. We didn't know who he was, but we were both there when it happened. There was an excitement in the air that made him seem like someone we could believe in. He shimmied up the drainpipe to the cheers of the people gathered in the plaza and climbed onto the roof of City Hall. Everyone held their breath. We watched on pins and needles. The moment he set foot on the roof, everyone let out a sigh of relief and sent up a loud cheer. He shouted out slogans, and they echoed them. As did I, as did Yoon. As did all of the people on top of the stone wall outside Deoksugung Palace, on the stairs leading down to the subway, in the branches of the gingko trees planted along the streets. Where have all of those people gone?

| | |

The instant Yoon told me that Miru's mother was hanging up on her before she could even finish saying hello, I felt like I'd been hit over the head. She said it was obvious that Miru's mother was hanging up. I had been thinking all along that something was wrong with their phone or that they kept missing my calls. Why had it never occurred to me that her mother was deliberately hanging up on me, and that there was nothing wrong with the telephone line?

| | |

Sunday. I went to the room at the bottom of the stairs where Miru used to live. I don't know why it took me so long to think of going there. Someone else has moved in. A forty-year-old woman with a limp. She seems to be living there alone. The woman, who has a lot of wrinkles around her eyes, never even heard of the name Miru. She said the room was empty when she came to look at it, and that she signed the rental contract and moved in right away—all of which took place last spring.

"Did she have a cat?" she asked.

"Yes, its name is Emily."

"I'm still finding cat hair," she said.

She didn't seem to be upset about it, so I told her it was a long-haired cat. After I left, I climbed back up the stairs and just stood there, staring off into space. Where had Miru gone with Emily? How could she move without saying a word to us about it? I felt as if we were strangers to each other. The woman came slowly up the stairs, carrying her trash.

"You're still here," she said.

She set down her trash bags and asked, "Did Miru plant those?"

She pointed at the green, overgrown lily stalks. They were at ground level, but I had planted them so Miru could see them from inside her room. When she first moved in, the place was so dark that I had decided to plant flowers in the yard for her.

"Please tell your friend that I'll take good care of her flowers. When I moved in last spring, those lilies really brightened up the room. I wondered who had planted them. I felt so happy the whole time they were in bloom. I asked the owner, and she said the previous tenant had planted them. So that was Miru!"

The woman nodded politely to me as if I were Miru herself.

| | |

The phone in the office often rings in the middle of the night. Sometimes I am woken up by the rings and cannot get back to sleep. When I unzip my sleeping bag, the sound vibrates in my ear like *a sympathetic resonance. It rings and rings the whole time I am slipping out of the sleeping bag, like a snake molting, and walking over to the phone.*

Once, I picked up the receiver, and a young female voice said, "I have to find Jisu."

"Excuse me?"

"Jisu." Her voice sounded urgent. "I said I have to find Jisu."

Why on earth would she be calling a magazine company in the middle of the night to say she needs to find Jisu? I knew she had the wrong number, but she sounded so desperate that I could not hang up on her. I started to tell her that I didn't know any Jisu, but then I heard the beep beep of the dial tone. She had hung up. I put the receiver back in the cradle and was about to return to my sleeping bag when the phone rang again. I thought I should at least tell her that I did not know who Jisu was and picked up the phone, but it hung up immediately. I guess Miru was not the only one. A lot of people were searching for someone. In other places as well, places I'd never heard of, there were probably other phones ringing off the hook in search of someone.

| | |

Another call came, and I thought it would be the same desperate-sounding woman—the one who was looking for Jisu. I stayed in my sleeping bag and let it ring. I thought it would stop eventually, but it didn't. I frowned, slipped out of the sleeping bag, and picked up the phone. It was Yoon.

"Can I come over?" she asked calmly.

I was usually the one who said that to her. I looked at my watch. It was three in the morning. I could hear her breathing over the phone. I hadn't heard from her all day. I had tried calling her sometime after midnight, but she hadn't picked up.

"Is something wrong?" I asked. "I'll be right there."

"No," she said. "I'll go to you."

I felt like the wind was knocked out of me.

"I won't keep it a secret," she said. "I'll tell you everything."

My hands started to sweat. I didn't have to ask. I knew she was calling to tell me about Miru.

—*Brown Notebook 9*

Chapter 10

Us in the Fire

The signal changed, and I crossed the street. Hail struck the asphalt and the tops of cars with a sound like glass breaking. On the other side, people were huddled under the bus stop shelter. The blank looks on their faces vanished at once. As if to mock them as they stood there stranded and looking nervous, the hail eased up and then stopped completely. It had come and gone in an instant, like a brief dream during a catnap. Rays of winter sunlight wedged their way back down between the buildings as if it had never hailed at all. But the people at the bus stop did not budge. They looked up at the sky in doubt and eyeballed me as I walked past.

The school was empty. It was winter vacation and the weather was freezing. Myungsuh was already waiting for me in front of the auditorium. He must have been cold, because his face was deathly pale. No scarf or gloves, either.

"Did you get it?" I asked him.

He nodded. "But why do we need Professor Yoon's office key?"

"I brought Miru's diary."

He was usually quick to give me a smile, but this time he looked at me blankly. I braced myself. I had promised myself I wouldn't stammer when I told him about Miru.

"Let's go to his office first."

He started to walk ahead of me, but I grabbed his arm. He wouldn't take his hands out of his pockets. I took off my glove, put it in my bag, and slipped my hand into the pocket of his coat. When I held his hand, he seemed to flinch.

"I called you again last night, didn't I?" he asked.

I gave his hand a squeeze instead of responding. I wanted to tell him it was okay, but I had already said those words too many times. It was okay that he called. He could call me any time, any hour of the day or night. So long as I knew where he was calling from. But often, when I asked him where he was, he had no idea. Sometimes it sounded like he was going to say something, but the line would suddenly disconnect. *When would we be okay again?* My hand was too small to wrap around his.

On the way to Professor Yoon's office, he turned to look back at the zelkova tree. I looked back, too. Usually surrounded by students, the tree stood alone in the winter air. I remembered the day I had stood in this same spot and looked back to see Miru walking beneath the tree with her bag over her shoulder and a book in her hand. Her walking hunched over with her shoulders rounded as if staring at her own heart. Her white cotton jacket and flared skirt with its pattern of white flowers against a dark blue background. In a flash, I remembered how her skirt had floated up in the breeze, and

I squeezed Myungsuh's hand hard. Maybe he was thinking about her at that moment, too.

I kept my hand in his pocket until we got to Professor Yoon's office and he needed to take out the key. Even though I knew the office was empty, I knocked on the door anyway as he was fitting the key into the lock.

When we stepped into the office, we were hit with a musty smell. The chilly winter air and the dampness overwhelmed us at first. Myungsuh shut the door and turned on the light. Like a curtain opening, the dim office brightened, and the outlines of books came into view. The books stared blankly down at us. I looked at Professor Yoon's desk on the other side of the stack of books. I could still hear him saying, "Come right in," the way he had the first time I had knocked on his office door long ago. If only he would poke his head out from the other side of the books and say, "Have a seat over there . . ."

"No one's here," Myungsuh muttered, though he had known that on the way in.

I went over to the desk. Normally littered with open books and manuscripts, it was spotless. I pictured Professor Yoon straightening up his things and ran my hand over the surface. Dust coated my palm. I had only meant to touch his desk, but I started dusting it with my bare hand instead. When that wasn't enough, I grabbed a tissue. A cloud of dust rose up from the box. Myungsuh went to the sink installed in one corner of the office and turned on the water. The long-unused tap creaked. He turned the water off and then on again with more force. Water gushed out. He stepped back, brushing off the drops that had splashed onto his clothes, and bent down. Beneath the sink was a pail with a dry cloth inside it. He held the cloth under the tap, wrung it out, and came over to me. Without saying a word, he wiped down the desk that I had been dusting with my hand.

"Give it to me," I said. "I'll do it."

He ignored me and focused on cleaning Professor Yoon's desk. He looked like he had come expressly to clean the desk. I watched as the white cloth grew dusty, and then I propped open the window. A cold breeze rattled in.

"It's a good thing they left his office untouched," I said.

"He might come back someday," he said. "I heard they still haven't accepted his resignation."

Someday . . . I murmured the word to myself. He finished cleaning the desk and then removed the cushion from the chair and cleaned the chair, too. He beat the dust out of the cushion and put it back on the chair before giving it a few more firm pats with the palm of his hand. He looked haggard. He had called me the night before, sometime after four in the morning. He must have been drinking, because I could barely understand him. I had asked him where he was but couldn't make out his answer. This sort of thing had been happening more frequently, and even though it was the next day, I couldn't bring myself to ask him what had happened. He would probably just say the last thing he remembered was boarding the subway and that he must have fallen asleep.

"Aren't you cold?" he asked me.

"Very."

After he was done dusting Professor Yoon's desk and chair, he closed the window that I had just opened and peered out between the blinds. No one would be out there.

With his back to me, he asked, "Why did you bring me here?"

"To add Miru's diary to the bookshelf."

I opened my bag, took out Miru's thick diary, and went to the shelf where the books stood with their spines facing in. He let go of the blinds and looked at me.

The first thing that had caught my eye when I visited this office for the first time were those old books that looked like they would crumble at the slightest touch—the books by writers who died young. Holding Miru's diary, I ran my hand over them, still shelved with their spines to the wall so neither author nor title could be seen. I felt like they were speaking to me but I couldn't understand a word they were saying. I remembered how Professor Yoon asked me, "Are you wondering why I shelved them that way?" And I unconsciously turned to look at the desk. Myungsuh was standing there looking my way, his face frigid with cold.

"Would you like to do it?" I asked.

His gaze moved to Miru's diary in my hand. "Have you had it the whole time?"

"I went to Miru's grandmother's house. Remember when you tried to call me in the middle of the night, but I wasn't home? It was that day."

"How did you find the house?"

"I met Miru's mother and went with her."

He stood there quietly.

"I'm sorry I didn't tell you."

I couldn't bring myself to tell him, so I had gone to meet her on my own. Afterward, I had sat in front of the telephone until late into the night before finally calling him. He and I were like twins. I had lost Dahn, and now he had lost Miru. He came over to me and took her diary. We were probably both picturing her hands, the scarred hands that recorded what she ate, leaving nothing out. I even pictured myself, as if that me were another being entirely, staring in fascination, having never seen someone who wrote down everything they ate with such devotion. All those days we spent writing stories in her journal. Whenever we were together, our faces would grow flushed with our love for each other. When Miru started filling her diary with the stories of people who had disappeared, we should have paid more attention. Those diary entries were Miru's distress calls. Myungsuh leafed through the diary and ran his hand over the pages. Then he handed it back to me.

"You do it," he said.

The diary must have been the reason Miru's mother didn't hang up that morning when I called. She usually hung up the moment I said Miru's name. But I could not resist calling their house whenever she came to mind. I knew her parents didn't want to talk to anyone about her, but I didn't know what else to do except to keep calling. Then, one morning, several months after my last failed attempt at making contact, the moment I heard Miru's mother say hello, I quickly said, "Don't hang up!"

"Please, don't hang up," I pleaded. During the silence that followed, my fingers felt like they were splitting apart.

"Who is this?" She finally broke the silence.

"My name is Jung Yoon."

"Jung Yoon?"

"Yes," I said quickly.

"So you're Jung Yoon."

I got down on my knees, the phone gripped in my hands.

"I read the diary you all wrote," she said, referring to it as "our" diary, rather than as "Miru's" diary. "It's at her grandmother's house."

"Please let me speak to Miru," I said.

All of my strength drained out of me. It was like I already knew that I would never hear Miru's voice again.

"Please put Miru on," I begged.

Her mother sighed.

"Where is she?" I asked.

The phone went silent.

"Please don't hang up."

"She's dead."

I didn't comprehend her words at first.

"She starved herself."

Finally, it sank in.

"Do you hear me?" she said. "She's gone."

I stared blankly out the window at Namsan Tower in the distance. I felt like it was tipping over and crashing down on me.

Miru's mother said she'd had no idea that Miru had gone to live in the empty house her grandmother left to her. Likewise, Myungsuh and I had been too caught up in the frenzy happening in the streets to know where Miru was. While he and I were asking if anyone had heard from Miru, she was alone in her grandmother's house. I wanted to hear more, but her mother said, "It's all in the past now," and hung up. A few days later, she called me back. When I answered the phone, she addressed me affectionately as "Yoon-ah." It felt natural. She told me she was going to Miru's grandmother's house and asked if I wanted to join her.

I went to the station in the city where Miru's family lived, as her mother instructed. A man who looked like a hired driver came up to me and asked if I was Jung Yoon. I followed him to where Miru's mother was sitting inside a silvery gray car. She was dressed all in black. I started to get in the front, but she motioned for me to sit next to her in the backseat. Emily was stretched out on the rear dash but didn't seem to remember me. Miru's mother and I didn't say a word to each other on the way to the countryside. Only when the car banked around a sharp curve did she look directly at me. Maybe it was all the black clothes, but her face looked pale. She took my hand— I had been holding on tight to the seat to keep from sliding each time the car took another turn. Her face was blank, but I could feel her warmth and strength as she tried to protect me. I stared straight ahead. Though I didn't look at her directly, I could sense Miru's features in her profile: the same nose, forehead, and lips. The long, graceful neck. It was like looking at an older version of Miru. When the curving mountain road finally straightened out, she gently let go of my hand. She glanced at me now and then but mostly stared out the window until we arrived at Miru's grandmother's house.

The house sat at the foot of a mountain. The village was tiny—only three scattered houses.

"I guess she wanted to live here like her grandmother." Miru's mother spoke for the first time since leaving the station.

"One of the neighbors told me they saw her wearing a hat and baggy pants, carrying a hoe, and working in the yard and the vegetable garden. They were shocked. They thought it was her grandmother's ghost at first."

The house was exactly as Miru had described it. It was as familiar to me as if I had already been there. In the court-yard stood the persimmon tree, plum tree, and cherry tree, and in the cupboard were the brass bowls and brass spoons and chopsticks. In the shed, the farming equipment and tools were neatly organized, and hanging on the wall were all of the things that Miru's grandmother had used or worn during her life. Her hat, her rubber boots, her raincoat. This must have been the place Miru's grandmother had built after com-ing south alone during the war with Miru's newborn mother on her back. The place that looked just like the childhood home she could never return to. The place where Miru's older sister injured her knee and was never able to dance again. Where Miru spent her final days alone. I stared at the base of the plum tree. That was where, on the day of the accident, Miru's sister held a branch like a ballet barre and gave her final performance.

"The house is going to be knocked down." Miru's mother's hollow voice floated on the air. "That's why I asked you to come. I wanted you to see it. Since this is where she spent her final days."

I pictured a young Miru fitting every pointed object she could find into the padlock and chanting *open, open, open*.

Miru's mother opened the front door of the empty house and turned to look at me. As I turned my gaze away from the plum tree and started to walk toward her, she stepped inside.

"She had an eating disorder," Miru's mother mumbled. "Miru blamed herself for the fact that her sister couldn't do ballet anymore. Her anorexia started when she refused to eat until her sister was out of the hospital."

I pictured how Miru used to write down everything she ate.

"Once it starts, you can't stop it. Even when she got as thin as a bamboo skewer, she would start crying and not stop. I don't know where she got the strength. She used to shake the walls with her crying. She would get better for a while, and then it would flare up again. Even after she started middle school, she was still in treatment. Sometimes we had to force-feed her through a tube when she refused to eat. After she turned fifteen, she stopped having relapses, so we thought it was over."

I'd had no idea. I wondered if recording everything she ate was her way of battling the part of her that didn't want to eat. Miru's mother went into a room on the far side of the living room. I peeked inside. The floor was scratched, wallpaper torn, wardrobe cracked, and windowsill chipped.

"Here." Miru's mother knelt down and traced her fingers over the scratch marks. "Emily did this."

I felt numb, unable to take in what had happened to Miru, but when her mother pointed out the claw marks, I burst into tears. Was Emily all she had as she was dying? I stepped into the room and stroked the scratched wardrobe. Some of the marks were distinct, others faint, and others very long. I pictured the cat's tiny claws. Emily. I hurriedly wiped my eyes and stood next to Miru's mother. We stared down at the scratched floor.

"We had no idea Miru would be here in this rundown place. I made a mistake. I should never have sold that house in the city. She begged us to let her live there with you. Back then, we didn't think it was good for Miru. At the time I thought that if she moved back into that house, she would never get over what happened to her sister. I was in so much grief that I couldn't pull myself together. I didn't have the strength left over to look after Miru. After we sold the house, Miru never spoke to us again . . . You said your name is Jung Yoon?"

Miru's mother's eyes looked unfocused. She was using my full name, as if she had just learned it for the first time and had never called me *Yoon-ah*.

"Yes," I said.

"I was a bad mother. Especially to Miru."

She opened the wardrobe and took a box down from the shelf.

"These belonged to her."

The box held her diary and a bundle of folded letters with bits of tape on them.

"We took down everything she had taped to the wall."

They were letters Miru had written to Myungsuh and me, and to Professor Yoon. She had never sent them.

"Will you take them?"

Miru's mother looked at me quietly. I bit my lip and nodded. There was nothing more I could do—nothing but stand there and watch as her mother wrapped the box in a carrying cloth.

On the way back to the city, Miru's mother suddenly said, "We had her cremated and scattered her ashes there." She kept tying and untying the knot on the carrying cloth, so I could not tell where "there" was. She told me Miru had grown so thin that she barely looked human. I turned to look out the window; there was nothing but mountains. "Her body was as light as a snowflake," she said. Her voice grew faint in my ears. My vision grew hazy until the trees on the hillsides blurred. While Miru was alone in that empty house, while she was refusing to eat, while Emily was clawing the floors, what was I doing? Looking back on it now, I was running around in the streets every day with Myungsuh, my cheeks red with excitement, lost in a sea of a million people. While he and I were banding together with strangers, locking arms and singing, and marching on City Hall, Miru was rustling like a leaf alone in this empty house at the foot of the mountains, writing endless letters to us and taping them to the walls.

When we arrived back at the station, Miru's mother did not get out of the car. She wouldn't even look at me. I stepped out of the car, unable to ask if I could take Emily with me. I hugged the box containing Miru's diary to my chest and headed toward the station, but I kept glancing back at the car. It showed no signs of leaving. I walked a few more steps and looked back again. It was still there. My own mother's face came to mind just then. Mama, who felt sorry for dying. Mama, who sent me away when she found out she was sick.

I turned and ran back to the car, stumbling over my own feet in my urgency to reach her, worried they might take off before I could get there. I knocked on the window. Only when the window began to roll down did I start to breathe again.

"Please open the door," I said.

Miru's mother looked at me with her empty eyes.

"Please," I said.

She pushed it open. I set the box on the ground, leaned inside, and hugged her. Her dry cheek brushed against mine.

"I'm sure Miru was very sorry," I said. "I'm sure she would tell you if she could."

"Thank you." She patted me on the back. "Thank you for not asking why I left her there."

I bit my lip. I was in no place to ask her that question. I, too, had abandoned Miru.

"Go now." She pushed me away. "Let's never see each other ag—."

Her throat locked up and she couldn't get the last word out. She struggled to regain her voice. I got into the car and closed the door behind me. It saddened me to think there were relationships like this. Relationships like the one between me and Miru's mother, where we could not help but say, *Let's never see each other again*, despite just meeting for the first time. We sat in the car for a long time, unable to part ways. When I did not get out, the driver retrieved the box. We ignored the annoyed looks from pedestrians who had to walk around the car. Finally, Miru's mother broke the silence and asked, "Will you take the cat?"

I cleared my throat and squeezed the books together to make room on the shelf. I was about to slide the diary between the books when Myungsuh, who had been standing there watching, said, "Yoon, wait." I paused and looked at him. He pulled something from an inside pocket of his coat. It was a folded letter.

"Let's put this in there, too."

I stared at it. Had Miru sent him a letter? As if guessing my thoughts, he said, "I wrote it." I thought about how I had written Dahn a letter six months after learning that he had died. In the letter, I invited Dahn to see the pavilion at Gyeongbokgung Palace with me. Myungsuh had not said a single word about Miru after finding out that she was dead. All he did lately was pass out drunk in random places and call me from a pay phone in the middle of the night. I felt a little relieved that he had written her a letter. I opened the diary so he could add his farewell letter to Miru.

"Would you like to read it?" he asked.

"No."

I must have sounded too firm. He stared at me for a moment.

"It was meant for her," I said.

"What are these?" he asked.

As he was slipping his letter into the diary, he looked at the other letters pasted onto the pages. They were once taped to the walls of Miru's grandmother's house. Letters that she had written to us but never sent. Letters I had pasted one by one into the blank pages of her diary. The page he happened to open to contained a postcard addressed to Professor Yoon. A single faded leaf was glued to the back of the postcard; the silhouette showed through. He gazed down at Miru's handwriting.

"You shouldn't read them," I said. He looked at me. "She would have sent them if we were meant to read them."

I had debated for a long time before pasting each of the letters and postcards Miru had written in the house into her diary. Initially, it seemed like the right thing to do would be to give the letters to Myungsuh and Professor Yoon, as well as to read the ones she had addressed to me. But she never sent them, and now there was no way of knowing whether she had meant for us to read them. I had left the box Miru's mother gave me on my desk for a month. From time to time, I would run my hand over the postcards and letters she had written to the three of us. Then, late one night, I decided to seal them within the diary that Miru had carried with her everywhere, and I pasted the letters onto the blank pages. As I did so, I knew I had to add this to Professor Yoon's shelf, the one that held his collection of books by young writers who died before the age of thirty-three. It was difficult not to read those letters while touching each of them in turn. Her sentences swirled before my eyes. I thought I spotted something about planting seed potatoes in the ground. Letters addressed to me contained Dahn's name. I would start to read, only to look away, spread on the glue, and paste the letter facedown onto the page. Even so, I accidentally read *I'm sorry I didn't keep my promise* and a few more sentences about the days we'd spent walking around the city. One letter, addressed "Dear Myungsuh," mentioned riding a sled one winter and falling into a river. I saw lines that looked like they were quoted from books she'd read. "His daily life was the suffering of a person who loves the internal, and writing was a form of prayer for salvation."—Kafka. "Cast a cold eye / On life, on death. / Horseman, pass by!"—Yeats. "Lived, wrote, loved."—Stendhal. One of the postcards contained a poem by Jules Supervielle: "Behind three walls and two doors, / you never think of me. / But no stone, no heat, no cold, / not even you can stop me / as I make and remake you / to my liking, inside of myself, / just as the seasons make forests / on the surface of the earth." One of the letters looked like an apology to Professor Yoon.

Calmly and without a word, Myungsuh placed his farewell letter to Miru inside her diary. I closed it and shelved it spine-first between the other books. He gave it a pat. We stood there for a moment looking at Miru's diary mixed in with the other books. He put his hand in his pocket. I put my hand in my pocket. He raised his left hand to scratch his head. I raised my left hand to scratch my head. He looked at the floor and stomped his feet twice. I looked at the floor and stomped my feet twice. Finally, he looked at me.

"Why are you copying me?" he asked.

"To make you laugh!"

But he didn't laugh and just stared at me.

"Jung Yoon," he said. "Don't try so hard."

"No, we have to try," I said firmly. "We have to."

He stood with his back to the bookshelf. I stood beside him with my back to the shelves as well.

"Move in with me," I said.

My words wandered among the shelves and returned to me like an echo. He didn't say anything. My phone had rung at three in the morning a couple of nights earlier. Emily, who had been lying right next to the telephone, was startled by the vibration and hid beneath the desk. The call was from Myungsuh. I asked where he was, and he said he didn't know. He was drunk, and it was hard to understand him. Without meaning to, I yelled at him to sober up and find a building or landmark nearby. The last thing I heard him say was "Hongik University." I layered on some clothes and was on my way out of the room when Emily followed me to the door. I told her I would be back soon and pushed her inside. I could hear her clawing at the door as I tied my shoelaces tight. It was below zero, and the wind was bitterly cold. I wrapped a scarf around my neck, pulled on my gloves, went downstairs, and hailed a cab. I assumed he had called from somewhere near the campus. I asked the driver to go slowly around the main road in front of the university. The bars were still open, their lights blazing, and people were stumbling out to the street to hail cabs. Why had he gone there? I couldn't find him on the main street, so I got out of the cab. I picked a block and started walking down each of the alleys. But even after searching each brightly lit alley, I could not find him. I wandered through the streets calling his name as alley cats ran and hid at the sound of my approach and trash blew around in the wind.

I must have combed through those streets for over an hour. I finally found him behind a dark stairwell near Sanwoolim Theater. There was a phone booth there. I walked right up to him, but he didn't recognize me. There was blood on his forehead, as if he'd run into something, and the back of his hand was injured. He could not have done all that drinking on his own, and yet there he was, alone. I had no idea how he managed to dial my number in his condition. His body was freezing cold. But he had still managed to fall asleep. The bottom of the staircase was covered in a thick sheet of ice. Icicles dangled overhead. He could have passed out and never woken up. I had to help him up somehow and get him into a taxi, but the alley was hidden from view, and he was laid out flat, which made it hard to handle him. I thought of how he had once found me barefoot in the middle of downtown, my shoes and bag lost in the melee, and carried me easily on his back. I took off my scarf and wrapped it around his neck and then covered his body with my jacket. I rubbed his cold hands to keep them from freezing and waited for someone to walk by so I could ask for help. As I did so, I thought, *We have to stay together and never part, not even at night.*

I managed to get him back to my room, but even by the afternoon, he was still not sober. I gave him something to eat, but he immediately threw it up. Emily curled up in a ball and kept her eye on the two of us. He didn't sober up until evening. He asked what he was doing in my room. Instead of answering, I said, "Move in with me." What had I said when Miru asked me to live with her? I'd told her I needed time to think about it. I pictured the look of disappointment on her face. He stared at the back of his injured hand and said nothing.

Myungsuh stepped away from the bookshelf.

"Let's get out of here," he said.

"And go where?"

"To see Professor Yoon."

"Now?"

"He asked us to come see him."

When he started to walk away, I grabbed his arm. He leaned against the bookshelf again. Miru's diary was right behind us. Someone came up the stairs in the hallway outside and walked quickly past the office. We listened to the sound of the person's shoes retreating. Whoever it was would have no idea that he and I were standing in Professor Yoon's closed office. Nor that Miru's diary was shelved there.

"Move in with me," I said again.

He looked down at my hand on his arm.

"We have to live together," I said forcefully. "We have to."

He held his breath.

"Let's live together. Emily, too. Eat together, brush our teeth together, wake up in the morning together, read together, go to sleep at night together . . ."

I trailed off. As I listed the things we should do together, memories of days past flashed before my eyes. I lost all strength in my hand, and he caught it as it dropped. Those days had happened to us by chance, with no warning or expectation. He, too, seemed to be thinking about the days we had spent in that empty house with Dahn and Miru. Dahn had written that the memory would stay with him forever, and that he would always be able to find his way back without getting lost. *That must mean it wasn't a dream.* He also said he and Miru had agreed that he would illustrate her diary. *Sometimes I think about that promise she and I made to each other.*

That day will come. Someday, I mean. Someday, when we meet again, I'll illustrate the stories the three of you wrote.

We left the school and walked to Jongno 3-ga to catch a bus to Professor Yoon's house. We walked in silence. When a cold breeze hit us, he took his hand out of his pocket and readjusted my scarf. Then he rubbed his hands together to warm them up and placed them on my cheeks. By the time we got to Cheongnyangni Station, transferred to a bus headed for Deokso, and found seats in the very back, a light snow was starting to come down.

"I can't wait for the years to pass, Jung Yoon," he said in a hollow voice. "Can't wait to be older, when I will understand, even if I can't forgive. Can't wait to become strong."

The village where Professor Yoon lived was white with snow like something on a Christmas card. The snow must have been falling the whole time Yoon and I were on the bus. It had stopped by the time we got off and started walking to the village, but then it started again. There were no footprints on the snow. Yoon held on to my arm and asked if I knew where the professor lived. I had gotten directions over the phone from both Nak Sujang and the professor, but it was my first time going there. Yoon fretted over whether we would find it in all that snow. The snow crunched underfoot with each step. I promised her we would, and she smiled.

"The snow really does crunch," she said, and stomped on it to hear the sound it made, as if she had never walked on snow before. "Listen! Crunch, crunch, crunch!"

She walked ahead so I could hear it, her tracks following her in the snow, then she stopped and waited for me to catch up.

"Look at that," she said.

She was pointing at the footprints we had just left. Mine were big, and hers were small. I liked walking in the snow and leaving footprints with her. I would happily walk anywhere in the world with her. With the snow crunching in our ears, we made our way along the winding path. The snow was piled high on top of an old tree that had fallen during the last typhoon. Birds alighted on the snow-laden branches and took off with a flutter at our approach.

"It feels like we're just going deeper into the mountains," Yoon said.

I had just been thinking the same thing, but I reassured her, saying, "It's just a little farther."

As we went around yet another bend, I started to worry, too. But just then, the village unfurled below us. The rest of the path looked like someone had just swept it clean.

The village was surrounded by mountains and completely blanketed in snow. There were only a few houses. The whole world had turned white. The path continued on like a line on a map. We traced it with our eyes. It meandered down the mountain and into the village, widening and then narrowing again. The swept path stood out clearly against the snowy landscape. It came to a stop in front of a house.

"That's it," Yoon said. "That must be where he lives."

We followed the path down to the village. Just as Yoon had predicted, the house at the end was the professor's. The front gate was open, and the professor was standing in the courtyard. The snow was piled high and white inside the courtyard as well. Leafless, snow-covered trees towered overhead. Inside the gate stood a sturdy-looking bamboo broom, the same one that must have been used to sweep the path we had just walked down. The professor watched silently as we approached. When we were standing in front of him, a dog came flying out of a doghouse on the other side of the yard. It was a big yellow dog. Before even greeting the professor, Yoon was scratching the dog's back as it wagged its tail. The dog lowered its ears and went to the professor's side. "It's big," the professor said," but very friendly."

Professor Yoon reached out his hand to pat Yoon on the shoulder, but she suddenly plopped down on the snow. I thought at first that she had tripped on something. Her shoulders were moving up and down, and then she burst into tears. Startled, I tried to help her up, but the professor said, "Leave her be." Once, long ago (now that I write those words, "long ago," it feels like something ancient) in Ilyeong, I had watched Yoon cry. She had looked as if she'd just dunked her face in the river. Once her tears started, she always had a hard time stopping, to the extent that I wondered how she was able to hold them in in the first place. Her eyes swelled up at once.

The professor already knew about Miru. I didn't bother asking how he knew. I wish the only things that ever happened to us were ones where you could ask how and why. He said he had received a letter from Miru's mother. Her mother had refused to see me. She took Yoon to Miru's grandmother's house and wrote a letter to the professor, but she wouldn't even call me. When I called him to get the key to his office, he must have already known about Miru. That must have been why he asked me to come see him and to bring Yoon. By the time Yoon stopped crying and we went inside, it was growing dark. The professor's house was furnished very simply: a chair and coffee table in the living room, a table and four chairs in the kitchen, and a desk and a chair in the bedroom. I sat on a long bench set beneath the living room window and looked out at our footprints in the snowy courtyard. The professor went to the kitchen, brought out a thermos, and poured a big mug of quince tea for Yoon and another for me. He looked out the window and asked Yoon if she was done crying. Yoon wrapped her hands around the mug and nodded.

"She brought me that tree," the professor said. I assumed he was talking about Miru. "We planted it together. She said it's crab apple."

It occurred to me that he might have been the last person Miru saw before going to her grandmother's house.

"The flowers bud in the spring," he said, "and after the leaves fall off, the apples come in. If the tree is still alive by the end of summer, we'll get to see some bright red crab apples before autumn."

Yoon and I sat next to each other and looked out at the tree. Snow glittered on the branches.

"Back in my twenties, when I was your age," the professor said. "I received a letter..." He leaned back against the sofa, his eyes fixed on the snowflakes dangling from the crab apple tree outside the window. "It was from a woman I used to know."

He turned to look at us. His steely eyes wavered for a second. Yoon set her mug down.

"There was a key in the envelope. I hadn't seen her in several years, so I was quite puzzled. There was a piece of paper wrapped around the key. I unrolled it to find a date and a hand-drawn map. It was the middle of winter, just like now. I didn't recognize the location on the map. At the time, I had completed my army service then went to the United States for several months to take a writing program at a university, after which I was spending the winter at my parents' house in the country. Not everyone had telephones back then. I had no idea what the key or the date meant, and I stewed over it for several days. I think I even wrote her a reply, filled with questions, but the snow was too heavy for me to get to the post office. In the meantime, the date in the letter came and went. It wasn't until several days after the snow had stopped that I realized I was supposed to have gone to see her by then. I came to my senses, shoveled my way out of the snow, and caught a train to the city. The map led me to Oksu-dong—I had never been to that part of the city before. I wandered around for a while, trying to find the house on the map. The ground was frozen, and the air was cold. I don't know how many times I slipped on those steep streets. At one point, my feet went out from under me and I fell on my back. My heart sank. What was she doing living in such a poor neighborhood? When I first met her, she lived in the wealthy neighborhood of Hannam-dong. She invited me over to her place once, and afterward we started to lose interest in each other. Or rather, she still liked me, but I lost interest. I can't explain what it was exactly. I guess I thought we were from two different worlds. When I started my army service, I didn't bother to tell her. I also didn't respond to any of the letters she sent me. She tried to visit me once when I was in the service, but I was gone on leave. After a few missed meetings, I stopped hearing from her. It was heartbreaking to see that she was living in one of those steep hillside slums. I started to hurry. Finally, I managed to find the house on the map. It was a small tenement building crowded with families at the end of a tiny alley on top of the hill. I rang the doorbell and knocked on the door, but no one answered. I took the key out of the envelope and put in the lock—it fit. I opened the door and peeked in. Shoes were lined up neatly beside the door and everything was in order, but no one seemed to be home. No one answered when I called out, so I took off my shoes and went inside. I called out again.

My voice echoed through the empty house. I tried opening each of the doors, one after the other. There were two rooms, one bigger and one smaller. I even opened the door to the bathroom, which looked like it had not been used in a while. No one was there. It was empty except for the chill in the air. I couldn't just hang around in a stranger's house, so I left. I locked the door behind me and went down the stairs. But something was tugging at me, and I kept glancing back as I walked down the alley. Then it hit me. The weather was freezing, but I broke into a cold sweat. I thought, It can't be, and I ran back up the alley, slipping and sliding the whole way, all the while praying I was wrong."

The professor paused. His eyes were red and swollen. He looked like he didn't want to finish the story. He glanced up at the two of us, nodded, and began again.

"I went back to the house and unlocked the door, but all I wanted to do was leave. I stood in the entrance for a moment and stared at the door to the bigger of the two rooms. When I had opened it before, it felt different from the other doors. It had only opened partway, like there was something behind it. I had poked my head into the rooms but didn't go all the way inside. I wasn't sure if it was even her house, and just because the key she'd sent me fit in the lock didn't mean I could go barging into someone else's bedroom. I wondered again whether I should leave. I was afraid. I cleared my throat and clomped over to the bedroom without taking off my shoes. I kept hesitating, and finally, because I thought I might back down, I pushed the door open fast and looked behind it. I was right that the door had bumped into something. I can't believe I'm telling you this, but it was her. On the wall behind the door. Hanging by her neck."

No one said anything for a moment. We watched the snow-covered courtyard grow dark. Then Professor Yoon continued.

"I'll never forget what I saw that day. I think that's why I never married. The memory has faded, but it never goes away. That's why I am not going to tell you two to get over the things you have gone through. You should think about them and then think about them some more. Think about them until you can't think anymore. Don't stop questioning the unjust and puzzling. Maybe if I had gotten there by the date written in her letter, I could have saved her. But then again, maybe her death was already planned, and all she wanted was for me to find her. Human beings are imperfect. We are complicated, indefinable by any wise saying or moral. The guilt, wondering what I'd done wrong, will follow me my whole life like my own shadow. The more you love someone, the stronger that feeling is. But if we cannot despair over the things we've lost, then what does it all mean? But . . . I don't want that despair to damage your souls."

The dog went out to the courtyard and sat in the snow beneath the window. The professor opened the window and stuck out his hand to stroke the dog's neck. His touch was gentle. Then he sat up straight, as if something had occurred to him, and he said, "Get up. Let's go into the mountains."

Dusk was falling. Why the mountains at this late hour? Yoon gave me a look. She seemed to be wondering the same thing. The professor grabbed some long poles that were propped up next to the front gate and handed us each one. He took one for himself as well and led the way. As we walked out the front gate carrying poles, we looked both ridiculous and resolute. The small village was completely blanketed. A few of the houses sat empty. On the way out of *the village and into the mountains, we saw no sign of anyone else out and about. Our legs sank deep into the snow as we followed the professor. The professor stopped in a part of the woods filled with old pines. I had never seen anything like it. The snow-covered trees stood in the darkness like people gazing down at us. It was so beautiful that I felt like kneeling before it. The professor brushed the snow off a branch that was touching the ground. Yoon stood below an old tree that measured more than two arm spans around and tipped her head back to look up.*

"Help me dislodge the snow," Professor Yoon said. "Since spending the winter here, I've learned that if it snows again when the trees are already covered, the branches can't bear the weight and will snap right off. Let's work together to clear the branches before it snows again."

Some of the branches were already broken. He raised his pole and used it to lift a branch. Though he barely nudged it, the snow poured down; flakes fell on our heads. Yoon and I followed suit and raised our poles into the branches to knock the snow loose. We moved hesitantly at first but soon became absorbed in the task. Though it was after dark, the snow reflected enough light for us to see. Each time we cleared one of the younger pines, the flexible branches snapped upward. Some of them knocked the snow off higher branches when they sprang up like that. Despite the cold, sweat broke out on my forehead and slid down the sides of my face. The professor collected the broken branches that were buried in the snow. One by one, I made my way forward until I lost sight of Yoon. When I looked back, she was hard at work shaking the branches, oblivious to me as well. The professor worked behind us for a while but then stopped and watched us in the dark. My whole body was wet with sweat. I had no idea how long we had been at it. The trees that had bowed under the weight of the snow rose up into the night sky. Even though she was out of breath, Yoon kept moving to the next tree. The mountains filled with the sound of our labor. I paused to look up. The stars glimmered in the frozen night sky. How long had it been since I lifted my eyes to look at the stars? It must have been past midnight. I didn't see the professor. I looked around but did not see him. Worried, I stopped and ran downhill. My spine was slick with sweat. The professor was sitting beneath an old pine cleared of snow. I asked him if he was okay. He smiled faintly. I sat beside him and listened to Yoon breathing hard as she shook the snow-laden branches. The sound of her pole knocking against the trees echoed through the mountains. I started to call out to her, but the professor stopped me.

"Leave her be," he said. "She'll stop when she's ready."

—*Brown Notebook 10*

I'll Be Right There

What is the furthest I shall reach
in life, and who can tell me? Whether
I'll still be a wanderer of the storm
and living as a wave in the pool,
and whether even I'll still be the pale,
spring-cold, spring-wind-trembling birch?
—Rainer Maria Rilke, from *The Book of Hours*

"I would like to tell you about a man named Christopher."
I pushed my glasses up and looked around the classroom. Their bright eyes were all fixed on me. I had been invited to speak at a women's university as part of the chapel service. I took my glasses off and set them on the table. Their bright eyes blurred. The students in the back row were reduced to silhouettes. I could tell they were wondering who this Christopher was, just as we all had back when Professor Yoon told us the story. I looked at their puzzled faces and smiled to myself. I can tell I am getting old whenever young

people strike me as endearing. But getting old isn't a bad thing. Getting old means that the subtle envy I feel for those passing through youth, and the waves of loss that wash over me when I see the way they seem to glow, will abate and leave only the hope that they will make their way forward freely, unimpeded by anything.

"Have any of you heard of Saint Christopher?"

I picked my glasses up from the table and put them back on. Their sparkling eyes once again poured into my own.

When Myungsuh called to tell me Professor Yoon was dying, I didn't go to the hospital for three days. I was ready to leave, but the phone had rung a second time: it was Nak Sujang. After college, he had left to study architecture at a university in Pennsylvania, where the real Fallingwater is located. Since then, he had returned and was running an architectural design firm not far from where I was living. He must have heard the news about Professor Yoon from someone else and called to tell me about it. Everyone's telephones—those of us whose lives were connected through Professor Yoon—must have been ringing off their hooks. When I heard it again from Nak Sujang, the news finally sank in. He suggested that we go together and offered to pick me up in his car, but I told him that a guest had stopped by right when I was getting ready to leave for the hospital and that I would go later. He started to ask about my "guest" but instead said he would see me there. After we hung up, I sat at my desk for the rest of the night. I stared at the clean surface of my desk for a while before spreading out the documents that I had been collecting for a long time to send to Dahn's older sister. I pored over them closely. They were from an NGO that was investigating suspicious deaths. Reading about people who had died before their time was painful. How was I to accept the fact of so many people driven to sudden and riddling deaths? I picked out the documents that pertained to unexplained deaths in the military and spent the next day photocopying them to send to her. My plan was to convince Dahn's family, who were unable to overcome the shock and pain of losing him and who still refused to talk about it, to petition for a reinvestigation into his death.

Though postponing my visit to see Professor Yoon in the hospital would change nothing, I avoided going anyway. It felt less like he was in the hospital and more like he was handing me a blank sheet of paper and asking: *What are you doing with your life?* I suppressed the guilt that welled up inside of me and did everything I could to put it off. I knew that the moment I went, I would be accepting Professor Yoon's death as a fait accompli. Outside the window, the snow was still coming down. I wanted Professor Yoon to turn his back on death and return to us, the same way I had once turned back in defeat while making my way through a blizzard to see him. I spent two days in this standoff with myself. By the third day, my tightly wound nerves loosened, and a strange sense of relief came over me. Then, by the evening of the fourth day, as if to defeat my desire to let time slip by without having to hear that Professor Yoon had died, I got another call. The moment the phone rang, I knew it would be Myungsuh. And I knew what he was going to say.

"He's not going to last the night."

Professor Yoon had once said that knowing you are alive means knowing you will soon change into a different form, and that that is the source of our hope. All beings, from human beings to the most insignificant creatures, experience a moment of radiance between birth and death. A moment that we call youth. When Myungsuh called me for the second time in eight years and told me Professor Yoon would not last the night, when he said my name and then nothing more, the memory of those long-forgotten words, *Let's remember this day forever,* came rushing back to me like a school of salmon swimming up a cataract.

I took the elevator to the ward where Professor Yoon had been admitted and walked toward his room, my footsteps echoing loudly in the hallway. Once I started paying attention to it, the clacking of my shoes grew louder until it filled my ears and I could hear nothing else. It was so unbearable that I had to stop for a moment. At the other end of the hallway, someone was leaning against the wall. He straightened up when he saw me. It was Myungsuh. Even from that distance, I recognized him at once. I took a step toward him but hesitated and stared at him instead. He stared back at me. We started walking slowly toward each other until we stood face-to-face in the middle of the hallway.

"You came," he said.

He was wearing a suit. His eyes locked on my face. I gazed back at him. I started to plunge headlong into memories of meeting him for the first time, so I stood up straighter and shifted my gaze down to his necktie and the oatmeal-colored button-down shirt he wore beneath a navy suit jacket. The photos I had seen of him in newspapers and magazines always showed him with his camera. He had become a photojournalist. I had learned, either from a newspaper I subscribed to or from randomly coming across it in a magazine, that he went into photography, rather than writing. There had even been an interview with him about a train trip he took with an installation artist across the East Coast of the United States. In the accompanying picture, Myungsuh was down on one knee taking photos. Beside him was a backpack the size of a small child. The reporter wrote that he tried to pick up Myungsuh's backpack, but it was too heavy for him to lift. He described how Myungsuh had run as fast as a tiger up to high ground with that heavy pack on his shoulders so he could get a photograph of an oncoming train. The article even said that the scar tissue in his knees, which formed from years of kneeling to take pictures, was as hard as caked-on layers of dirt. The first time I stumbled across his picture in the papers, I couldn't take my eyes off the page, but over time I got used to seeing him. In his photos, Myungsuh looked like he was constantly on the move, which was probably why it seemed so strange to see him in a suit.

"Let's go," he said.

He walked ahead of me. When I turned the corner, I saw the familiar faces of old friends. They stood together in pairs and in groups; one stood by himself, lost in thought and staring down at his shoes. Some greeted me with nods, while others reached out to pat me on the shoulder. One asked reproachfully, "Yoon, what took you so long?" Myungsuh kept walking one step ahead, guiding me to Professor Yoon's hospital room door. There, he turned to look at me. He took his hands out of his pockets and rested them on my shoulders.

"Prepare yourself."

He started to say he would wait outside the door but then changed his mind and suggested we go in together. The moment I entered the room, I understood why. I grabbed Myungsuh's hand. Professor Yoon was encased in a kind of glass-sided iron lung. His face and arms lay outside the glass. Breathing and feeding tubes hung from his nose and throat. His body was so swollen that there was no trace of the old Professor Yoon, who had been as thin as a plaster skeleton. I stared at his arms where they lay outside of the glass, away from his swollen body, at his hands lying motionless at the ends of arms so riddled with marks that there was nowhere left to insert a needle. Only his hands were as I remembered. His fingers were rough, but in the light, the skin was as translucent as a baby's. His fingers were as slender as the wooden holder of a dip pen. My hand longed to touch Professor Yoon's hand but held on tight to Myungsuh's hand instead.

"Talk to him," Myungsuh said, his eyes locked on the professor's face. "He can hear you."

He could still understand us in his condition? I didn't move, so Myungsuh went to Professor Yoon's side and said, "Professor, Jung Yoon is here." The professor did not react; his face was motionless. It was hard to believe he was even breathing. His eyes, which were once sharp yet kind, remained shut. Someone nudged open the door and gestured to the aide by

Professor Yoon's side. The aide left, and it was just the three of us in the quiet stillness of the hospital room. I reached out and took Professor Yoon's hand. His skin felt loose but warm.

"Open your palm," Myungsuh said quietly.

I thought I felt Professor Yoon's fingers move. I did as Myungsuh said and held my hand open beneath Professor Yoon's wizened fingers. His fingers curled and moved gently over my palm. *All . . . things . . . must . . .* My eyes widened, and I stared down at his fingers, which had turned into a pen against my hand. He wrote on my palm: *All things must come to an end.*

More old friends came to the hospital to see Professor Yoon and stayed instead of returning home. Myungsuh and I stayed, too. I took a cab home in the evening to refill Emily's food and water bowls and rushed back, but Myungsuh would not leave the vicinity of the hospital room for even a moment. I alternated between staying at Myungsuh's side and joining the others, who were gathered in the hospital cafeteria and coffee shop. I kept my hands in my pockets and hoped that someone would start talking and never stop. I didn't wash my hands, either. We ordered food and let it grow cold, drank alcohol on empty stomachs. After three days, Professor Yoon passed away. The sky was overcast that day, and a snowstorm struck around dusk. Snowflakes coated the hats and shoulders of people coming to visit. I was standing outside the hospital room with Fallingwater, who came by in the mornings and evenings, when we were told that Professor Yoon was gone. I walked down the long hallway away from his room, my heels clicking, took the elevator to the ground floor, and walked behind the building. My knees threatened to buckle. In an out-of-the-way spot away from people's eyes, I leaned back and stared at my shoes. They said that Professor Yoon had not allowed anyone to get near him for the first three years of his illness, but then he must have sensed his death was near because he called his older sister and asked her to take him to the hospital. They said that even after he was hospitalized, he wanted to be left alone, and it was only after it was too difficult for him to speak that he allowed us to be notified. Despite being only half conscious, he had traced messages on the palms of everyone who visited him. He wrote *Just as I came into being, so must I pass out of existence* on the hand of the person who saw him before me, and *That's where the stars are* on Fallingwater's hand, and *Do the flowers not bloom and fade* on the hand of the person who had tried to visit Professor Yoon one night but drove in circles instead, and *They are always shining there* on Myungsuh's hand. What would he have written on Miru's and Dahn's hands, if they had been there? Professor Yoon's final tracings were: *Bury my ashes under the tree.*

After he quit his post at the university, Professor Yoon never returned to his office. We assumed he continued to write poetry, but none of his writings were ever published. He passed the time at his cottage by tending to the trees in the mountains, planting things in the earth, and sharing the fruits of his labor with us whenever we visited. His last request was to be interred "under the tree," but he had not said which tree, or even which kind of tree. As a result, what we talked about the most during his three-day wake was, to our own surprise, trees. An oriental oak in Uljin on the east coast was mentioned, as well as a six-hundred-year-old white pine in Hyoja-dong in Seoul. Fallingwater told us that the tree was no longer there. That it had fallen one year in a storm. He said people in the neighborhood tried everything they could to save the tree, but to no avail. After it was removed, other pine trees were planted around the site. People listed off the names of arboretums around the world. Everyone had a tree that was special to them: pine, oak, wild cherry, Japanese torreya, Chinese parasol tree. All throughout the funeral, we whispered names of trees to one another. One person described an enormous silver magnolia growing in a field overlooking the water in a certain small village in Namhae on the southern coast. One day, five hundred years ago, a fisherman from the village had caught the biggest fish anyone had ever seen. He found seeds inside the fish's stomach and, without knowing what they were, planted them in the earth nearby. That spring, the seeds sprouted and grew into the enormous silver magnolia. The more we talked about trees, the more we found that we knew the same trees by different names, depending on where we were born and where we grew up. When that friend brought up the silver magnolia, Fallingwater said, "Don't you mean a Japanese magnolia?" He even brought in a book to quibble over it. Silver magnolias were common near the southern city where that friend had grown up. Those who grew trees but had never seen a silver magnolia added to the confusion by continuing to call them Japanese magnolias. We became so engrossed in it that we forgot we were at a wake. After someone brought up the oriental oak in Uljin, someone else countered with an oriental oak in Andong. They said that if a scops owl flies to the tree in the spring and hoots, there will be a good harvest that year, and someone else said that the oriental oak in Uljin grew from a sword that a Goryeo Dynasty general had stuck in the ground after losing in battle. Professor Yoon's wake was like a classroom filled with students of trees. The discussion went on and on: ibota privet, guelder rose, Japanese yew, Korean fir. I pictured the crepemyrtle beside my mother's grave. The long branches extended well past her grave, and when the bright red blossoms were in bloom, you could see where she was buried even from a great distance.

In the end, Professor Yoon was buried in the mountains near his cottage where he had spent his final days. Everyone had a different opinion, but that was the chosen spot. We buried him beneath a pine that was more than two hundred years old. It might have been one of the same pines that Myungsuh and I had cleared of snow until we both collapsed from exhaustion. Back then, it had been too dark to see anything, but when I looked around in the daylight, I saw that the woods overlooked a river that led to the sea. In the back, flanking the site like a folding screen, was a lush stand of Korean pine and Japanese cornel. The urn that held Professor Yoon's ashes was set in the earth beneath the tree; we took turns scattering handfuls of soil on top. When it was my turn, the moment my hand closed around the cold earth, all of my words deserted me, leaving only one: *Goodbye*. After the funeral, we sat in a bar until dawn, drinking aimlessly, and started to piece together the words Professor Yoon had left on our palms. We argued late into the night about which parts should come first and which should come later; one person fell asleep right there in the bar with his face pressed against the table. When we put Professor Yoon's last words in order, they spelled out: *My Christophers, thank you for being a part of my life. Do not grieve for me. All things must come to an end—youth, pain, passion, emptiness, war, violence. Do the flowers not bloom and fade? Just as I came into being, so must I pass out of existence. Look up to the sky. That's where the stars are. They are always shining there, whether we are gazing up at them, and whether we forget, and long after we die. May each one of you become one of those shining stars.*

When I finished telling the story of Saint Christopher, one of the students raised her hand. Since the time I had been given was short, I had not planned on taking any questions and was getting ready to step down from the podium. But I put my glasses back on and nodded at the student who had her hand up.

"Thank you for sharing the story. So, does that mean that we are Saint Christopher? Or are we the child he carries?"

Long ago, Professor Yoon had asked us the same question. Whenever I find myself in one of those moments where the past seems to be repeating itself in the present, I stop thinking of time as moving in a straight line. Seated next to the girl who asked the question was my cousin's daughter, Yuseon. While the three of us were having lunch on Sunday, Yuseon had paused in the middle of picking up a perilla leaf with her chopsticks and said, "There was an announcement at school that you're going to be the guest speaker at chapel. Is that true?" My cousin said, "If they announced it, then of course it's true!" Yuseon, who was the spitting image of my cousin, cocked her head to one side. I could tell she didn't believe that her aunt—the one who went to the public bath with her, the one who always missed her dental appointments because she hated going and would get phone calls from the nurse, the one who was always quick to grab the last piece of fruit left on the plate when they ate together—was the one invited to speak at chapel. Yuseon said, "That's strange. They usually only invite famous people . . ." Then she added, "I hate going to chapel. I usually skip it. Is it okay if I don't go?" So I had assumed she wouldn't be there. When I saw her sitting there, looking so bright-eyed next to the girl who'd asked me that question, I felt a little awkward. To her, I was just an aunt who combed her hair for her or swapped clothing. The girl who slipped and slid over the linoleum in her haste to help me trim Emily's claws looked so grown-up seated amongst the other college students. Judging by the way they smiled at each other, I assumed that she and the girl who'd asked the question were friends.

I stood up straighter and prepared to give my answer.

The day Myungsuh, Professor Yoon, and I had gone into the mountains to dislodge snow from the trees, it snowed again sometime in the night. Myungsuh and I left the village the next morning to find that the trees in the mountains were once again covered in snow. On the bus back to the city, Myungsuh said he would move in with me. When I got home, I moved my things around to make room for him. But he never showed. He even stopped calling in the middle of the night from wherever he had collapsed while wandering around the city. When I got tired of waiting for him to call and went to the magazine company where he worked part-time, he came running out to meet me. He showed none of the foot-dragging of someone who did not call and did not keep his promises. The company where he worked was in the first ten-story building to go up in Gangnam, the new district south of the Han River. Nowadays, ten stories doesn't seem like much, but back then, it was the tallest building around. Nearby was a royal burial ground covered in pine trees; I called him from a phone booth at the entrance. He appeared so quickly that it was hard to tell whether I had hung up the phone and come out of the booth first or he had come out of the building and shouted to me from across the distance first. He threw his arms around me before there was a chance for things to get awkward. We walked around the royal burial grounds three times. I didn't bring it up, but he promised again to move in. He said he would bring his things over in three days. But three days went by, and he never showed. Four times he said he would move in, only to break his promise. Each time, I went back to his office building, and he ran out and hugged me just like before. The hugs lasted longer and longer. On the night of his final broken promise, he came to my place. That time, he did not hug me. He just stared silently down at his feet. Together, we gazed out at Namsan Tower shining as always in the distance. I think I asked him what he was afraid of. I was surprised by his answer.

"If we live together, we'll just hurt each other. It'll turn ugly."

I understood what he meant by hurting each other, but I didn't know what he meant by ugly. I thought maybe I'd misheard him and asked him to repeat what he had said.

"If we start this way, you'll never get anywhere and you'll never accomplish anything, because of me."

"I don't understand," I said.

"I'll isolate you from others. You'll be like an island, cut off from everyone else. I'll end up making it so that people can only know you through me. I'll want you to not have any other relationships, and I'll try so hard to keep you by my side that it will turn us both ugly."

"Then why did you agree to move in?"

"Because I want to live with you, too."

I shivered in the cold and glared at the lights of the tower. Back then I did not understand, and did not want to understand, what he was saying to me.

Whenever I refer to a certain time as *long ago*, I feel like I am walking somewhere. Maybe those things that we realize only after so much time has passed that we can describe them as *long ago* are what we are made of.

On that night long ago, the boy I thought I had known better than anyone else seemed like a complete stranger. It was as if he was gone and I stood alone. I bit my lip and realized that

I could no longer fathom his heart. Having thought that he was all I needed, I felt pathetic. He said my name, but I didn't answer. He reached out his hand, but I didn't take it. Was he trying to tell me that being with me had turned ugly? A crack ran through my heart, and a thin sheet of ice formed over it.

He turned me around as I glared at the tower and tried to say something to me, but I would not hear it. I left him on the cold, windy rooftop and went inside. Which of us was in the right? I could hear him calling my name and knocking on the door, but I did my best to ignore him. I sat at my desk and resisted the urge to go back outside. The book of poems that we had found in the bookstore where we took refuge from the riot police during a demonstration was lying facedown on my desk. I turned it over and flipped through the pages in defiance of the sound of his knocking. Line by line, I read the poems that I had already memorized after countless readings. I read them out loud to drown out the sound of his voice. I have no idea when he finally left. I fell asleep with my head on the desk, the book of poems on the floor.

And him?

When I opened the door and stepped outside, the roof was covered in snow.

He's gone, I thought.

When I realized he was gone, my knees nearly buckled. I looked around for any trace of him and found his footprints overlapping one another in front of the door. He must have paced back and forth there as it continued to snow. I placed my feet inside his crushed footprints and followed the tracks.

They led across the roof and down the stairs. At the entrance to the building, his footprints overlapped again, the snow tamped down until it was hard and gleaming, as if he had been pacing back and forth a long time. The footprints continued down the hill below. They led me in the direction of Miru's old house. Near the house, his footprints crisscrossed again and turned back. Maybe he had stood there lost in thought, or had stared up at the house that was now occupied by other people. I stood in his prints and looked up at the house in the morning light, and then I, too, turned back. I'd thought that if I followed his tracks long enough, I would be able to find him, but they became impossible to follow. They were the only prints at first, but as the morning progressed, other people left their tracks as well, until finally a garbage truck passed by, covering them all with tire marks. I stared for a long time at the spot where the truck had erased his footprints, and then I headed back home. There, I threw some things in a bag and took the train to my father's house in the country. I spent the rest of the winter at my father's side.

But it was not yet over between us.

On a day when the snow, which had been falling for over a week straight, was piled as high as a grown man, Myungsuh showed up at my father's house. He had walked all the way from the city. His toes were frostbitten, and his cheeks were blistered. "Why did you do that?" I asked. He took my scolding without a word. "You'll go to this length, but you won't move in with me?" He didn't answer. He stayed in my father's

house with us for three days. He went into the mountains
to clear the snow from the pine trees just as we had at Professor Yoon's house, played games of *janggi* with my father,
and even followed him to my mother's grave. When he left, I
bought him a train ticket and saw him off at the station for
fear that he would try to walk back to the city. Myungsuh,
who had not said a word the whole time we were sitting in
the waiting room, called out my name at the turnstile where
his ticket was being checked. I looked over at him, and he
said that after I returned to the city, we should finish what we
had started at Namsan Tower. I asked what he meant, and he
mumbled, *hugging strangers . . .*

One day, after winter passed and spring had come, I saw him
standing in front of Myeongdong Cathedral. He was holding
a sign that said "Free Hugs." I didn't think he would go so far
as to make a sign. We had arranged to meet each other there,
but I couldn't bring myself to approach him. Our plan was
to first hug a hundred strangers and then reconsider what we
would do with our lives. We had agreed to start at Myeongdong Cathedral. I had gone there countless times in search of
him. I waited and watched him from a distance. To this day,
I cannot explain why I hung back instead of hurrying to join
him. What should I call the peculiar resistance that spread
through me when I first saw the "Free Hugs" sign? People cast
sidelong glances at him and his sign as they walked by. Some
even stopped and stared. Not only did he not hug anyone, he
looked as if he himself felt awkward, like he didn't quite know
what to do with himself. A foreigner walking past went up to

him and gave him a hug. When the person squeezed him, his arms hung awkwardly at his sides. He stood in that spot for three or four hours. No one else approached him, nor did he approach anyone. But he didn't look like he was waiting for me. When I saw him drop his sign, as if in defeat, I left.

How eagerly I used to wish for someone to tell me I would someday be able to painlessly accept everything that had happened to us.

Even after he visited me at my father's house, we didn't break up. We kept making promises and planning to see each other, right up until eight years ago. As if we couldn't *not* make promises. So many promises that we never kept and didn't remember. Promises idly made on top of promises unkept.

Putting off our breaking up by promising to see each other again.

After Myungsuh had found out what happened to Miru, he resumed his habit of telephoning in the middle of night with no idea of where he was or how he got there, so I got calls from him every night. I think the first thing I asked him each time was *Where are you?* Just once, he had stated the name of a town known for growing apples. I headed to the intercity bus terminal and waited for the first bus of the day so I could hurry to where he was. There, we rented bicycles and rode along a narrow path beside an apple orchard. Stuck our hands out to pluck apples wet with morning dew. Crunched into those fresh apples and laughed. That day, nothing bothered us, as if we would always be moving forward together. But it didn't last. Before long, he was back to being unable to say where he was calling from. I would go out in search of him. Sometimes I found him, and sometimes I didn't. Once, when I had barely managed to find him, I made him laugh by telling him that anyone who calls at four in the morning must be a North Korean spy. Then one night, the call came not from him but from a stranger. The man on the phone said that Myungsuh had climbed over his wall and fallen asleep in the yard. He said Myungsuh didn't look dangerous, so he had shaken him awake and asked him questions until he was able to get a phone number out of him. That was how he got my number, he said. But if I didn't go and get him right away, he would have to call the police. I asked where he lived. It was Miru's old house. I ran through the dawn air to get Myungsuh. When he saw me, he called me Miru. Though I can't remember, I'm sure there have been times when I looked at him and called him Dahn, too. Was that maybe the night we stopped making any more promises to each other? When we stopped saying, *I'll be right there?*

A few days ago, I went to visit my father in the nursing home. In the bus on the way to the train station, the person sitting next to me had a newspaper open to a picture of Myungsuh. It was an article about one of his photo exhibits. Since I couldn't take my eyes off the newspaper, the person handed it to me when he got off the bus. I opened it up and murmured, "Emily, these are great photos," as if she were sitting right next to me. The title of the exhibit was Embracing Youth. The photos were of young people hugging each other in countries all over the world, including pedestrians on Arbat Street in Moscow. The article said that he had spent three months on the road to take a thousand photos of young people hugging each other. He must have left right after Professor Yoon's funeral. In response to the reporter's question, "Why, of all things, photos of young people hugging?" he had said, "Sometimes I'm troubled by self-destructive urges, but seeing young people hug each other helps me to overcome them." He added that of all the people in the world, the people of Moscow were the least inclined to smile, but even they couldn't help but grin when they saw young people hugging each other on Arbat Street. He added that he himself had hugged a hundred young people he didn't know on that very street.

Did he feel the same way I did?

Sometimes I feel like I am falling apart, like I am bombarded. I push away the fear and sluggishly make my way to my desk and write, in order to fight off the mysterious anxiety that paralyzes my senses. I stared at his photo, at him saying that he had hugged a hundred young strangers, and I felt so sad that I had to turn away and gaze out instead at the noonday city flashing past the bus window. Staring back at me were the ghosts of us from days past, trudging through the city with our loneliness and our dreams of *someday*.

That day, at chapel, another student raised her hand. She asked, "Looking back on your twenties, what would you most want to say to those of us who are going through our twenties now?" I made eye contact briefly with Yuseon, who was seated amongst the other students, as I looked over at the student who had asked the question. She must have been shy because her voice trembled. Without even having to think about it, I said, "I hope you all have someone who always makes you want to say, *Let's remember this day forever.*" The students oohed and aahed, and then laughed at each other's reaction. I laughed with them. "Also . . ." They'd thought I was done but they quieted down again. "I hope you will never hesitate to say, *I'll be right there.*"

The day after the veterinarian told me that Emily, who was now so old she could barely move, had inoperable stomach cancer, I was woken in the middle of the night by the faint sound of a ringing telephone. The faint ringing seemed to grow louder, as if drilling straight into my eardrums. I reached out and brought the receiver to my ear, and an unfamiliar voice asked if Jungmin was there. I said no, but the young man suddenly burst into tears and pleaded with me to please put Jungmin on the phone. I set the receiver down without hanging it up. After a while, I picked it up again, and the boy was still crying. He didn't seem to care whether I was listening or not. He just needed time to cry into the telephone. Once he stopped crying, he would feel a little better about the situation with Jungmin. Emily got up from where she had been curled up in a ball on the nightstand, slowly climbed onto my stomach, and stretched out. By now, even grooming was difficult for her. When I asked the veterinarian if there was any chance Emily could make it through surgery, she said that Emily had lived a surprisingly long life already and did I need to put her through that? I took Emily home instead. I stroked the scruff of her neck until I heard the phone beep—either the boy had stopped crying or the call got disconnected—and I placed it back in its cradle. I couldn't get back to sleep, so I worked at my desk for a while before opening the bottommost drawer. I took out envelopes, printouts, a dictionary of Chinese characters, until I reached the box at the very bottom that contained Myungsuh's journal. I had sealed it inside that box as I was coming to terms with his absence. I opened the box and took out his journal.

So much I wish I'd done differently. Bursts of guilt—*If only!*—that haunt me at every turn. Suddenly understanding those old feelings in unexpected, unrelated situations. Things that will remain incomprehensible or unanswered regardless of what lies ahead of me.

Would the day ever come when I could tell him that I'd finally gone to Basel, to Peru? That I had stood before Arnold Böcklin's *Isle of the Dead* in the Kunstmuseum Basel and whispered Miru's name, then looked around wildly because I thought I heard her say, *Yes?*

Etched in the earth in the Nazca desert plain at the foot of the Andes mountains, invisible at human eye level, are inscrutable geometric figures that can be seen only from the sky. You have to be at least three hundred meters in the air to see them in their entirety. They say the images were left there by the Nazca people fifteen hundred years ago. Because they had no domesticated animals, the people who made the glyphs did all of the work with their bare hands. The figures include hundreds of long lines formed by removing bits of gravel to expose the lighter sand beneath: giant birds whose wings are so large that, if they were given life and took to flight, the shadows might cover much of the plain; strange and beautiful creatures that I do not recognize. They are engraved in the plain like codes scratched out by someone's fingers. How did the Nazca leave these enormous glyphs before anything had been invented that could lift them into the air and enable them to look down? It is believed that the fifteen-hundred-year-old images were able to last this long because, despite being at a latitude where you would expect to find lush tropical growth, the area is very dry. It had not rained in the last ten thousand years. I couldn't fathom that length of time. The word "dry" seemed like an understatement for a place that had not seen rain in ten thousand years. My travel companions and I viewed the glyphs from a helicopter. Zigzags, stars, plants, and grids of inestimable size, circles, triangles, squares, trapezoids—the glyphs went on and on without end. They did not just cover the vast and desolate Nazca plain but stretched farther away, across islands, past deep ravines and streams, around the curves of the Andes. Hundreds upon hundreds of connected lines. There was an enormous triangle with its top lopped off and a bird that looked as if it was flying south. Then one in particular caught my eye: a fifty-meter-long spider etched in the sand.

Would I have ever guessed back then that I would one day gaze down at a fifteen-hundred-year-old spider drawn in the desert? At the spider glyph in the Nazca plain of the Andes mountains, where I had arrived after flying for eight hours, changing planes in Los Angeles, and flying for another twenty or so hours, Dahn returned to me, as real as anything. Dahn—who had once taken me all the way to my mother's grave despite his fear of spiders. At that moment, a corner of my heart that had been lightless and cold as ice suddenly cracked, and a single ray of light from a morning star rushed in and shined on it. It felt warm. Quietly, so no one could hear, I whispered his name. Dahn's face floated over the fifteen-hundred-year-old spider engraved in the desert floor. I murmured to myself, *Don't be afraid*. And *I'll never forget you*. It was then that I finally realized I was not made up only of myself. Everything I saw and everything I felt was also part Dahn. And part Miru. And partly their unfinished time that I was living.

The morning light stretched across my desk while I flipped through page after page of his journal. Emily summoned up the strength to jump onto the desk and curled up next to me as I was reading. *Don't worry, Emily* . . . I mumbled, unsure of what I was telling her not to worry about, and scratched her behind the ears. She gazed at me for a moment and then sprawled out like a puddle on top of the desk. Myungsuh's journal had sat sealed and unopened for almost as long as we had been apart.

Everything in it seemed new. Despite having read it so many times that I thought I had the pages memorized, I felt like I was reading it for the first time. I turned over the final page and slipped the brown notebook out of its black dust cover. The last time I had done this, when I had sealed his journal almost eight years ago, was still fresh in my memory. Into the cover, I slipped the letters Dahn had sent me, my belated replies that I'd had nowhere to send, and the slim book of poems by Francis Jammes that Myungsuh and I once read together in a bookstore while a demonstration raged in the streets outside. They didn't fit. I took the book out, unfolded the letters, and started slipping them between the pages instead, but after a moment, I just sat there, feeling at a loss. Where was Miru's diary now, the one I had shelved in Professor Yoon's office with the books by writers who had died before the age of thirty-three? Who was reading the book of poems by Emily Dickinson that Dahn had snuck onto the base? For all I knew, they were nowhere to be found. I flipped Myungsuh's journal over to slip it back into the dust cover, and paused. There was something written on the very back. I sat up straighter as I read it: *I want to grow old with Jung Yoon.* It was Myungsuh's handwriting. Had this been written here all this time? These words had been sealed away for the last eight years? I set the journal down and sat unmoving as the morning sunlight finished its trek across my desk. Emily quietly opened her eyes and looked at me. Eyes still blue despite her old age. "Don't worry, Emily . . ." I murmured as I filled my fountain pen and answered the sentence it had taken me eight years to find:

I'll be right there.

Author's Note

I'll Be Right There is a story of young people living in tragic times. It is also the story of people who find themselves separated, despite their love for each other, because they carry wounds that are too deep to overcome, and who struggle to come back together. Their story takes place in the 1980s and early 1990s in South Korea, which is also when I was going through my twenties and early thirties. The long dictatorship of the Park Chung-hee regime had collapsed, and what took its place was not freedom but a new dictatorship headed by Chun Doo-hwan. At the time, South Korean youth, including university students, were protesting in the streets and being fired upon with tear gas nearly daily in their quest for democracy and freedom. That period of unrest lasted about a decade. Young people would rally against the government one day only to disappear mysteriously the next, while others committed self-immolation in the streets in protest. And young men who had led demonstrations later died suspicious deaths in the military during their compulsory service. If it were not for the sacrifices of these young people who fought and struggled for change, South Korea would not be what it is today. It is this history that forms the setting of *I'll Be Right There*.

However, in this novel, I do not specifically reveal the era or elucidate Korea's political situation at the time. This was a deliberate decision on my part as a writer, because I believe that what happens to the characters in *I'll Be Right There* is in no way limited to South Korea. Everything that happens in this novel could happen in any country and in any generation. I believe that no matter how rough the world becomes, there will always be teachers and students learning from each other, and even when savage and violent powers obstruct our freedoms, there will always be earnest and heartfelt first loves and friendships being born. While writing, I was focused on and absorbed in giving expression to those moments. I believe those are the moments that define our lives. We may be the protagonists of tragedy, but we are also the heroes of our most beautiful and thrilling experiences.

KYUNG-SOOK SHIN, the author of seventeen books, is one of South Korea's most widely read and acclaimed writers. Her best seller *Please Look After Mom* has been translated into more than thirty languages. She has been honored with the Man Asian Literary Prize, the Manhae Prize, the Dong-in Literary Award, the Yi Sang Literary Prize, and France's Prix de l'Inaperçu, as well as the Ho-Am Prize in the Arts, awarded for her body of work for general achievement in Korean culture and the arts.

SORA KIM-RUSSELL is a literary translator based in Seoul. Her translations and writings have appeared in *Words Without Borders, Azalea: A Journal of Korean Literature and Culture, Drunken Boat, Pebble Lake Review, The Diagram*, and other publications. She teaches at Ewha Womans University.